MAN ON THE RUN

BY

SUZANNE FLOYD

June 2014

# COPYRIGHT

I dedicate this book to my husband Paul and our daughters, Camala and Shannon, and all my family. Thanks for all your support and encouragement.

# CHAPTER ONE

Bored with the reruns on television, I flipped through the channels so fast I barely saw what each one was offering. "If you'd pause on each station, you might find something you want to watch." Mom spoke up from across the room where she was reading. I thought she was engrossed in the story, and not paying attention to what I was doing. Apparently I was wrong.

When the host of America's Most Wanted came on the screen, I took my finger off the remote button. Maybe he would have something interesting to say. Within minutes I was captivated by the story he was telling. Fifteen years ago, a man named Warner Franklin had blown up several houses in his neighborhood over a disagreement with his neighbors, killing several people before disappearing into the wilderness in New Mexico. "He's still out there," the host announced gravely, "He's a survivalist, and the FBI speculates he could be living in the forest anywhere around the country, but they feel he would stay in the west or southwest." A picture of the man at the time of the explosion came up on the screen along with a computer generated picture of how he might look now, fifteen years later.

"I've seen him," I gasped. "He's here in Arizona, in our forest."

Mom looked up again, resting the book in her lap. "Who's that, dear?"

"That man," I pointed at the television. "I've seen him in town." She squinted at the TV, and I handed her the glasses sitting on the table beside her chair. Without them, she can't see three feet in front of her.

"Hmm," she stared at the picture on the screen. "I don't know. That could be just about any man with a beard." She chuckled. "It sort of looks like how I imagine The Hermit would look if I ever saw him." We've always been aware someone was living deep in the woods surrounding our small town. There were occasional sightings of an old man with shaggy gray hair moving silently through the forest, but few people have actually seen him up close and personal. No one knows his name; he's just The Hermit, capital letters.

As a teenager, I'd spent many hours scouring the forest looking for the illusive man. I'd taken a lot of ribbing from the other kids over my obsession, and never saw more than a shadowy figure moving silently among the trees.

"Do you think that man's been in the store?" I pointed at the television. Mom and I own the General Store in Flanagan's Gap, one of many small towns in Northern Arizona surrounded by national forests.

"Oh, I don't know, maybe. This time of year, strangers are beginning to come in. People camping out, here on vacation, things like that. A lot of men don't bother shaving when they go camping. They all look alike once half their face is covered with all that hair. It's hard to tell what they really look like."

"That's the point of wearing a beard. It's a good disguise," I argued.

"I don't think a fugitive from the FBI would risk going into any town, especially a small one where strangers stand out. They don't want to get caught." She picked up her book again. The show went on to another story, but that image was burned into my memory.

Fugitives have been known to hide in plain sight, living anonymous lives until years later someone sees their picture, recognizing it as a neighbor. Why does she find it so hard to believe one could be hiding in the forest surrounding our town since we all believe The Hermit, a man we've never seen, is out there? A fugitive could also explain the petty thefts we've been experiencing in the last few months, I thought. I planned on keeping my eyes open.

My sleep was fitful that night; Warner Franklin trampled through my dreams, first as The Hermit we've all heard about most of our lives, then as himself blowing up the town.

Feeling foggy-headed the next morning, I stumbled to the

kitchen to start the coffee. Maybe caffeine would clear out the cobwebs. "You're up early, dear." Mom came in while I tapped my fingers impatiently on the counter, waiting for the coffee maker to do its job. "Didn't you sleep well?"

"Bad dreams," I mumbled. "This stuff with that fugitive and The Hermit kept rattling around in my brain."

She patted my hand, setting a cup in front of me. "Maybe I can help you with that. I know why that man looked sort of familiar," she chuckled. "He's been in the store. Well, not the man on the TV, of course, just someone who looks similar. He's much younger than the man the FBI is looking for, though. He would have been a child when that man killed his neighbors. The Hermit is much too old to be either of them." Mom considers anyone younger than her a child; that means the man she'd seen in the store could be anywhere between five and fifty-five.

Letting the subject marinate in her mind over night, she came up with the answer that had eluded her last night, and satisfied her this morning. "You're sure it isn't the man on TV?" I asked.

"Yes, dear, he was in just last week for some supplies. I tried to strike up a conversation, but he isn't very talkative. He must be camping in the area, and just needed some supplies. He sort of looks like that fugitive. His hair is long, and he has a beard. He was kind of scruffy and dirty like he's been camping for a while, but he didn't smell bad. People working out in the sun all day smell worse than he did. But like I said, he is much too young to be the man the FBI is looking for. He was polite, but didn't stop to chat like most folks do," Mom finished. This settled the question in her mind. The subject was closed as far as she's concerned, but I was far from convinced.

Polite and quiet weren't in the FBI description of Warner Franklin. Loner, standoffish, even anti-social were better descriptions, but mostly dangerous. "No one said anything came up missing after he was here?" I asked. I didn't know what to think now. If he was in during the morning, I wouldn't have seen him since I'm teaching in our homeschool co-op at that time of day. I know I've seen someone who resembles the man the FBI is looking for though, and I don't think he's all that young. "Do we have three men living out there in the forest now?" I wondered out loud. "If this keeps up there will be as many people living in the forest as there are in town."

Mom chuckled. "I'm sure we don't have anything to worry about. Whoever was taking things has probably moved on. I'm certain that nice young man had nothing to do with the thefts going on lately".

That's so typical of Mom, I thought. I don't think she's ever had an unkind thought about anyone. "I'll keep an eye out, just the same." My stubborn streak reared its ugly head.

~~~

Two weeks later, Megan Riley stomped into the store, grumbling about something. Usually the most even-tempered person I know, she was all out of sorts this morning. We've been best friends almost from the cradle. Our moms were pregnant at the same time, and we were born fifteen days apart. She's older; an old joke between us.

"You know I'm the first person to help someone out when they're in need," she stated without any greeting. "If that old man needs food he should ask, not just come into our homes, taking what he wants." She herded her two-year-old twins in ahead of her.

"Who are you talking about?" I leaned down to give the two boys a hug before they went in search of my mom.

"The Hermit, that's who, and he isn't as old as we always thought."

"You actually saw The Hermit?" I couldn't believe her luck. It's been my fantasy, not hers, to see this illusive figure. He's like our own personal Big Foot, part myth and part reality. But he's called a hermit for a reason. He wants as little as possible to do with other people, and civilization in general.

"Saw him? We stared at each other like two deer caught in

4

a car's headlights." She heaved a sigh. "I forgot the twins' toy bag, and had to go back to get it. I was only gone a couple of minutes, and he was already helping himself to the leftover stew; eating it right out of the bowl with his grubby fingers no less! Can you believe the nerve of the man?" She shook her head, her blond curls bobbing around her face. "Once he got over his surprise at being caught red-handed, he ran out the back door, pulling a pair of Jack's jeans off the line as he ran past. He was moving pretty fast for an old man when he ran into the forest."

"What'd he look like? You're sure it was The Hermit?" I had my doubts, but I didn't say anything.

She shrugged. "Since I've never actually seen The Hermit, I can't be positive it was him. But who else could it be? I always thought he was just a harmless old man who wanted to be left alone. But this guy looked mean; he even snarled at me before he turned tail and ran. The twins were right beside me; I was scared he was going to do something to us."

"Do you think he's watching the town so he knows when no one's home?" The thought was scary indeed. The man the FBI is looking for is dangerous. "Should we start locking our doors?" It's a foreign concept to lock our doors, but what if it was the fugitive, and not The Hermit?

"He certainly thought it was safe for him to go into my house," she continued to complain. "He's never been this bold before." In my mind, this was confirmation that it wasn't The Hermit. It could very well be the man the FBI was looking for. How could I go about proving it though?

Mom came out of the back room with Joshua and Caleb, each holding an edge of the apron she always wears when she's working in the store. "These two little guys have been carrying on a conversation with each other, but I can't understand a word."

"Welcome to my world," Megan laughed, finally relaxing after her scare. "Dad says it's 'twin speak,' most twins have some version of it. They'll be ready for school before I can understand them. I keep telling them to talk like Mommy and Daddy; but they just laugh, and jabber away to each other."

Students in our homeschool co-op began clamoring into the store where classes are held in a back room, halting talk of Megan's visitor.

~~~

By the end of the day everyone in town had heard about what happened in Megan's kitchen, and Sara Flanagan called a town meeting. "Calm down folks, don't everybody talk at once." She pounded the gavel on the podium, trying to call the meeting to order. As the last of the line of our small town's founding father, Sara is the nearest thing we have to a mayor. The crowd slowly quieted down, and she turned to Bill Wheeler. "What have you got to say?"

At six feet two inches, he towered over Sara's diminutive frame. "I don't mind sharing what I got with those less fortunate than me. But I think they should ask, not just take." A mummer of agreement rose from the crowd until Sara pounded the gavel again. People in Flanagan's Gap have always been willing to help their neighbors, but what happened this morning is unacceptable.

"The Hermit always left something in exchange for what he took." Sandy Bridges added. "Why's he stealing things all of a sudden?" That was the question in everyone's mind. It was everyone's complaint. "He's always been careful not to get caught. Why is he taking chances now?" It was the consensus of most people in town that The Hermit was behind this rash of thefts. After that TV show, I had another explanation, but nothing to back it up, so I remained quiet.

As far back as I can remember people would come home to find a beautiful wood carving sitting on the table or front stoop. Food would be missing from the refrigerator or cupboard, or an article of clothing would be missing from the clothes line. We always knew if he took something, he left something behind. No one in town considered it stealing because of what he left in exchange.

As in most small towns, we trust each other; rely on each other, only businesses lock their doors at night. Now paranoia is creeping into our way of life.

"What does Jack have to say, Megan?" Sara asked. "Has he seen The Hermit lately?" Megan's husband Jack works for the Forest Service, and knows the forest like the back of his hand. He's probably the only person in town who has actually spoken to The Hermit.

Standing up, Megan shook her head. "Since this all started, Jack's tried to find him, but he hasn't been able to locate him. His shack still shows signs of life, but The Hermit was never there when he stopped by. He's kind of worried about him." She and Jack were high school sweethearts, and were married as soon as she had her degree. Their identical twins just turned two a couple of weeks ago.

"He should be worried about his family," Bill grumbled. "He could have hurt you and the twins this morning."

"Jack's been working in the forest for the past week. He doesn't know what happened." Megan defended her husband.

Everyone vented their anger over all the missing food and clothes, but no one had a suggestion how to stop it. Instead of once or twice a year, as it had been in the past, it was once or twice a month and escalating. After the first few times things turned up missing without the usual exchange, people had called the sheriff's department without getting much satisfaction. David Graham, the deputy in charge of our area had a profound suggestion: "Lock your doors." Now why didn't we think of that? I thought sarcastically No one was interested in calling him this time.

At eight-thirty, the meeting broke up. It was time for social hour. Our town meetings are held in the church hall. People bring a dessert or snack to share.

"I don't understand why he's stealing more food than he used to," Megan said. "Until now, he only took things he couldn't grow or catch for himself. Now he's taking all sorts of things. Last week, he took a bag of potato chip from Betty's house. What's with that?" Taking potato chips is akin to taking the Crown Jewels as far as I'm concerned, but I understood the urge. It's almost an uncontrollable need to have the salty, crispy munchies. He's never felt the urge to have them before though, so why now?

"Why is he just taking things, and not leaving something in return?" she continued to grumble. Several years ago, he left a beautiful carving on the counter in Mom's kitchen. It's one of her prized possessions, and now sits in a place of honor on the shelf behind the cash register in our store.

"Maybe he's getting too old to hunt and fish, and do his carvings," I suggested. "That could be why he's taking more now." Or maybe he's not the one taking things, I thought. This sounds more like a criminal than The Hermit.

# CHAPTER TWO

School would be officially out in a few weeks, but that wouldn't ease my schedule any. We try to keep the kids busy and out of trouble during the summer, along with keeping up the skills they've learned during the school year. We also have a community pool everyone chipped in to have built several years ago. Parents volunteer as life guards. Mom and I also have a craft workshop for anyone who wants to join. The craft projects are sold in the store to tourists when they come through.

An internet search regarding Warner Franklin hadn't been helpful. Since the television show aired, there had been numerous 'sightings' all over the country, but he was still on the loose

It had been a month since Megan caught the man in her kitchen; no one reported any problems since. Although that was a good thing; I was a little disappointed. I certainly didn't want anyone getting hurt, but I was hoping to get a glimpse of this man myself. Was he Warner Franklin? Or someone we don't know about? Where was The Hermit? Did Warner Franklin do something to him? Had they both moved on? Mom hadn't said anything about seeing the 'young man' in the store again either. I didn't know what to make of all this.

"You're just bored, dear," Mom told me as she placed a plate of her special French toast in front of me. "You need to add a little excitement to your life." The fact that she can pick up on my moods so quickly never fails to amaze me.

Bored? I thought. I need some excitement? What were people trying to tell me? "I'm just feeling a little restless," I tried to explain. "It happens every year when school is about to end." I tried to laugh off the mood. "Once summer activities are in full swing, I'll have plenty to occupy my time." Being shopkeeper, teacher and crafter leaves me very little free time for excitement, even in the summer. But was she right? Was I looking for something more in my life? Is that why I'm so interested in this fugitive?

Until now, I always thought there was plenty of excitement in Flanagan's Gap. We have satellite TV, high speed internet and even Netflix. During the summer our softball team plays against other teams in the area. Nearly everyone enjoys hiking in the forest. In the winter, we can go skiing or ice skating on the pond once it freezes over. It might not measure up to what passes for excitement in the big city, but we manage just fine.

If you want to go to the show or the mall or even do some major shopping, you need to drive forty-five miles to Prescott. Something I haven't done for a long while, I silently admitted. Maybe I did need a little R and R to get a right perspective on things again. I just didn't know when I could squeeze it in.

~~~

I've hiked the forest around Flanagan's Gap most of my life, all though it's been a while. Old trails are overgrown, new ones have opened up. I decided this would be a good time to get back into the habit, and do a little exploring while I'm at it.

"Tell me again, what are we doing out here?" Megan said, puffing slightly to keep up with me. She left the twins with Mom to join me in a hike. "We haven't gone hiking much since we came home from college. Why the sudden interest now?"

"It was a long winter; I've been feeling a little cooped up lately," I countered, evasively. "Besides, the exercise will do me good. I'd like to get rid of the pounds I gained over the last school year."

She snorted. "You don't need to lose weight. What you need is some outside interests, not exercise." By that she means I need a boyfriend. I can't argue that point, but the pool of single men in Flanagan's Gap is pretty shallow. Maybe this summer a cute, eligible man will swim into our little pond and decide to stay.

Turning my thoughts back to the task at hand, I continued walking deeper into the forest, hoping to find something to indicate someone other than the casual camper had been there. I figured a hermit or a fugitive wouldn't stay close to the usual camping sites.

"What are you looking for?" I wasn't paying attention, and didn't answer until she raised her voice to get my attention. "Becca, I asked what you're looking for?"

"Um, nothing." I tried for an innocent expression, but failed miserably.

"You are such a liar," she accused, laughing at me. "Now tell me the truth. What are you looking for? Why are we really out here?"

"I just want to make sure it's safe for the kids before summer break starts." That much was the truth, just not all of it. I didn't want the kids out here if there was any chance of them running into an armed and dangerous fugitive.

"There's plenty out here that's dangerous, but most of these kids have lived here their whole life. They know to watch out for snakes and wild animals. The newer kids have all been instructed on what to watch for. You've been acting squirrely for the past month. What's really going on?"

I had to tell someone or I'd bust. Continuing to walk through the tall trees and underbrush, I filled her in on the man I'd seen on "America's Most Wanted." "What if he's the guy that's been stealing things?" I finally asked.

"Are you kidding me?" She gaped at me in disbelief. "How long do you think he's been out here? How dangerous is he? Why didn't you tell someone?" Her questions spilled over each other, not giving me a chance to answer.

"Mom doesn't think it's the same man. She thinks he's too young."

"You mean she's seen him, too? Why didn't you say something before?" she asked again.

I lifted one shoulder in a shrug. "It was just speculation. I didn't have any proof. I still don't."

11

Suzanne Floyd

"That's why we're out here today, right?" I nodded, unable to deny it, but I didn't say anything. "You need to let the town know. You should tell Jack. He can keep an eye out for anyone suspicious." She looked around, her brown eyes a little spooked at the thought of a fugitive so close to town. "Do you think that's the guy who came in my house?"

I didn't have an answer for that. "Jack hasn't seen anyone out here?" I asked instead. Surely if he had, he'd tell her. He wouldn't take any risk with her or the twins.

"You know how busy they all get with fire season starting," she shrugged, "but if this guy's been out here for years, Jack would have seen him. He would have told me, or someone."

There was a silent rebuke in her words, heaping on the guilt. I should have said something at the time the man came into her kitchen. What if it really was the fugitive? But if he was just one of the many homeless people in the country, looking for something to eat, I could have been accusing an innocent man. I didn't want to be one of those people calling the FBI with false leads.

We hiked for another half hour without seeing any sign of human habitation outside of the established camp sites. Maybe we hadn't gone far enough into the forest, I thought. This guy was a survivalist; he wouldn't stay where the casual hiker could find him. Neither would The Hermit; he wanted to avoid people for a different reason. I didn't even know where his shack was.

Disappointed, we headed back. "Be sure to ask Jack if he's seen anything suspicious," I told her as we parted ways. "The petty thefts that started a couple of months ago might be when he moved into our area." The fact that the thefts had stopped after Megan caught him in her house could mean he'd moved on.

"Jack hasn't seen anyone suspicious out in the woods," Megan reported later that evening. "If anyone has been living out there for fifteen years, they're really good at hiding

12

themselves."

"What about The Hermit? Could they be the same person?"

She laughed. "Come on, Becca. We've heard that story since we were kids; our parents heard about him before that. You said the FBI has only been after this guy for fifteen years." I released a disappointed sigh. Maybe she and Mom were right. I just wanted it to be true to stir up some excitement for myself.

"Jack agrees you need to find..." She paused, searching for the right word.

"A boyfriend?" I asked when she stumbled over what to say next.

She ignored my comment, continuing like I hadn't said anything. "He has Saturday off, and suggested the two of us go to Prescott for a girls' day out. He volunteered to watch the twins. That's an offer I can't refuse. We can go shopping, or see a movie, just relax."

It sounded wonderful. "On the way home we can stop, and pick up some supplies for the store," I said. "We're running low on a few things."

"You are such a workaholic," she accused with a laugh. "We're going there to shop for us, not the store."

"You know how hard it is to get some of the suppliers to come all the way out here. We can have fun, and still pick up some things. I'll drive."

"That's a wonderful idea," Mom said when I told her about Megan's suggestion. She never objected when I took time off from the store. "You work too hard, and need some fun in your life." She was hinting at the same thing Megan had. They all thought I needed a boyfriend. I'm just not sure where they thought I was going to find this elusive man.

The average age of males in Flanagan's Gap is over forty-five, and most of them are already married. The next largest age group was somewhere below ten or over sixty. I wasn't looking in any of those groups.

"Maybe you should find a teaching job in Prescott," she went on. "You could have a social life, and still come home on the weekends." This was a subject she has visited on a regular basis since I graduated from college.

Dad died while I was junior in college. I wanted to drop out, and come home to help her with the store, but she wouldn't hear to it. "You need to finish your education. If you still want to come home then, I won't stop you," she told me at the time. Every now and then she has second thoughts. Flanagan's Gap isn't exactly a hot bed of opportunities.

Getting my teaching degree was the right thing to do, and so was coming home. I can't always convince her of that though. The homeschool co-op I started for the few kids in town has been a hit. We now have fifteen students ranging from kindergarten to high school.

Of course, my pay check is nearly nonexistent. Mom and I live mostly off what we make in the store. Whatever people can give me for teaching is extra. Fortunately, our bills are almost as nonexistent.

~~~

Saturday morning I was excited about the day ahead. Maybe we could plan a day out every couple of months. Megan needs time to herself, too. It wouldn't hurt Jack, or the twins, to do without her for a few hours.

I'd forgotten all about the possibility of a fugitive living out in our forest. Almost forgotten about him, I amended. "Be careful today, and don't talk to any strangers," I warned Mom without thinking about my words until she laughed at me.

"Yes, Mommy," she laughed. "How do I wait on our customers if I can't talk to strangers? This time of year we have as many strangers as we have townsfolk coming through," she reminded me. Even as small as it is, Flanagan's Gap is becoming a tourist destination; something we've worked hard to achieve.

Because I hadn't said anything more about the man on TV, she'd forgotten about him, and I didn't bring him up again. If

14

she did start to believe me, I didn't want her to be afraid over a possible mistake on my part.

I tucked the list of items we needed in the store into my purse. It would be the last thing we did before heading home. It was longer than I expected, and would take me a while to get everything.

Later Megan and I were laughing and joking as we left the restaurant. I'd only had one glass of wine with lunch, but I felt like I drank the whole bottle. Maybe I am taking life a little too seriously, I thought. Linking arms, we headed back to the craft sale in the square. I'm always looking for ideas to use in the craft workshop.

As always a large crowd milled through the courthouse square. Prescott's Arts and Craft Fairs are a popular attraction, bringing people from all over the state. Suddenly I stopped, gripping Megan's arm. "It's him!" I stared at a man walking across the square away from us. He was lost in the crowd before I could get a good look at him, but I was certain it was the man I'd seen on television. Or was I? There was something different about him.

"Who are you talking about?" She looked at me like I'd lost my mind. There were so many people it was hard to see across the square, let alone pick out one particular person.

"Sorry, my imagination has run amuck again. Maybe I should have skipped that glass of wine." I tried to laugh it off, even as I scanned the crowd hoping to see him again; but he was gone.

"Are you still looking for that fugitive? I thought you gave up that idea."

"Yeah, I did, sort of." I heaved a sigh, frustration welling up in me. "I really need to get a life, and stop watching all those real life crime shows," I joked.

I tried to put the image of the man out of my mind, but he kept intruding on my thoughts for the rest of the afternoon. Had it really been him, or just someone with a beard and longish hair, letting my imagination fill in the rest?

15

By the time I got the supplies we needed from the warehouse store, and headed back to Flanagan's Gap, dusk had settled over us. I finally decided it couldn't be the man the FBI was looking for. He wouldn't come into a large city for fear of being recognized. If the man really was hiding out near our town, he probably figured a small hick town like ours would be safer for him.

Jack and the twins were waiting on the front porch when we pulled up in front of her house. "Mommy!" Jacob and Caleb were still at the toddling stage, and couldn't make it down the steps from the porch on their own. They did a little dance beside their daddy waiting for her to come get them.

"You'd think I'd been gone a year," she joked. "I guess absence really does make the heart grow fonder."

"Who is happier to have you home; Jack or the twins?" Relief was written in every fiber of his being.

She chuckled, "Probably it's a tie. He's never had to deal with both of them by himself for an entire day. It does them all good." She leaned across the seat to give me a hug. "Relax tonight, kiddo, and don't think about anything beyond the fun we had." I knew what and who she was talking about. "Let's plan on doing this again in another month."

"Looks like you just about cleaned out the store, Becca," Jack called to me. "Are you going to need help unloading?"

"Mom and I can get it, but thanks for the offer. Enjoy having your wife home." I laughed. He looked so frazzled I almost felt sorry for him. Some men take for granted that a woman can handle a house, kids, and a job with one hand tied behind her back until they have to do it alone.

Mom was waiting with the big cart a few minutes later, ready to help unload the back end of my truck. I really had gone overboard on my buying spree. We wouldn't need to get supplies again for a while.

"Tell me all about your day," Mom said as we started stocking the shelves in the storeroom. "Did you see anyone you know?" She always expected to see a familiar face when she went to town.

Her comment conjured up the image of the man walking across the square. I'd only had a fleeting glimpse of his profile. There hadn't been time to see if it was really the man from TV, or even guess at his age. Was I doomed to see his face every time I saw a man with a beard and long hair?

"Only Megan," I joked. "I bought a few extras," I stated the obvious, while changing the subject. I didn't want to bring up the man I'd seen across the square. "They had some new items I thought we could try out." People usually wait for us to restock our shelves so they don't have to go to town. It was a good arrangement for them and for us. They didn't have to make the long trek into town, and our store flourished.

~~~

As a small town that caters to the tourist trade, some businesses have to stay open on Sunday. Our General Store is closed though, a throwback to days gone by when stores were only open on Sunday in case of an emergency. Flanagan's Gap is lucky to have our own church and a full-time pastor. Those who don't attend here, go to one of the other towns for services. Of course, Pastor Curt Watson wears a different hat during the week when he and his wife, Judy, run one of the three restaurants in town.

Today is the beginning of our summer schedule; it's "Bar-B-Cue Sunday." Everyone brings a side dish, and the hunters among us supply the meat that's roasted over an open pit. Everyone is welcome, including any tourists who want to join in. After we've eaten our fill, the softball team from nearby Hilltop will be over for the beginning of the summer season. It's a ritual everyone from the surrounding towns takes part in.

Sitting on the bench waiting for my turn at bat, Mom tapped me on the shoulder. "There's the young man I told you about," she whispered.

My stomach felt like it had turned upside down in my body. It was the man the FBI was looking for, yet it wasn't. Something was off; I just couldn't put my finger on what.

17

"What's he doing here? Where did he come from?" I wasn't aware I'd spoken out loud until she answered.

"He's here for the same thing the rest of us are," she laughed. "Maybe he lives in Hilltop, or one of the other towns around here."

She had a point, but if he lived in one of the other towns, why did he come to our store instead of shopping there? Our store is larger than most in the other towns; but they do have some sort of general store. It was my turn at bat, and I didn't have time to consider the issue further.

We take softball seriously in Flanagan's Gap. I needed to concentrate on what I was doing instead of looking at the man across the field. The first two pitches were way off base, and I managed to hold steady, not reaching for them. When the third pitch came at me, I swung with all my might. I even surprised myself when I connected. The ball flew out to center field, and I made it to second base before I had to stop.

By the time I crossed home plate, nearly twenty minutes had passed since I saw the bearded man. Once again he had disappeared before I could get a good look at him. Something nagged at the back of my mind. It could be the man I'd seen on TV. It could also be the man I'd seen in Prescott; then again, maybe not. I just couldn't grasp what was different. Probably just the fact that it had been a computer rendering, and not an exact picture, I told myself. If he lived in Hilltop or one of the other small towns nearby, as Mom suggested, he wasn't as interested in softball as the rest of us. He hadn't stuck around for the entire game.

Megan is our official scorekeeper, as well as in charge of first aid in case someone gets hurt during the game. While she's busy with those duties, everyone takes turns watching the twins, and the other little ones. Mom enjoys playing surrogate grandma to all the children in town since I haven't given her any grandchildren of her own. Too bad everyone is so interested in my love life, or lack of one. It only points out what I considered one of my own inadequacies.

The game went into extra innings, but finally the Flanagan's Gap Elk pulled out a win. We celebrated with homemade ice cream and fresh iced tea and lemonade on the front lawn of the church. "Did you see the man I was talking about?" Mom asked when she put her dish into the trash. "He can't be the man you saw on that show." She brought my thoughts back to the bearded man.

"Why not?" Maybe she could supply the missing piece I couldn't figure out.

She laughed. "He's too young. He would have been a teenager when those crimes were committed."

I wanted to give myself a head slap because I hadn't seen the obvious. She was right. From the brief glimpse I'd gotten of the man, he did look much younger than the fugitive the FBI was looking for. My imagination must be playing tricks on me, I told myself. I can't accuse every man with a beard of being a fugitive. Most men in Flanagan's Gap had some type of facial hair; but not that many had beards, long hair, and were grubby. No one had complained of clothes or food missing since Megan caught the man in her kitchen, so maybe whoever was stealing these things had left the area. With most of the town at the game today, would things turn up missing? Time would tell.

I couldn't decide if I was glad or disappointed this wasn't the man the FBI was looking for. Hunting for a fugitive certainly would have added the excitement everyone said was missing in my life.

# CHAPTER THREE

Summer vacation finally arrived; no more classes until the fall. We had a week off before crafting classes would begin. With Mom minding the store and no classes I felt at a loss with nothing on my morning schedule. At the last minute I decided to do a little exploring. Pulling on my hiking boots, I loaded my fanny pack with energy bars, nuts, my small first aid kit, two bottles of water, sun screen and bug repellent. It was a big fanny pack.

I clipped my smart phone to the waist band of my jeans. With GPS I was assured I wouldn't get lost. It's easy to get turned around out in the wild. If I did find anything indicating someone was living in the forest, I wanted to be able to pinpoint exactly where. I twisted my long, straight hair into a knot on top of my head, put on a hat to keep the sun off my face and headed out.

"I'll be back in time for lunch," I called to Mom. My long walking stick was in the umbrella stand by the front door. A walking stick comes in handy when navigating the ups and downs of the trails, and checking around the underbrush for snakes. When Megan went with me, we hadn't gone very far before turning back. Today I wanted to check further into the forest for any signs of someone actually living out there.

No matter how many times I tell myself I'm going to give up on this quest, (I shy away from the term 'obsession'), I still find my mind conjuring up the drawing of Warner Franklin I'd seen on TV. He's an experienced outdoorsman and a survivalist. He could live off the land for years, and no one would ever know he was around. If that's the case, I argued with myself, why has he been stealing things in town where people could see him? I didn't have the answer to that, but I wanted to check out our little piece of forest just in case. I don't want anything to happen to the families living in

Flanagan's Gap or the tourists who help support our town.

"Do you have your whistle?" Mom called before the door closed behind me.

Turning back inside, I grabbed the whistle hanging beside the door. "I got it. Thanks." I slipped the lanyard over my head. Her chuckle followed me out the door. She has always maintained that a shrill whistle is a good defense against almost any wild animal. With their acute hearing, the shrill sound hurts their ears causing them to run away. I'm not sure if she's tested out her theory, and I don't want to be the one to find out it doesn't work. I also don't want to be without the whistle just in case it's the one thing that will chase away a bear.

There was plenty to indicate people had been in the forest recently. Unfortunately, most of it was trash left by careless hikers and campers; in other words, tourists. I'd brought a trash bag with me, and began cleaning up the forest floor as I walked. That wasn't what I'd come out there for, but as long as I was there, I might as well pick up the trash. If someone was hiding out here, would they be careless enough to leave something behind for me to find?

How far did the average hiker go into the forest? I wondered. Since coming home after college, I haven't had a lot of time for hiking, or anything else for that matter. The Forest Service explored all parts of the forest, but did they go into the deep back woods? Or did they just watch for fires from their lookout towers? I'd have to check with Jack.

"Hi, Becca." Thinking I was alone in the forest, the sound of another voice not far behind me sent my heart into overdrive. Jumping and whirling around, I raised my walking stick over my shoulder like a baseball bat ready to strike out at an assailant.

"Whoa there. It's just me." Chad Baker held up his hands in surrender. Seventeen and already over six feet tall with a build that promised to send the girls nuts, he smiled at me, but didn't come any closer. "I saw you come out here, and decided to see what you're up to. Sorry I scared you." He didn't look very sorry. In fact, he looked like he thought it was funny.

Chad had been my student the first year his family moved here before transferring to the public school forty-five miles away. He was more interested in sports and girls than learning, and there wasn't enough of either to hold his interest here. The only time I see him now is if he comes into the store or during the summer. "So what are you up too?" he asked a teasing grin tugging at the corners of his mouth. He knew exactly how badly he'd scared me.

"It's called hiking, Chad. You might want to try it some time. Why did you follow me?" I wasn't sure if I should be afraid of him, or if he really was just curious about where I was going.

He shrugged. "Didn't have anything better to do." He kicked at a fallen log. "There isn't a whole lot to do in Flanagan's Gap." He seemed more like a bored little boy than the world weary teenager he was trying for.

"Maybe you just aren't looking in the right spot. Have you thought about giving your folks a helping hand around the farm? I'm sure they'd appreciate it."

The Bakers moved here from California when Chad was in eighth grade. I'm not sure what the stereotypical Californian is, but they do fit the profile in my mind. Rex and Nancy are leftovers from the hippie era. They started a little organic farm, and set up a windmill to produce most of the electricity for their home.

Chad groaned at the mention of working on the farm, and I coughed to cover the laughter bubbling up in my throat. "I don't want to be some kind of farmer," he grumbled.

"Well, how about a job in town? Did you look into something there? People always need help with something."

He'd walked up beside me, towering over my five feet three inches. I took a step back to move him out of my personal space. "Give me a break," he groused. "I just got out of school. I want to hang out for a while."

"And you're already bored with 'hanging out'," I made air quotes in a joking manner. "That tells me you need to do something constructive, or you're going to get into trouble." Our little burg can't officially be classified as a town, probably not even a village. With a population of full time residents of six hundred, more or less, including men, women, children and even a few cats and dogs, everyone has to pull their own weight. During the summer, the population can swell to over fifteen hundred when the summer people and campers arrive. It can get really busy then.

"Everyone has to work to get by in this world, Chad. In most small towns, everyone wears more than one hat or there aren't enough people to fill all the jobs. Nothing gets done if you sit on your rump."

He groaned again. "You sound like my teachers in town."

"In case you haven't noticed, I am a teacher. I also run the general store with my mom; have a craft workshop this summer, and play on the softball team. That keeps me busy and out of trouble. Have you thought about joining our softball team?" I started walking deeper into the woods, hoping he'd get tired of following me, and go back to town.

"Softball is for girls," he scoffed. "I play baseball in high school."

"That's a sexist attitude, or maybe it's just that you don't think you'd be any good at softball, and don't want us old folks showing you up." Maybe offering him a challenge would do some good.

"You aren't old, Becca; you're just a couple of years older than me." One minute I thought he was making fun of me; the next it seems he's flirting with me. I let the comment go, and kept walking, letting the silence stretch out. I didn't know what more I could say.

"Where are you going?" he finally asked when he became uncomfortable with the silence. "Are you looking for something?"

"Just trying to get some exercise," I answered. I'd never

get rid of him if he thought I was looking for something in particular. "I'm joining the hiking club as one of the leaders. I need to reacquaint myself with the different trails. As with most small towns in the west, Flanagan's Gap got its beginnings as a mining camp. There are plenty of old shafts and tunnels in the area. I don't want anyone falling into one. Besides, the hikes are a good way to reinforce some of the things the students learned in science. I also want to make sure we won't be running into any wild animals close to town." That speech definitely sounded like it came from a teacher.

His eyes grew large as he turned around in a circle looking into the dense woods. "Wild animals?" His voice squeaked, and he cleared his throat to make it work properly. "What do you mean wild animals?"

"You've lived in Flanagan's Gap how long?" I asked, trying hard not to laugh at him. "You should know by now there are wild animals out here."

"Sure, deer and coyotes. They aren't dangerous." His head was swiveling around like he was at a tennis match.

This time I laughed out loud. I thought he'd lost a little of that big city sophistication in the years he'd lived here, but I guess I was wrong. "Even the deer and coyotes can be dangerous if they feel threatened. There are also snakes, javelina, elk, wolves, and bears out here. You aren't living in Los Angeles anymore." More than once, bears have wandered into town looking for a free meal from trash dumpsters. But even a bull elk or a big deer can be dangerous.

"Maybe we'd better head back to town." He turned in a circle again, trying to decide which way town was. Panic drained all the color from his face. If he'd been out here alone, he wouldn't know how to find his way back.

"Did you bring a compass? Your cell phone with GPS? Anything?" My frustration escaped on a sigh when he kept shaking his head. "Did you even bring some water?" Again he shook his head. "A teenager without any electronics; what's up with that?"

24

He kicked his toe in the dirt. "Mom took my cell phone away from me. She said I didn't need to "stay connected" in the summer."

I could only shake my head. "Tell your mom I said the next time you decide to go hiking, you need to have your cell phone with GPS with you. How did you think you were going to find your way home?"

"You know the way, don't you?" By now his cocky attitude had disappeared, and true panic clouded his dark brown eyes. For a minute, I thought he was going to pass out.

"Yes, of course I do. But I also brought my phone, along with other items you should have when you go hiking." I turned around. "Come on. Let's go home." This hadn't turned out the way I wanted. Next time I go looking for fugitives in the forest, I'll make sure I'm not followed.

When we walked out of the forest, the ball park was on the right and Main Street was straight ahead. Chad's sigh of relief was audible when he sighted the familiar buildings. "You won't say anything about this, will you Becca?" His reputation was on the line now.

"It will be our little secret. But the next time you decide to wander into the forest, make sure you know how to find your way back. I don't want to have to head up a search party to go looking for you."

"Maybe I could join the hiking club with you. I think I'd like that." He looked at me with something akin to hero worship. Just what I need, I thought.

"We'll see. Go help your folks with the farm for now. I have to help Mom in the store." I left him standing in the middle of the street. I could feel his gaze on my back. Had I just created a groupie for myself? I certainly didn't want him to get a crush on me. Everyone thinks I need a boyfriend, but I'd like him to be a few years older.

Frustrated by my aborted exploration, I headed home, entering our house behind the store. I hadn't been gone long, but it was still warm enough that I needed a shower before I went to work. I was going to have to figure out a way to do my exploring without a partner next time.

An hour later Chad was back with an air of false casualness, and a big smile on his young face. "Hi Becca, Mrs. Dutton, Mom sent me in for..." He sputtered to a stop while he tried to think of something she would need from the store.

I waited to see what he'd come up with. Rex and Nancy Baker grow nearly all of their own food. They also have chickens and a small herd of goats. Last year they started making goat cheese and butter. Nancy is now experimenting with a line of lotion and soap made with goat's milk. Anything beyond what they can use themselves, she brings to the store for us to sell.

"Does she have anything for us here at the store?" Mom asked giving him the excuse I wasn't going to offer. I wanted to kick her, but I'm not into parental abuse.

"Yes! That's what I meant to say. I think she has some eggs and butter." At least he hopes she does, I thought. I'm not sure how he's going to explain to his mother that she needs to bring those things to us.

"Tell her we're always happy to get anything she wants to bring in." Mom smiled at him, expecting him to leave. He just stood there grinning at us.

Before the silence could get extremely awkward, the bell over the door jangled and blonde-haired, blue-eyed Misty Taylor came in, giving us a reprieve. "Hi Chad." She batted her long lashes at him. If she came in to buy something, she forgot all about it the minute she saw him. Mom and I were suddenly invisible. The uncomfortable moment was avoided as they walked out together.

"Ah, young love," I laughed. "I wonder if Chad will even remember to tell Nancy she needs to bring some things for the store."

"Did Nancy really send him here, or was he looking for a certain young storekeeper?" Mom asked. She raised one eyebrow, a big smile on her face. "It looks like you just dodged a big case of puppy love." I swear, sometimes she acts all wrapped up in her own little world and other times, like now, she picks up on the smallest details.

"I ran into him when I was hiking this morning," I hedged. "We walked back together." I'd promised not to tell anyone he'd been unable to find his way back to town, so I wouldn't.

"Is that why you came back so fast? I'd say you made quite an impression on him," she laughed.

"And I'd say he quickly forgot all about it when he saw Misty." I laughed with her. I was grateful that pretty little Misty wandered in when she did to distract Chad.

I've never considered myself attractive, just passable; average. At five feet three, I'm not tall or short. I have hazel eyes and brown hair, nothing outstanding there either. I keep my hair shoulder length so I can pull it back in a ponytail and out of the way.

Between the two of us, Megan has always been the real looker. Until Jack laid claim to her heart in high school, the other boys were always after her. I was the plucky sidekick who went along for the ride.

~~~

For the next two weeks, I stayed busy getting the craft schedules and supplies lined up. Just because it was summer, and there was no school didn't mean we had time on our hands. The pace seemed to heat up along with the temperature.

Megan and the twins were in every day helping out when she wasn't working with her dad in his office. Like me, she came back to Flanagan's Gap after graduating from college. She works with her dad as a Physician Assistant, as well as teaching science in the co-op.

As the only doctor for the small towns around Flanagan's Gap, Doc Granger has always been a busy man. Megan had been able to cut his work load considerably. After her mom had passed away while we were in high school, he had buried himself in his practice. Now he was beginning to find the same "outside interests" Megan was suggesting for me. Maybe there was hope Mom would find someone also.

Thoughts of the possibility of a fugitive living close to town had to be put on the back burner of my mind, but occasionally those thoughts would intrude. I still wanted to do a little exploring on my own; there just weren't enough daylight hours to do it.

After that day in the store, Chad and Misty had become an item. You rarely saw one without the other. Chad even joined our softball team. He likes showing off his talent to his lady love. Seeing them together always brought a smile to my face and my heart.

The man Mom pointed out during the first game of the season was becoming a regular, staying longer with each game. I tried to study him from a distance, but it wasn't easy. He kept to himself, sitting away from the other spectators. He rarely spoke to anyone. Flanagan's Gap is a friendly town, but we also respect the privacy of others. If he didn't want to talk to anyone, we wouldn't force ourselves on him.

I wished now I had recorded the episode of "America's Most Wanted" so I could go back and study the picture of the fugitive. Nothing new had turned up about him on the internet, and the sightings from around the country had died down. Either the FBI was stymied as to his whereabouts, or they had bigger fish to fry.

Those crimes had been committed fifteen years ago. He'd be in his fifties, maybe even close to sixty by now. I needed to get closer to know if he's that old. From where I was sitting though, he didn't look anywhere near sixty. "Crap," I muttered under my breath. I'd really wanted it to be him.

"What?" Jack looked at me.

Color flooded my face. Until then I wasn't aware I'd spoken out loud. "Nothing, I just remembered something I needed to do. It's not important." He returned his attention to the play on the field, quickly forgetting about me.

Today the man stayed until the game was over, and I saw my chance. If I couldn't talk to him, I'd follow to see where he was going, and what he was doing. If he didn't have something to hide, why was he so standoffish? Where did he live? "I'll meet you at home," I told Mom. "Can you take my bag with you?" I didn't wait to hear her answer.

Like he knew I was coming after him, he hurried away from the ball field, disappearing into the forest like a ghost through a key hole. Standing at the edge of the trees, I looked around for any sign of which way he'd gone. There were no foot prints, no broken branches; nothing was disturbed to give me a clue. "How did he do that?" I asked the trees.

I kicked at a fallen branch, disgusted with myself, and turned back to the ball field. I was going to have to be a little more inventive or sneaky if I intended to follow him. Why didn't he want me to catch him? I asked myself. What's he got to hide?

The answer to that is easy, I thought. He's a wanted man. He might not be the man the FBI is looking for, but he has another reason to hide. So why has he started coming to our softball games? I wondered. Why not stay hidden in the forest? My thoughts were going in circles. I couldn't decide if he was the man I'd seen on TV or not. The Hermit hadn't been around in months either. What was up with that? Where had he gone?

"Where did you run off to?" Megan asked. People were still milling around the field.

I shrugged. "I thought I saw someone I knew." I didn't look at her, hoping she couldn't read my thoughts.

She laughed at me. "You are such a liar," she accused like she had that day we went hiking. "You went after that guy across the field. You think he's the criminal you saw on TV. What did you think you were going to do if you caught up with him? Didn't you say he's armed and dangerous?"

"Mom still thinks he's too young to be the fugitive. She said he was polite and shy. I just want to know if I've made all this up in my head."

Before we could continue the conversation, Chad and Misty stopped next to us. They were holding hands. "When are you taking the next nature hike?" Chad wanted to know.

"I'll be taking the little ones out tomorrow," Megan said. "Do you want to join us?"

"I was hoping Becca was going." His face turned pink, and his gaze didn't quite meet mine. It seemed like there was still a little bit of hero worship going on. "She really knows what she's doing."

I coughed into my hand. "Um, I think I'll go out on Wednesday. Do you both want to go along?" I hoped he was including Misty. I didn't want to encourage him in any way.

"That'd be great," Misty spoke up. "I tried to tell him I know what I'm doing, but he thinks it's best if we go with a trained guide." Her blue eyes never wavered from his face. More than one person here has a serious case of hero worship, I thought. Misty has lived in Flanagan's Gap all of her sixteen years. She knows the forest as well as anyone in town. I kept that thought to myself though. She obviously didn't want to embarrass Chad.

"Come on, Slow Pokes," Mom called to us. "The ice cream is melting." With a last look at the forest where the man had disappeared, I followed the others to the ice cream social getting set up in the shade of the tall trees. Several women prepare homemade ice cream each week, and the men take turns cranking the old fashioned ice cream makers while the game is being played. It's always ready to eat by the end of the game.

For the next several weeks the mystery man failed to show up at our games, leaving me guessing about his identity. Just like The Hermit and the fugitive, he'd disappeared.

~~~

With the older kids, I could go deeper into the forest on our hikes. I kept hoping I'd see something to indicate someone had been living out here. I didn't know where The Hermit's cabin or shack was. Jack never told anyone.

"Do you think The Hermit has moved deeper into the forest?" I asked Megan. She had joined me on a hike with several tourists. I kept my voice low, so they didn't hear what I had to say. They might not take kindly having a hermit close by.

Megan laughed. "If he moved any deeper, he'd come out the other side. As it is, Jack is the only one who even knows where his shack is." She confirmed my suspicion that none of the other rangers knew where The Hermit lived.

"Are there wild animals out here?" A lady asked, her voice shaking slightly with nervous energy.

I wanted to say, 'Duh, lady, this is the forest. What do you think you're going to find?' Chad spoke before I could put that thought into words. "Becca is a good guide. She isn't going to let anything happen to you." A couple of the men looked skeptical, their eyes skimming over my average, slightly out of shape frame. Fortunately, they kept their thoughts to themselves.

Since they seemed to be a little worried about their surroundings, I decided it was best to keep the walk close to town and cut it short. No one complained; they appeared glad to get back to civilization. Or what passed for civilization in Flanagan's Gap. They weren't impressed with our little town any more than they were with the forest. Why did they come here if it's too primitive for them? Within minutes, they were on their way out of town.

"Well, they weren't very impressed with us," Megan chuckled. "Maybe they should stick with the bright lights of New York City where they came from." I'm grateful most of the tourists who come to town are a little more friendly, and not quite so "sophisticated" when they come here. Some even decide to stay, helping to grow our town.

Most of the tourists don't mind that many of our stores close on Sunday. I should qualify that by saying the parents don't mind. Teenagers have no reference to that concept, and spend a lot of time grousing about having nothing to do. That's why we do our best to include visitors in all our activities.

One visitor who still didn't join in was the bearded man. When he bothered to come to the games, he usually left before the game was over. I couldn't help but wonder why. Was he aware I tried to follow him? If so, he knew I couldn't follow him while we were still playing. Sneaky little devil. I guessed I'd have to be just as sneaky. I wasn't sure how, though.

The start of the week gives us some respite after a busy weekend, with weekenders headed home, and people who work in the bigger towns headed off to work. It's a good day for me to do a little deep forest exploring. "I'll be back before noon," I called to Mom. "I have my whistle."

"What's got you so interested in hiking again? I thought you'd given up on finding The Hermit." I'd been hoping to avoid this discussion. Maybe I can still distract her.

"I've put on some weight, and want to take it off. I'm not going to wear my swim suit until I do."

"Oh, pooh. You aren't overweight. Men don't want to hug a skeleton; they want something they can hold on to."

"Well, these extra pounds haven't helped me at all," I laughed. "I need to try something different. Maybe if I'm a skeleton, Mr. Right will notice."

She shook her head, her salt and pepper hair bobbing around her face. "Have you thought about applying at one of the schools in Prescott? Mr. Right might be waiting for you there."

I'd walked into that one, I told myself. Lately, this has been her mantra. Get Becca a job somewhere else so she can find her man. "No, Mom, I'm not moving to Prescott. Who would run the co-op? I enjoy what I'm doing, and I like to think I'm doing a good thing. I've seen what the public schools are teaching, and I'm not impressed. You're not getting rid of me, so give up. Okay?"

She walked over to me, giving me a hug. "I'm not trying to get rid of you. I just want you to be happy." She kissed me on the cheek.

"I am happy, Mom. This is my home; this is where my

friends are." I decided to turn the tables on her. "Am I standing in the way of you finding a new Mr. Right?"

"Oh, go on your hike." She gave me a playful shove towards the door. Her cheeks were tinted pink. Maybe I had hit on a touchy subject.

Laughing, I headed outside. The sun was just edging over the mountain tops, giving them an ethereal glow. It was still early enough that the temperature was comfortable. If I don't have anyone suddenly tagging along, I should be able to go farther into the forest than I have so far. Maybe today was the day I'd finally get some answers.

The old adage "Be careful what you wish for," played in my head several hours later.

# CHAPTER FOUR

After trekking through the forest for an hour, all I had to show for my time was a bag full of trash, sweat running down my back, and two sore feet. Maybe I needed some new boots. So far, all I'd seen was a small herd of mule deer, a couple of javelina rooting around for food, and a bear. Luckily, it was going in the opposite direction, and wasn't interested in me. Thank you, God. My hair was plastered to my head under my hat, and my pony tail lay heavy against my neck. If there was something or someone out here to find, they were doing a very good job of staying hidden.

I still had an hour's hike back to town. Just a few more minutes, I bargained with myself, then I'll head back. I kept walking, which had become a limp by now. My feet really hurt. "I can't take another step," I spoke out loud. Fallen trees were scattered around the forest floor, and I sank down on the closest one. I guess the little bit of hiking I'd done since school let out hadn't done me that much good. Sitting there, I surveyed my surroundings. Sunlight filtered through the tall trees leaving a lace-like pattern on the ground. Small wild flowers poked their heads through the fallen needles.

Pulling my cell phone off my waistband, I started taking pictures of the purple, yellow, and pink flowers at my feet. Identifying all the different kinds of flowers growing in the forest could be a school project this fall. Looking up at the canopy overhead, a sun beam shot through the branches. At that moment, it looked like arms of pure light reaching down to embrace me. I sat captivated for a long moment, enjoying the feeling. As soon as I snapped the picture, the light shifted. The image was gone.

My feet no longer hurt, I felt rested after just a few minutes. At that moment, I felt like I could walk for another hour into the forest, but that would mean two hours to get back to town. I couldn't guarantee my feet wouldn't start hurting again long before that happened.

Somewhere close by, the snap of a branch breaking when stepped on sounded as loud as a gun shot in the silence of the forest. Whirling around, I looked over my shoulder to see where the sound came from. Was a wild animal there? Had the bear come back looking for a tasty morsel? Or was it another kind of wild animal, the two legged kind, and ultimately more dangerous than any animal in the forest?

At the edge of my vision, movement captured my attention, but when I turned my head, all was still. Would a wild animal be smart enough to know I was looking for it and stand still? Or were only humans cunning enough to lie in wait for the opportunity to pounce on their prey? My heart was beating so hard I imagined my shirt was moving in and out on my chest. If someone or something was out here with me, I was sure they could hear it pounding.

My only defense was my walking stick and whistle. This might be when I get to test out Mom's theory about the shrill sound driving away wild animals. I hoped that was what was out here. I didn't think a whistle would frighten off a predator of the human kind. I clicked several pictures of the trees all around me. Maybe the camera's eye would pick out something my human eye didn't see.

Switching from my camera app to maps, I saved the coordinates of my location. I wanted to be able to find this spot again. Like you're really going to come out here again, my thoughts mocked me; not very likely, at least not alone.

The forest was eerily silent as I started back to town. Even the birds and small animals sensed danger of some kind was near. I decided to take a different trail than I used coming in. Maybe something will indicate what or who was out here with me. I better not find out Chad followed me, and was trying to scare me. It wasn't a comforting thought, but it was better than thinking it was the fugitive or even a bear.

It didn't take me as long to get back to town as it had to get deep into the forest; probably because I was really trucking it. Fear overrode curiosity, and I didn't stop to look for anything indicating someone was living out there. I knew there was, just not who or what. I was going to find out where Chad had been this morning. If he was out there trying to scare me...well, I'm not sure what I would do to him, but he wouldn't be doing it to anyone else any time soon.

I burst from the forest at the same spot the bearded man had disappeared on Sunday. Everything looked so normal, tears prickled behind my eyes. Until that moment I hadn't admitted to myself just how scared I'd been. Chad and Misty were having batting practice on the ball field. Megan was playing with the twins in front of her dad's office. Even Mom was outside enjoying a few minutes between customers.

I wasn't sure what those pictures would show; I just knew I had to see what the camera's eye had captured. Chad and Misty waved as I hurried past. He didn't seem the least bit worried that I might have seen him in the forest. So it probably wasn't him, I told myself. Megan called to me, but I kept going. "I'll be right back. I need a shower." I hurried off before anyone else could sidetrack me. Pictures first, I thought, then a shower.

Opening up my laptop on the desk in my room, I plugged in my phone, downloading the pictures. "Oh. My. Gosh! How had I missed that?" I was probably sitting right over where it had been partially buried by pine needles and forest debris. It had blended in so well, I hadn't even noticed it. I stared at the screen for several long seconds, unable to believe my eyes. Each picture of the flowers was now overpowered by something else. "I have to show this to someone," I spoke out loud in the empty room. But who? There was no police department in Flanagan's Gap. Until the petty thefts started, we'd never had a problem with crime. Since this was in the forest, my best guess was I should let Jack know.

The last series of pictures proved I hadn't been alone in the forest. As I'd snapped the pictures, he had turned away. The camera captured enough to prove it was a man, not an animal, watching me. The longish, dirty hair could belong to the man who came to our softball games, or it could be the fugitive from the TV show. It could even be The Hermit. From the vantage point of the pictures, I could make out his beard, long hair, and floppy hat, but little else. Darn!

It didn't matter who it was. What mattered was the body lying practically beneath my feet. It looked like the animals had gotten to the exposed part of the body. There wasn't enough left to tell if it was a man or a woman. That would take someone with a lot more knowledge of bodies than I had. I wasn't sure what was still buried under the pine needles and dirt.

I saved the pictures before unplugging my phone and turning off the lap top, to head back outside. The shower would have to wait a little longer. At least I could tell Jack where to find the body.

"Where is it, Becca?" This was the log I'd sat on, but the only things here now were the flowers, what was left of them anyway. Someone had trampled on them after I left. "Are you sure this is the spot?"

"Yes, I sat right there! Look at the picture. These are the flowers. Someone was here after I went back to town. I also recorded the coordinates. This is the place. A man was standing behind me in those trees. If he hadn't stepped on a branch, I never would have known he was there."

"Well, whatever was here, it's gone now." Jack turned away from me, studying the forest. "The Hermit's shack is farther into the woods, but he wanders all around. I wonder if it was him." He sounded sad, like he'd just lost a friend. For a minute, I thought he was going to dismiss what was in the picture as some sort of trick of light. I should have known better. Jack was one of the most fair-minded people I've ever known.

"Those were real bones from a real person. What do we do now?" I asked. Jack looked as confused as I felt. The worst crime rangers usually had to deal with was someone starting a forest fire or maybe poaching the wild animals. A murder hadn't been committed in Flanagan's Gap in the entire history of the town. Technically this hadn't happened in town, but it involved everyone. No one would feel safe any longer.

"This is the jurisdiction of the FBI." He gave a weary sigh. "Since the body disappeared, I'm not sure what they'll do about it though. I guess I'll turn it over to the sheriff's department, and let them decide whether or not to call in the feds." He didn't sound any happier about that option than he had about calling the FBI. He shook his head. "I can hear Graham now, laughing at us. He'll probably say those bones have been there for years."

Deputy David Graham again, I thought. We all went to school together. Now David thinks he's a big deal because he's a deputy sheriff.

"If they've been here for years, why are they gone now?" I asked. "They didn't get up and walk off by themselves." Jack shrugged, but he kept his thoughts to himself. I could guess what they were though. His opinion of David matched my own. He only did as much work as was absolutely necessary, and only what would benefit him.

Reluctantly, Jack took the pictures to the sheriff's department, turning the case, if there was one, over to David. "I don't know why they don't transfer that idiot somewhere so he can learn proper law enforcement procedures," he grumbled unhappily. "He's no smarter than he was in high school. This doesn't mean I can't do a little checking on my own," he muttered after making the announcement at the emergency meeting Sara called that evening.

"For the time being," Sara advised, "we'll suspend any hikes with the club. We don't want to put anyone in danger. If anyone else goes into the forest, take precautions, not chances." Only two years older than me, Sara looked like she was a little overwhelmed. Along with the rest of us, she was walking in unknown territory.

As Jack had figured, David Graham wasn't impressed with the pictures. Since the body had disappeared, nobody expected him to forward the pictures to the FBI.

I silently vowed I wasn't going to let this get pushed under the rug. What the camera had been able to pick up wasn't a trick of light or my imagination. I hadn't imagined seeing the man watching me either. I have the pictures to prove someone else was out there. This weekend I'm not going to let the bearded man ditch me again, I vowed, even if it means I don't play softball.

~~~

My plans were thwarted, though, when the game was played in Hillside instead of Flanagan's Gap, and the bearded man didn't show up. Maybe he was raiding our houses while most everyone was at the game. By the time we got home it was late afternoon, but I was determined to do a little nosing around. I quickly changed out of my softball uniform into jeans and hiking boots, and headed for the forest.

"You aren't going into the forest, are you?" Chad came up behind me, causing me to jump with surprise, and just a little bit of a guilty conscience. Sara would probably consider my idea as taking chances.

I don't know where he could have gotten the idea I was going hiking, I thought, looking down at my jeans and boots. "Um, I just want to clear some cobwebs from my head."

"But it isn't safe out there." He had the same wild, frightened look in his eyes he had the day he followed me into the forest. "What if you run into The Hermit or that guy who was out there before? He saw you when you found that body. He might come after you."

"I'm not going to do anything dangerous. I'm just going for a little walk. I'll be back soon."

"You can't go out there alone," he insisted, pulling himself up to his full height. "I'll go along to protect you in case you run in to that guy again."

I couldn't stop the groan from escaping my lips. "Chad, I

was born here. I know these woods like my own living room. I don't need you to come along for protection."

"Just because you know where you're going doesn't make it safe. What if you run into some bad guy? You wouldn't stand a chance against him." His jaw was set in a stubborn line, and the muscle in his cheek was bunched up.

"Oh brother," I heaved a sigh. "All right, Chad, let's go home." I looked at the already darkening forest. "It's getting too late to do anything anyway. I'll see you later." Disappointed, I headed home. If Chad thought I was going into the forest on my own, I had little doubt he'd be right there to 'protect' me. I found that sweet as well as laughable. He couldn't find his way out to save himself, let alone both of us.

The summer schedule was finally in full swing, and I was busy enough throughout the week that I forgot about looking around for signs of Warner Franklin or The Hermit or the bearded young man. Reluctantly, I agreed with Mom that the man who had been coming to our softball games was much too young to be the fugitive, let alone The Hermit.

By Sunday afternoon I was ready to follow "the bearded man" if he showed up at the game. I wished I had something else to call him instead of 'the bearded man.' Even though I used that term only in my own mind, it was beginning to sound ridiculous. I decided to not play, giving me the opportunity to follow him if he left early. There were enough others to step up and take my place. Sitting with the crowd, I kept a close watch on the sidelines. My heart skipped a beat before rushing on when he finally sat down across the field from me. This was the day; I felt it in my bones. I was going to find out who he is, and what he's doing in our forest.

The Flanagan's Gap Elk were ahead in the seventh inning. He'd be taking off any minute now. I slowly made my way to other side of the field. When he stood up to leave, I planned on being right behind him. I didn't want to give him the chance to disappear again.

I was only a few yards behind him when he walked in

among the trees. Excitement bubbled up inside; he couldn't get away again. I stopped for a few seconds letting my eyes adjust to the dim interior of the forest. Looking around, I slapped my leg in frustration. "Crap! He's done it again." In a matter of seconds, he had managed to disappear. Where could he go that fast? Turning in a circle, there was no place he could hide, just trees and scrub brush. So where was he?

"Why are you following me?"

With a startled shriek, I whirled around. The bearded man was standing between me and ball field just a few feet into the edge of the forest. "I...I'm not following you," I stammered, hoping he couldn't read the lie on my face.

"Of course you are. You've been trying to follow me for a couple of weeks." His voice was more cultured than I expected for someone who lived the life of a hermit in the forest.

"Why are you hiding out in our forest?" I hoped I sounded far braver than I felt.

"Your forest?" One light eyebrow lifted slightly. "I wasn't aware this was private property. I thought this," he waved his arms around to encompass the entire forest, "was part of the national forest." His tone was condescending.

"It is part of the national forest, but it's also our backyard. We don't take kindly to people sneaking around, hiding out right outside our homes." The fractured sun beams didn't assist me at all as I tried to decide exactly how old he was and what he looked like.

"I wasn't aware I had to get your permission to camp out around here. I'm not breaking any laws." Defiance made his tone sharp.

"You are if you're the one taking food and clothing from our homes when no one's home."

"I haven't taken anything! I'm not a thief," he stated indignantly.

Ignoring his statement, I continued my interrogation. "What's your name? How long have you been living out here?" I didn't want to get close enough for him to grab me, but I wanted to get closer so I could actually see what he looked like. With the dim lighting of the forest and that full beard, he could be thirty or fifty. At the games, he always wore a ball cap pulled low over his eyes, not the floppy hat the man in my pictures wore.

"What's your name?" he countered.

"W...why do you want to know?" I was quickly losing ground and my nerve.

"Why do you want to know my name?" This was getting me nowhere fast.

The sun shifted just enough, casting a bright beam between us, like a spot light illuminating us. My breath escaped on a relieved sigh. He wasn't the fugitive, and definitely not The Hermit. He was probably only a couple of years older than me. But why was he living in the forest? Did he have anything to do with the body disappearing? I didn't know if I should say body or bones. What I could see in the picture was more bare bones, but they had belonged to someone; that meant it was a body.

"What's your name?" I asked again, this time without the accusation in my voice.

"You tell me yours, I'll tell you mine." A smart-aleck smirk lifted the corners of his mouth into the heavy moustache on his upper lip.

I was feeling anything but playful at the moment, and I bristled at his teasing tone. I finally gave a heavy sigh. The only way I was going to get any information out of him was to answer. "My name's Becca Dutton. My mom and I own the General Store."

"I know. Your mom's nice." The implication that I wasn't nice had the hackles on the back of my neck raising. He still hadn't told me his name, so I asked again, tapping my foot while I waited for him to answer.

He waited several beats before saying anything. Probably trying to decide whether to tell me the truth, I thought. "Griff

Tomlin," he finally stated grudgingly.

"All right, Griff Tomlin, why are you hiding out in the forest?" I wasn't successful in keeping the accusation out of my voice this time.

"I'm not hiding out. I'm camping out."

"Seriously?"

"Yes, seriously. What's wrong with that?" His hands were braced on his narrow hips now; his temper on the rise again.

"You've been camping out for…what five, six weeks now? Who does that alone?"

"Someone who likes to camp, and isn't afraid of his own company."

"So why do you come to our softball games if you like your own company so much?"

"Maybe I just like sports." I gave a snort of disbelief, and he asked, "Have you seen me mingling with the other people, trying to make friends? I don't need other people to make me happy. I'm just fine out here alone as long as people afford me the privacy I want."

Ignoring his jibe, I decided to switch tactics. "Have you seen anyone else out here? Maybe The Hermit?"

"Who's the hermit?"

"By definition, it's a person who rejects civilization and prefers to be alone. Sound like anyone you know?" I tossed the jibe right back at him.

"If that's the definition of a hermit, and there's one out here, how is it you know about him? If there is such a person, wouldn't that mean he hasn't made himself known to you or anyone else?"

I shrugged, "It's a story almost as long as my life. Answer my question; have you seen anyone else out here?" I was tired of his evasive tactics.

"Just snoops looking for things that are none of their business." The smirk was back. I wanted to smack it off his bearded face. There was something else in his expression, something I couldn't identify or define.

"Oh, for crying out loud! I'm not snooping. I'm looking out for myself, and a town full of people I care about. We've had some trouble in the past few months. I want to know if you're the one causing that trouble, or if it's someone else." I wasn't going to say anything about the possibility that Warner Franklin was in this neck of the woods.

"It's not me, but maybe it's your hermit." Now he was clearly making fun of me.

"It's not The Hermit," I snapped. "Did you go into Megan's house and eat her leftover stew?" I wasn't convinced he wasn't the thief plaguing our town.

"Who's Megan?"

"Darn it, answer my question." Frustration had me ready to swear at him as well as throw something.

A chuckle rumbled deep in his throat, and I stomped my foot wishing I had my walking stick so I could take a poke at him.

"No, I haven't been in anyone's kitchen in the last six months," he finally answered. "Does that make you feel better?"

"Six months? You've been out here that long?" I couldn't believe anyone would go "camping" for six months, I don't care how much they like their own company. That smacks of being a hermit to me.

"That's not what I said." He was teasing me again, and I could feel my temper on the rise. After several beats he continued. "I just said I haven't been in anyone's kitchen for that long. Now if you're through with this inquisition, how about going back to town, and forgetting all about me?"

"Not going to happen. I know you're out here, and I'll be watching for things to go missing in town. If that happens, I'll be back."

"What happened to the premise of 'innocent until proven guilty'?" His eyebrows drew together in a dark frown.

"When there's only one person out here, it's a good bet he's the guilty party."

"Did you forget your hermit? Maybe he's the one who's taking those things."

"Nope, it's not him. He doesn't work like that." Or maybe he's already dead, I thought. Those bones belonged to someone. I said a little prayer that it wasn't The Hermit. The whole town was attached to the man even though we didn't really know him.

"So you've met this elusive person? This hermit?" He continued making fun of me.

"I wish," I muttered. "No, I haven't met him, but everyone knows his habits. He doesn't steal things. That's more than I can say for some people." If he thought I was accusing him, so be it.

"I haven't…Oh, forget it. I don't have to justify myself to the likes of you. Go home, and leave me alone. I'm not hurting you or anyone in your town." He turned away, and within seconds he had disappeared in the dense foliage.

"How does he do that?" I asked the empty forest. I took several steps in the direction he'd gone, but there was nothing I could follow. No footprints, no broken branches; nothing. Dressed for the softball game in shorts and a tank top and not jeans and boots, I couldn't very well go after him, even if I knew where he'd gone.

The silence of the forest enveloped me, giving me an eerie sense that I wasn't alone. The usual chatter of birds in the trees, insects buzzing around, and small animals scurrying in the underbrush was missing. Unwilling to be caught by the fugitive, I turned back to the opening leading to the ball park. My heart nearly stopped beating. A dark figure stood between me and the way out. It couldn't be Griff Tomlin; he'd gone in the opposite direction.

"W…who are you?" I tried to sound brave, but my voice cracked. "What do you want?"

"Stay away, stop snooping around." His voice was a gravelly growl, like it was rusty from lack of use. Before I could think of anything to say, he melted into the forest without another word. I was left alone, and feeling very unsafe in my own backyard.

# CHAPTER FIVE

Monday morning I wasn't any closer to figuring out what to do about Griff Tomlin, or the other man, than I'd been when I walked out of the forest yesterday. Maybe Griff Tomlin wasn't dangerous or a thief, but that didn't explain who he was, and why he'd been hanging out in the forest this long. I didn't believe for a second he was just 'camping out'.

My next question; was the guy watching me that day I found the body, and again yesterday the same person? My guess would be yes. He was upset that I'd been snooping in the forest so much lately. With the sun at his back, his face had been in the shadow, I didn't think I could describe him. He definitely had a beard and longish hair, but I couldn't say what color his hair was. The FBI certainly wouldn't take me seriously with so little information.

At least now I knew there was someone besides The Hermit and Griff Tomlin living in our forest. Instinct, or something close to it, told me this other person was infinitely more dangerous than either of the others. Before I said anything to the sheriff or the FBI, I needed to get more information, more of a description.

I also want to know if that body was The Hermit. If so, how did he die? Who killed him? I wish now I'd made an effort to get to know him. Maybe he was just a lonely old man who needed a friend. I dismissed the fact that he didn't want to be around people. I was feeling guilty on so many levels.

~~~

"Do you think you could describe the man you caught in your kitchen well enough for Mom to draw him?" I asked Megan while I waited for my turn at bat the following Sunday. I couldn't believe I hadn't thought of that at the time it happened. Mom was an amateur artist, and at the risk of sounding biased, she did beautiful work. With Megan's description, maybe we could figure out if it was the fugitive, Warner Franklin, in our forest.

"You're still on that kick?" She frowned at me. "You're just like Jack. He's still obsessing about that body you found. You're obsessing over that fugitive." She gave a put-upon sigh. "He's afraid it might be The Hermit. He really liked that old guy. You both need to let the sheriff's department handle things."

"What are they doing about it?" I argued. "Jack said they weren't very concerned since the body mysteriously disappeared. David probably thinks I made the whole thing up." I hadn't said anything about seeing the dark figure last Sunday when I followed Griff Tomlin. I hadn't said anything about talking to him either. "David should have called in the FBI," I added, knowing full well they wouldn't have done any more than David was doing. No one believed me even though they had the pictures I took.

"Well, do you think you could describe him to Mom?" I asked again, wanting to get back on topic.

She gave a slight shiver. "I'll be seeing that face in my nightmares for the rest of my life. If it will make you feel better, I'll come over tomorrow, and see what she can do. Right now, it's your turn at bat." She nodded her head towards the field, her blond curls bobbing around her face.

My mind wasn't on the game, and I struck out. Not something I normally do; I can usually get on base, if not make it clear around. Our team was behind by two runs.

When I flopped down beside Megan again, she gave me a sympathetic smile. Fortunately she didn't say what she was thinking. What I already knew. I needed to concentrate on the game.

Was she right about the fugitive? I wondered. Was I trading one obsession for another? The Hermit and Warner Franklin were both experts at avoiding detection. While I was in college, I'd forgotten about The Hermit. After coming home though, I had taken up the search again, just not as publicly.

"Oh, by the way, your friend's here again." Megan broke in on my thoughts, her brown eyes twinkling with mischief, drawing my mind back to the present.

"What are you talking about?" I looked around. Was she talking about Chad? He'd been here for the entire game since he was playing. Probably everyone in town knew about the little crush he had on me, even Misty. She was smart enough not to be upset about it though. If she was busy, Chad followed me around like a puppy.

"Over there," Megan nodded at the other side of the field. "Isn't he the one you've been trying to follow into the forest? Is that where you secretly rendezvous after the games?"

My cheeks heated up at her teasing. Maybe I should have told her why I'd followed him. I certainly didn't want her, or anyone, thinking I was chasing some stranger who was "camping out" in the forest. "I was just trying to figure out if he's the one who has been taking things. What if he'd been the fugitive?"

"Becca, use some common sense." She sounded frustrated with me. "If he was hiding from the FBI, do you really think he'd come to our softball games? If he was stealing from us, he wouldn't want to draw attention to himself by coming to our games either. Besides, he isn't much older than we are. The guy who was in my house was more our parents' age. So," she concluded, "he's too young to be either the fugitive or The Hermit."

Unfortunately, our team lost. I hadn't been any help, but I didn't hurt the team again. I managed to keep my thoughts on the game where they belonged. I wasn't surprised to find Griff Tomlin gone before the last out. Today I wasn't going to follow him. He'd just melt into the forest like he had in the past. I wasn't particularly interested in meeting up with the dark shadow again either. I couldn't suppress the shiver that traveled up my spine at the thought.

~~~

Two days later, Deputy David Graham came striding into

the store. He usually had a puffed up opinion of himself and his position. Today was no different, except he acted all serious. His thumbs were hooked in the belt loops of his uniform pants, emphasizing his self-important swagger.

"Mrs. Dutton, Becca," he gave a polite nod in our direction. "I have a few questions about those pictures you took in the forest." The muscles in his arms bulged, stretching the fabric on his sleeves until it was ready to rip. His neck was the size of a small tree trunk. Wasn't sure how much time he spent at the gym, but in my estimation he needed to slow down a little.

"What do you need to know?" I stayed behind the counter, not wanting to get in the way of any flying buttons from his shirt when he took a deep breath. He must deliberately buy his uniforms one size too small to show off those muscles.

"Where were you when you took them?"

"In the forest." I wanted to say, "Well, duh," since it was rather obvious where I was. "I believe Jack gave you the coordinates when he brought you the pictures." I'm not sure what else he expected me to add. I couldn't tell him anymore than I told Jack.

His scowl darkened. "I need to know exactly what you saw. Who else was out there?"

"I thought I was alone until a branch snapped behind me," I said, explaining what I saw and did that day. I'd given the pictures to Jack, and I know he'd turned them over to the sheriff's department. "What's going on? Why are you interested now?"

"I need to see your camera." He ignored my questions.

"I took the pictures with my cell phone."

He held out his hand. "I need that."

I bristled at his ultimatum. "I'll show you the pictures on my phone, but you can't have it." I started to draw it out of my pocket.

"It's evidence. You'll need to turn it over."

"Evidence of what? I'm not just giving you my phone."

"What do you have to hide?" His rusty colored brows

drew together in a straight line above his light blue eyes.

"I don't have anything to hide, but I'm not just giving you my phone."

He flexed his arms to make himself look bigger, more intimidating, and I swear I could hear a few stitches pop. If he did that too many times, his shirt would fall right off his body. I almost laughed at the image, but wisely coughed instead. Insulting him would only make matters worse.

"She can forward those pictures to you," Mom suggested, always the cool head in any difficulty. "Will that help you, Deputy Graham?"

Deputy Graham? I thought. Was she playing on his self-important attitude? The man grew up in Hillside, and was only a year older than me. We'd known each other most of our lives. I wasn't about to act like he was some sort of big wig.

"I need the original pictures to make sure they haven't been tampered with." He wasn't going to back down.

Well, neither would I. "So you think I faked the pictures?" I snapped. I wanted to get right in his face, but I still wanted to stay out of popping range of those buttons in case they didn't hold.

"Now, Becca, I didn't say that." He was suddenly all conciliatory, realizing he'd pushed me a little too far. "I just need to check these things out."

"You can check things out all you want, but unless you get a warrant, I'm not just giving you my phone. I didn't do anything wrong. With your attitude, I don't know how you ever get anyone to cooperate with you.

"Sounds a little like a guilty conscience talking, Becca."

Before I could launch myself over the counter at him, Mom stepped in again. "David, maybe you need to take it down a notch. Accusing someone of wrong doing for no reason has never gotten you what you want." She sounded like she was scolding one of the little kids that come into the store. She really did know him well.

Red crept up his thick neck at her reprimand, and he

kicked at the floor for a minute. I knew exactly how he felt. Any time I got too big for my britches, Mom was able to take me down a peg.

"Can I see the original pictures, Becca?" Such a difference, I thought. I still wasn't going to just hand him my phone. Knowing him as I do, he'd act like he was looking at it, and walk right out the door.

"I'll be glad to put them on a memory card for you. I took a few pictures of the flowers, and the figure behind me."

"Then where were you when you took the picture of the body?" he scowled at me.

I'd just explained this to him, but I'd go over it again; a little slower this time. "I was sitting on a log because my feet hurt from hiking so far. The flowers were pretty, and I thought they would make a good school assignment. It wasn't until I looked at the enlarged picture on my laptop that I saw the body, the bones," I corrected.

"So what do you think happened to them when you went back with Jack?"

"Gee, I don't know. Maybe they got up and walked off." Sarcasm dripped from my voice, and I got pleasure from the red that crept up his neck again. "Someone, probably that shadowy figure behind me, came back after I left, and moved them. The flowers were tramped flat when we came back. I know I didn't do that. Why so interested now? You didn't seem to care when Jack brought you the pictures."

"Have you noticed anyone else in the forest lately? Maybe a stranger?" He ignored my questions again.

"There are a lot of strangers in the forest this time of year. It's summer so there are tourists and campers here all the time. You should know that." I could feel Mom's eyes on me, and knew what she was thinking. I wasn't about to tell David about the bearded man, Griff Tomlin, I silently corrected. I don't know why I was suddenly protective of him; I just knew I couldn't sic David on an unsuspecting stranger.

"Has The Hermit been around lately? We haven't heard of

anyone spotting him for a while." His tone had changed from accusatory to cautious.

Mom and I looked at each other, then shook our heads. "He hasn't been around for several months," she said, equally cautious. "I've been concerned because someone usually has...contact with him in that length of time."

David chuckled, sounding almost human for a change. "You mean food or clothes haven't turned up missing, and someone has a new statue." Flanagan's Gap isn't the only town The Hermit had visited in the past. I could almost feel the small carving sitting on the shelf behind me. How many others were around?

"Yes, that's what I mean," Mom admitted. "But that hasn't happened for a long time. Do you think that body was his?"

David shrugged. "I guess we won't know unless it turns up again so it can be tested." I handed him the memory card holding the pictures minus the one of the sun beams. That one was for me and whoever I wanted to share it with. David wasn't one of them. He wouldn't see the arms of heaven the way I had anyway.

"What's this all about?" I pressed him again. He still hadn't given me an answer. "Why are you so interested now?"

Holding the card between two fingers, he tipped his head. "Thanks for this, Becca. Give me a call if you see anything suspicious." With the same swagger, he walked out.

"That turd! He got what he wanted, and just walked out without giving us anything."

"He's a policeman, Honey. They ask questions, not answer them," she chuckled.

"He's always done that, even in school."

"What exactly did he get from you in school?" One eyebrow rose slightly.

"My homework! He always promised one thing or another, but never came through after he got my homework." Indignation made my voice sharper than I intended. Mom laughed, but didn't comment.

"Maybe we should have told David about the young man who comes to our games," she added, looking out the window where David was getting into his car.

"No!" I spoke too quickly, too sharply. "You were right, he's much too young to be the man the FBI is looking for, or the man Megan saw."

She didn't argue or comment, just smiled that knowing little smile that says she knows what I'm really thinking.

"Do you think the FBI has sent out flyers, or whatever they send to other law enforcement agencies, to notify them this fugitive could be in our area?" A worried frown furrowed her brow.

"That's the problem," I said. "They don't know where he is. *We* don't know where he is. He could be here or anywhere."

"But you still think that fugitive is in our forest." It was a statement, not a question. "It can't be the young man who comes to our games though." She believes me now. She'd seen the pictures I'd taken of the shadowy figure in the forest. Had that convinced her?

"I don't know who it is, but I know someone else is out there." I guess I'm going to have another talk with Griff Tomlin again; my thoughts were in turmoil. Hopefully, this time he'll be a little more forthcoming.

# CHAPTER SIX

Since Griff Tomlin only came into town on Sunday for the softball game, I was going to have to wait for nearly two weeks before I could talk to him. The team was going to Payson for the game this week. So far, he hadn't gone to any of the away games, even the ones closer to home.

If I didn't want to wait, I could go to him. My stomach fluttered a little at the thought of going into the forest. I didn't want to run into that shadowy figure again after his warning. I wouldn't be looking for him, but how would he know that?

Leaving our homes and businesses unattended gave me very queasy feeling. Would the dark figured man take advantage of our absence, and ransack our homes? He hadn't taken anything since Megan caught him in her house nearly two months ago. Was that the reason he stopped? Or was he stealing from some other town? Was that why David had come looking for the pictures on my phone?

Wednesday was always a slow time for businesses in town. The weekend campers were gone and the next batch wouldn't arrive until Friday. "I think I'll go for a hike this morning," I called out to Mom. We don't open the store until noon on Wednesday. I would have plenty of time to look for Griff Tomlin, or someone else, and still be home in time to shower and help her in the store.

I wasn't going to be deliberately looking for Warner Franklin, I told myself. In my mind he was the dark figured man. Maybe when Mom and Megan finished the sketch of the man, I would know for sure.

Taking hold of what little courage I had, I filled my fanny pack with the usual items I take on a hike. "I'll be back before you open up. I have my whistle and walking stick."

"Maybe you shouldn't go into the forest until David or the Forest Service finds who else is out there." She came out of her room still wearing her robe. "If you were right all along, and it is that fugitive, he could hurt you." A worried frown clouded her normally happy face.

"I'm not looking for him, Mom. I want to talk to...the guy who comes to our games. If he's been in the forest for a while, maybe he's seen this other man. Or maybe even The Hermit." Everyone in town was afraid to voice the thought that the bones I'd found belonged to him.

She started to object, but I cut in before she could say anything. "David Graham isn't going to tell us anything even though the whole town is at risk if someone dangerous is hiding out around here. He'll apologize later if necessary, but that's all." Even I could hear the bitterness in my voice. David only did what was good for David.

Before she could argue further, I went outside. It was still early; the sun just coming over the tops of the trees. Stopping on the porch of our house, I drew in a deep breath of the pine-scented, cool air. At six-thirty the temperature was a cool seventy degrees, by mid-afternoon it would climb into the mid-nineties.

A few people were out and about, heading to work, or just getting ready for the day. If my luck held, Chad would still be sleeping, so he couldn't try to tag along. I didn't think Griff Tomlin would show himself if Chad was there.

"What do you want now?" I'd only been walking for ten or fifteen minutes when someone came up behind me.

With a startled squeal, I whirled around, holding my walking stick like a bat. That and my whistle were my only weapons. Griff laughed at my softball batting stance. "You think that's going to scare away a bear?"

My heart thudded noisily in my chest, and it took a couple of seconds to find my voice. "This isn't funny." I stomped my foot on the soft pine needles. "Why do people insist on sneaking up behind me when I'm out here?"

"Maybe if you'd stop sneaking around, people wouldn't feel the need to sneak up on you. I, for one, want to know why you keep coming out here looking for…What, exactly, are you looking for this time?"

"You. I have some questions."

"I don't have any answers; even if I did, I don't have to give them to you. Now, go back to town." He started to turn away.

"Wait! Please, wait." Before he could melt into the forest again, I needed to get him to listen to me. My breath came out in a sigh of relief when he turned around, his dark glare not quite so hard.

"Well, what's your question? I don't have all day." His foot was tapping impatiently on the forest floor, imitating my earlier action.

"What do you have to do that's so pressing? You're camping out, not going to work." My tone was waspish.

"Camping out is my work. Ask your questions, or I'll leave you standing here alone."

I tried to draw a calming breath. The man brought out the worst in me. "Have you seen anyone else camping or living out here? Not a weekend camper, but someone who has been out here even longer than you." I didn't know how else to phrase the question.

"Are you starting that again?" He sighed dramatically. "I stay away from people, and I like it that way."

"That doesn't mean you haven't seen someone. I'm not asking if you've made friends. I just want to know if you've seen anyone."

"Why? What's it to you?" Suspicion clouded his bearded features.

"Look, things have been happening that haven't happened before. I'm just trying to figure it out. I don't want anyone getting hurt."

"Yeah, like what things?" His anger had turned into curiosity, or was it suspicion.

"I'm not accusing you of anything. I guess I'm asking for your help. At least, your input." I started with the unexplained thefts, the man in Megan's kitchen, the fugitive the FBI is looking for, ending with the disappearing bones. "So if you've seen someone suspicious out here, I'd like to know."

"You thought I was suspicious, but I haven't done any of those things." The little I could see of his features had closed down sometime during my explanation.

"Okay, you're right. I'm...sorry."

He gave a humorless chuckle that didn't lighten the mood. "That was hard for you to say." Heat moved up my neck, and I narrowed my eyes at him in an attempt to cover my embarrassment.

Getting serious again, he gave me an answer. "I don't know anything about the thefts or anything else. You sure those bones weren't just some dead animal you stumbled across?"

"If it was an animal, why would someone take the time to move it after I left? Besides, you can make out the skull of a person hidden by the leaves and pine needles." I shivered, remembering the image on my laptop. "I didn't notice it until I put the picture on my computer, it was that well hidden."

"You said there's a hermit living out here. Maybe he's doing this."

"Or maybe those are his bones," I countered. "No one has seen The Hermit for a long time."

"Becca, where are you?" Groaning, I turned at the sound of Chad's voice.

"Give me a minute..." I turned back to Griff, but he was gone. The man could be a ghost or a figment of my imagination as quickly as he disappears.

"Becca, Becca," Chad kept yelling. I wanted to smack the kid.

"I'm right here. Stop yelling. What do you think you're doing?" Misty was with him when he came through a dense outcropping of brush.

"I was afraid that guy got you." For a minute I thought he was going to hug me, but he pulled up just in time.

"What guy?"

"I don't know; whoever's out here. The guy who moved those bones you found."

"Who were you talking to?" Misty spoke up. "We heard you talking to someone." She looked around, but of course Griff had vanished.

"Just some camper," I explained vaguely. "I thought maybe someone camping out had seen something."

"Did he?"

"No." I shook my head. "I didn't want to spook anyone so I didn't ask specific questions." I could have told him I'd been interrupted before I could get him to confide in me. If he knew anything, that is.

Once again, I hadn't been gone as long as I'd hoped when we came out of the forest. Mom was sitting on the front porch with a glass of fresh lemonade. "How was your hike? Did you find anything?"

"Just the usual assortment of campers." Chad and Misty were still with me so I didn't elaborate. I'd explain later, but there really wasn't anything to tell.

~~~

Despite the bones that had mysteriously walked away, most of the people in town had been lulled into a false sense of security because nothing more had happened. I knew better. That man was still lurking around in the forest. I didn't want to go to the game, but what would be my excuse? I'd seen a shadowy figure in the forest? I'd been warned to stop snooping? No one knew about that warning, not even Griff.

"There's that nice young man." The game had barely started when Mom pointed at Griff Tomlin sitting by himself, closer this time than he usually did. He was sitting on our side of the field now.

Feeling my gaze on him, or maybe he was watching me, waiting for me to notice him, he nodded, then turned his attention to the action on the field. If he smiled, I couldn't tell from this distance, and the fact that his face was covered with a heavy beard.

My stomach rolled nervously. What was he doing here? Why had he been looking at me? For the rest of the game I could feel his eyes on me every time it was my turn at bat. Was he deliberately trying to make me nervous? If so, it was working. Darn it anyhow!

"I think you have a fan," Megan teased, poking me in the ribs. She nodded down the row of people watching the game. Griff wasn't watching the game though. He couldn't make it any more obvious that he was watching me instead.

"Probably not. There are other people around us. Maybe he's watching you."

"Nice try," she laughed. "He hasn't taken his eyes off you since he got here. I don't think he's even aware what's going on anywhere else on the field, just where you are."

True to form, he left before the game was over, but he stayed longer than usual. My thoughts raced, trying to figure out what he was up to.

Flanagan's Gap won the game, but just barely, no thanks to a couple of screw ups on my part. We'd celebrate with our usual ice cream social on the church lawn when we got home. Would Griff Tomlin show up for that, too? I wondered. It would be a first.

~~~

Any kind of celebration would have to wait though. Nearly everyone who hadn't been at the game was gathered in the street in front of our store. Someone had smashed out the front windows while we were gone. The door hung at a drunken angle on the hinges. I wished now that I had listened to my instincts and stayed home.

Mom and I rode with Jack and Megan to Payson, and I jumped out of the back seat before he even pulled to a stop. "Stay outside, Becca," Jack ordered. "He could still be in there."

"Bet me. That's my home and business." I shoved my way through the crowd, and into the store. The sight nearly brought me to my knees. Food was all over the floor, glassware was smashed, display cases were overturned, and clothes had been thrown into the mix. Whoever did this had used a hatchet or sledge hammer to smash everything in sight. Canned goods were broken open; the contents spread over everything. Nothing was left in one piece.

"Who would do this?" Mom stood in the doorway, her face ashen, and her hands trembling. Ever practical, she started to pick up the broken glass so no one would get cut. "No, Dora, leave everything just the way it is," Jack admonished gently. "We have to call the sheriff's office."

I snorted. "Do you really think David is going to do something if it requires anything that resembles real investigating?"

"He might be a muscle-bound, pompous jerk, but he can't ignore this." I followed as he walked through all the rooms in the store and our home. Nothing had been spared.

There were gaping holes in all the walls, in the store as well as our house. Nothing had been spared there either. Mom and I had talked about remodeling, but certainly not like this. Something sticky dripped over the sides of my bed, the mattress had been slashed open. My clothes had been cut up and thrown on top of the mattress. The case of my laptop had been pried open, the hard drive smashed on the floor destroying anything I had stored on it. Makeup was smeared on the bathroom mirror with obscene remarks. This guy, whoever he is, really hated me.

Mom's craft supplies were in ruins, knitting needles and crochet hooks broken, and yarn left in knots. Her colorful paints made bright splashes on the walls, contrasting with the black from the charcoal sticks. The picture she and Megan had been working on was shredded on the floor of the craft room. This had taken a lot of time. He knew we would be gone for several hours, and felt confident he wouldn't get caught.

I sagged against the wall as I came back in the store feeling like my life had spun out of control. "I wish I'd never seen that stupid TV show," I muttered. The front counter was in pieces, the cash register smashed. Where was the little carving The Hermit had left for Mom several years ago? Turning around to check where the shelf had been behind the register, I noticed something stuck to the wall. This guy had left a note on the back of a soup label. I must have made some noise, because as I reached out for it, Jack took hold of my arm. "Don't touch it, Becca. There could be fingerprints." We both leaned towards the wall to read what was written.

*"Stay out of the forest and stop following me, or you'll be sorry."*

"Of all the nerve!" My first thought was Griff Tomlin. Why would he do this? When would he do it? I amended my thought. He got to Payson shortly after the game started, and stayed until it was almost over. He didn't have time to drive back to Flanagan's Gap, and do this much damage before we arrived. Someone else had done this. My first guess was the dark figure I'd now seen twice in the forest; the fugitive, Warner Franklin. He knew I was looking for him.

"Go outside with your mom, Becca. Take care of her." His order gentled with his last words. "I've already called this in. They'll send someone out." He paused for a heartbeat. "Hopefully it won't be David." The two men had never gotten along, even in high school. David's swagger and self-important attitude didn't help.

Mom was in good hands. Megan and Doc Granger were making sure she was all right. I turned to some of those standing around. "Does anyone know who did this? Did anyone see anything?" I had to shout to be heard over the commotion. By now everyone from the game had joined the crowd, all talking at once.

"I was working at the station," Bill Wheeler spoke up, his booming voice quieting the crowd. Everyone wanted to hear what had happened. "That time of day on a Sunday there's never much traffic, so I was inside trying to stay cool. I was working on an engine, making a lot of noise myself. I didn't hear anything until something came crashing through the front windows. By the time I got over here, whoever did this was gone. I'm sorry, Dora." He sent her a gentle look. At any other time I might have paused to wonder if there was something going on between them. Now my mind was filled with what had happened to our store and home.

I looked at the others standing there. "Did anyone else see what happened?" My question was met with a sea of shaking heads.

Our store was at the end of a row of other small stores. The two closest to ours were also closed on Sunday. Bill's gas station was the closest one that was open.

A half hour after Jack's call, David came roaring into town, sirens blaring and bubble lights flashing. Typical, I thought, anything to draw attention to himself.

Getting out of his car, he hitched his gun belt up, puffing out his chest. He surveyed the crowd, before walking over to me. "What happened here?"

"Gee, David, I don't know. I think someone broke into our store. What do you think?" He hadn't even looked at the store windows.

Diplomatically, Mom stepped in. "When we came home from the softball game in Payson, this is what we found." She pointed at the front of the store. "Everything's ruined." Tears clogged her voice, and I wrapped my arms around her. Tears stung my own eyes, but I refused to let them fall. I wouldn't give Warner Franklin the satisfaction. Or let David Graham see any weakness.

David gave a low whistle as he walked into our torn up store. "Someone really did a job here."

"Took you long enough to get here, Graham," Jack snarled. "Why didn't you send someone else if you were so busy?"

"This isn't the only crime I have to investigate, Riley. It doesn't look like this is a matter of life and death. No one was hurt, right?" Our small county had a relatively low crime rate so what was he investigating. I don't remember when the last murder took place. Did those bones belong to a murder victim? If so, who? A chill traveled up my spine. If that was the case, why hadn't we heard about it on the news? It had been two weeks since I found them, only to have them promptly disappeared.

"Whoever did this, threatened Becca. Is that serious enough for you?"

"A threat?" David looked at me. "Why would anyone threaten you?"

"How would I know? I guess he doesn't like the fact that I found that body. Did you even investigate that?"

Ignoring my question, he turned away to survey the room again. "Is anything missing? Can you tell if he took anything?"

"In this mess?" I asked. "How am I supposed to tell if anything is missing? I could do a complete store inventory, and I still wouldn't have an accurate account. Everything is broken or smashed, pieces are everywhere. He even destroyed our home." I turned away when my voice cracked, tears threatening to spill over again.

After walking through the entire mess, David leaned against the wall much the same as I had. "Where's this threat you mentioned? He got nasty with your makeup, but I didn't see anything threatening."

"If you did some actual investigating instead of just giving lip service, you'd see the note," Jack snapped. "If it was a snake, it would bite you on the as…" Megan cleared her throat, stopping Jack from going too far. We hadn't seen her standing in the doorway surveying the mess.

Turning around, David saw the note still pinned on the wall, right where the man had left it for me to find. "So who is this you've been following? Are you stalking someone?" If he didn't have a dark scowl on his face, I would have thought he was joking. In truth, he sounded like this was my fault.

"No, I'm not stalking anyone! Hiking in the forest isn't a crime. It's something we've all done most of our lives. I want to know who moved that body and why. Who died out there? You don't seem very interested in finding out."

"I'm doing my job, and I don't have to report to you what I find. This is a criminal investigation, Becca. You need to stay out of it."

"Isn't threatening someone a crime, David?" Mom asked softly. She was standing beside Megan just inside the store. "I don't want anything to happen to my daughter." She had a way of saying something quietly, and making you feel about two inches tall when you were in the wrong. I hope that was how David felt right then.

"I'll look into it, Mrs. Dutton. I don't want anything to happen to her either. I'll call in the crime scene techs to take pictures and lift any fingerprints."

Would Warner Franklin be careless enough to leave prints behind? I wondered. I doubted he was that stupid. He'd avoided capture all these years for a reason. He certainly wouldn't want the FBI to know where he was. I was sure they would be a little more interested in this than David appeared to be if they thought Warner Franklin was behind it.

"You might want to have some of the men keep an eye on the place overnight," David suggested.

"What for?" I asked, defeat weighing down on me. "There isn't anything left to smash, and nothing worth stealing." Like most towns in the area, Flanagan's Gap was built around mining operations more than a hundred years ago. All the old buildings, including The General Store, were built over mining claims. Anyone who had lived in town all their lives would know that. I didn't think Warner Franklin would know to look underground for anything valuable.

"Do you know if there's any possibility that a fugitive the FBI is looking for could be in our forest?" Mom stopped David from leaving as soon as the crime scene unit arrived.

He turned slowly to look at her. She wasn't intimidated by the dark scowl on his face. "What do you know about that, Mrs. Dutton?"

"No one in this town is stupid, young man, and we don't live on the other side of the moon. We get news programs here right along with the rest of the world. We've seen articles in the paper and watch television. The FBI is looking for a fugitive, and he could be living out there." She waved her arm at the forest surrounding our town. "Now, please answer my question." I wanted to applaud the way she had taken him to task, but I figured that would be overkill.

"They don't know where he is, and they certainly don't know if he is anywhere near Flanagan's Gap." He turned a dark glare on me. "Stay out of the forest, Becca. Whoever this guy is, you've managed to get on his bad side."

While I sputtered my anger, he stalked out, letting the techs do their work. This wasn't my fault, but he wanted to place the blame at my feet.

By the time the crime scene unit left, there was an even bigger mess, but it didn't matter that fingerprint powder was everywhere. There wasn't anything salvageable anyway. They took the prints of anyone who could have been in the store for a legitimate reason; which means nearly everyone in town. I'm not sure if they thought one of our friends might have done this, or it was for elimination purposes. They didn't speak to anyone as they worked.

It was getting dark when all the police units cleared out. They carried out several items that didn't look familiar. Whatever it was didn't belong in our store. "What did you find?" I stopped an older man who seemed to be in charge.

"Just some evidence, ma'am; it's nothing for you to worry about." He might as well have patted me on the head, and sent me on my way.

"This happened to my home, my business. Everything is something for me to worry about."

"Deputy Graham will be in touch." He kept walking, placing whatever he'd found in the back of his van.

"You can stay at our place," Megan said, drawing my attention away from the man and his burden. "We'll tackle this mess in the morning."

"Everyone available will be here first thing," Sara said. "We'll have this straightened up in no time." Most of the town was still outside, watching the proceedings. A murmur of agreement passed through the crowd at her words. I'd been able to hold back the tears in front of David's almost uncaring attitude. But now, their kindness had them spilling over.

It was useless trying to lock up for the night. There was nothing left inside worth stealing. Besides, the doors would have to be replaced right along with the windows.

# CHAPTER SEVEN

Bright and early the next morning, the insurance adjustor arrived to survey the damage. "Woo wee," he exclaimed. "You got yourself one big mess." For the next hour he took pictures of the damage. "Anything taken?" he finally asked. "Or can you even tell?"

Mom shook her head sadly. "I don't think that was the purpose of this. Any valuables were stored elsewhere." On his way out the door, he assured Mom we'd have a check before the week was out. That was one less thing to worry about.

As soon as he was gone, everyone who didn't have to go to work was at the store with brooms, mops, and shovels. That's a major benefit of living in a small town; friends and neighbors pitch in to help in any crisis.

"It looks like you could use a little more muscle in here."

That voice had my heart pounding, and my head spinning. Cautiously I turned around, expecting to see a man with a full face beard standing behind me. The man standing there was a stranger. "I'm sorry, we aren't open today. Or for the next few weeks," I muttered.

A big smile lifted the corners of his mouth. "Hi, Becca."

"Griff?" I stared at the man in disbelief. He wasn't dressed as he'd been every time I'd seen him before. He'd even shaved off his beard. "Wh...what are you doing here?" The only thing that I recognized was his voice.

He grew serious then. "I heard about what happened. I thought I'd come lend a hand." He'd come in at the one time all day that I was alone.

"Oh, well," I couldn't think of anything to say for several beats. "Ah, you clean up nicely."

For a minute he was taken aback, then he gave a bark of laughter. "Yeah, I guess I do."

"What are you doing here?" I asked again. Would he

disappear when other people came into the room like he did in the forest?

"You need help," he stated simply. "I came to offer mine."

"How did you even know what happened?"

"Just because I've been camping out doesn't mean I don't know what's going on around me." A teasing grin tilted his lips into the moustache still on his upper lip. "Now, what can I do to help?" His answer didn't tell me anything, but I let it go, for now.

I looked around. "Pick your poison. There's plenty to be done." So far Griff had done his level best to avoid people. Why had he come to help out now when there would be lots of people around? "Why did you shave?" The question came out of nowhere, and was totally irrelevant to what was going on.

He shrugged. "I just figured it was time." It was another non-answer.

Before I could continue with my questions, Chad wandered in, interrupted us again. "Who is this guy, Becca? Do you know him?" His tone was protective and slightly belligerent.

I couldn't keep the sigh from escaping my lips at his poor sense of timing. Every time I try to have a conversation with this man, Chad intervened. "His name is Griff. He's been camping out. I met him when I was hiking."

"I've never seen him before." I stared at him for a long moment. He sounded like a jealous lover. What was up with that?

Griff held out his hand. "I've been to a few of the softball games, and saw you play. You're good." Grudgingly, Chad accepting Griff's outstretched hand. Mixed emotions warred on his young face. He wanted to accept the compliment, but wasn't sure he should. "Thanks, I guess."

Before the discussion could deteriorate further, Mom, Megan, and Misty come into the store from where they had been working in our house.

"Hello?" Mom stopped, looking at the three of us. The

tension was a physical thing sitting in the middle of the room. Then a smile broke out on her face. "It's nice to finally see your face." She walked across the floor still littered with items thrown from the broken shelves, her hand outstretched in welcome. Somehow she'd recognized him even when I hadn't.

"Um, hello, Mrs. Dutton." He took her proffered hand. "I came to help out."

"Of course you did." She smiled at him. "See, Becca. I told you he was a nice young man." It was a toss-up who was more embarrassed, Griff or me.

"You know this guy, Mrs. Dutton?" Chad wasn't any happier about that than he'd been to learn I knew him.

"Well, we've never exchanged names, if that's what you're asking. But he's been in the store a time or two, and of course I've seen him at the games."

"The name's Griffin Tomlin, Mrs. Dutton. I'm sorry for your troubles."

"Thank you, and thank you for coming to help. We can use as many hands as possible to clean up this mess." Sadness clouded her light blue eyes as she surveyed our shattered store.

Misty walked up beside Chad, taking his hand. "We need some help out back." She tugged on his arm to lead him away from further confrontation. We could hear his heavy footsteps as he clomped out. Hopefully, Misty could find out what had gotten into him.

"How did you find out about this?" For the moment, we were alone again. Mom had gone back to our house with Megan. Misty went outside with Chad to help load all the broken and ruined furniture into dumpsters. We could hear the whispered words between them, and he looked more embarrassed than angry when he stomped outside.

"I told you…"

"Don't give me that bull about knowing what's going on around you. If you were really camping out, you wouldn't know about our break-in."

"I like to keep tabs on the people around me. I saw the

70

deputy and crime lab guys here last night. I'm glad you weren't here when it happened." A cloud of worry swept across his rugged features. "Does that deputy have any idea who did this?"

I turned away. "I'm never quite sure what David Graham knows, or what he guesses at. So what are you really doing here?" I whispered. People were wandering through the store again working to clean up the mess so repairs could be started. I didn't want anyone to hear us. Chad's teenaged jealousy was still fresh in my mind.

"I just came to help out."

"Don't give me that!" I whispered harshly. "Before, you would disappear if anyone came near you. Now, you get in the middle of the whole town, you've changed your appearance, you're putting on a whole different attitude. What's going on?"

He shrugged, trying to put on an innocent face. "I just finished camping, and thought I'd help you out before I head home."

"And where is home?"

He shrugged again, his face closed down. I knew that look. I wasn't going to get any information out of him even before he said anything. "I'm in between places right now. That's why I was camping. I enjoy the outdoors, and didn't have any place special I needed to be."

He was the master of non-answers. "You sure you aren't a politician?" I turned my back on him. I didn't want to hear any more of his lies.

~~~

It had been a long day, and everyone was tired. We still had more broken furniture and shelves to remove. Our house still needed to be cleared out, but it would have to wait. I stared at the half empty rooms. The anger was gone, leaving behind an empty hole in my chest. How could this happen? Why would Warner Franklin do this? What had I done that upset him this much? I couldn't even say with any kind of certainty that he was here in Arizona.

71

Before I could wallow further in my pity party, Pastor Curt stepped up beside me. "I know this is hard, Becca, but no one was hurt. Things can be replaced."

"I know." I released a heavy sigh. "I just can't believe anyone would do this."

"Evil is everywhere in this world," he said. It was a theme he'd preached on many times. It had never hit home like this before.

~~~

"We might have something on that body you found," Jack announced at dinner that night. Mom and I were staying at their house one more night before the insurance company put us up in the local bed and breakfast.

I choked on the bite I'd just put in my mouth. "What? Who is it? Did you find the body?" My words came out garbled around my mouth full of food. Mom shot a frown in my direction, but didn't comment. We all wanted to know who had died in the forest.

"Some guy from back east decided to hike across the country, camping out instead of staying in hotels. The last time his family heard from him, he was in East Texas somewhere. That was over three weeks ago. He could have made it to Arizona by now, or he could be in New Mexico, or still in Texas. I sure wish that body hadn't disappeared."

I had to agree. That picture wasn't very helpful. I wasn't even certain the sheriff's department was doing anything to find it. David wasn't very forthcoming with information.

"Why would somebody kill someone camping out?" Mom put words to the question in my mind. "Why move the bones later?"

Jack gave a tired shrug. "The only answer I have to that, Dora, is whoever did it was hoping the body wouldn't be discovered. Until we find where it was moved to, we won't know who it is, or how he died." For now, we were assuming the person was a man, but it could be a woman.

Three days later, the FBI descended on us. And Griff

disappeared. Again. He was here one minute, the next he was gone, just the way he had done when he disappeared in the forest. What's with that? My stomach did somersaults, and I suddenly felt sick. Was he wanted? Is the FBI here because of him, and not Warner Franklin? Why else would he hide?

"Miss Dutton? I'm Special Agent Greene with the FBI." He flashed his badge and identification so fast I couldn't get a close look at them. "I would like to ask you a few questions." The man was in his late forties, maybe six feet two, and couldn't weigh more than one hundred sixty pounds. Unable to find my tongue, I nodded. "I understand you saw a man in the forest, someone who didn't belong there." Again, I just nodded. Was he talking about Griff? Would I turn him in? Should I? "What can you tell me about him?"

I leaned against the wall, finally able to draw a deep breath again. "I can tell you he did this," I waved my arm to indicate the destruction of the store. Until I knew otherwise, I was going with the premise that they were here about Warner Franklin and the destruction of our store and home.

"How can you be certain of that? Did you see him?"

"He left a threatening note. Didn't you see it? Isn't that why you're here?" At least I hoped that was why he was here.

His expression was blank for a moment before he continued, ignoring my question. "I understand you took a picture of him. What did you see before you took that picture? What does he look like? Can you describe him?"

"I assume you saw the picture I took, or you wouldn't be here. I can't tell you anything more than what the picture shows."

Still ignoring my comment, he pulled out a copy of the picture I'd seen on the TV show that started my whole obsession with Warner Franklin. "Is this the man you saw?"

"You don't listen very well, do you." It was a statement, not a question. "I saw that picture on television. I don't know if it's the same man I saw in the forest. He was in the shadows. By the time I snapped the picture, he had his back to me. I don't know what he looked like because I couldn't see anything beyond a shadow," I said, reemphasizing the point.

"Have you seen him anywhere else?" His questions were relentless.

"He may have been in town, but I can't be positive about that." I tried to explain about the thefts and the man in Megan's kitchen, but he cut off my explanation.

"You also found a body in the forest, but it disappeared before authorities could get there. Why did you take pictures of it instead of calling it in?" He switched topics.

"I didn't take pictures of a body," I stated emphatically. "I took pictures of some flowers. I didn't even realize the body was there until I got home, and downloaded the picture onto my computer. That's when I called Jack, Forest Ranger Riley," I corrected.

"I need to see your computer."

"It won't do you any good."

"Why is that?" he asked, suspicion creeping into his voice. He straightened up, stretching to his full height, probably hoping to intimidate me. One blonde eyebrow rose slightly.

"There wasn't anything left in one piece in our store or our home. That included my laptop."

"So you don't have the picture." He sounded resigned to failure.

This conversation wasn't going anywhere. "It's on my phone. I can give you a copy of it."

"I'll need your phone." He held out his hand like he thought I'd just turn it over for the asking.

Here we go again, I thought. "I'll give you a copy of the pictures, but I'm not turning over my phone."

"What do you have to hide?"

"Nothing. Am I under suspicion?"

He gave what I suppose he considered a smile, but it looked more like a grimace to me. "Should you be?" He answered my question with a question.

"Oh brother," Heaving a frustrated sigh, I decided not to

dignify that with an answer.

Agent Greene's partner hadn't bothered to introduce himself, and had remained silent until now. He poked Greene in the ribs, nodding at the others in the room. No one was working. They were watching the proceedings, tension climbing higher with each question. "Why don't we take this outside?"

"I don't think so." I wasn't going anywhere with these men. "If you have questions, ask them right here. I haven't done anything wrong, so don't try to say I have."

They weren't used to the average citizen opposing them. Most people were probably intimidated by the mere fact they were from the FBI. For a long moment, strained silence filled the room while we stared at each other.

"Becca, we need some…" Mom stopped in the doorway of the store when she saw the strangers. "Hello. Are you from the construction company?" Dressed the way they were, in business suits, that wasn't very likely.

"Mom, these men are from the FBI. They're here about the pictures I took of the body in the forest and the shadowy man."

Ever the polite hostess, she walked across the room, with her hand outstretched to welcome them. "I hope you can catch the person who did this. He threatened my daughter."

"We just have a few questions for her." Agent Greene's answer wasn't very satisfactory or clear. "We need to take her phone so we can examine those pictures."

"I'm sure Becca can send them to you without you confiscating her phone. She already gave Deputy Graham and Forest Ranger Riley copies. David Graham also has the threatening note the man left behind when he did this," she looked around at the mess. "Did he show it to you?"

"Um, no ma'am," Greene's partner answered.

"Then maybe you need to find him instead of trying to intimidate the victims." She gave them the same reprimand she gave any school boy who was misbehaving.

Agent Greene would have argued, but his partner was smarter than that. "Thank you for your help, Miss Dutton. Please send those pictures to my phone." He handed me his business card. "If you see this man again, call one of us immediately. Remember, if it's the man we're looking for, he is armed and very dangerous."

# CHAPTER EIGHT

As quickly as he'd disappeared, Griff reappeared as soon as the agents left. "Why did you vanish?" I confronted him, my fists braced on my hips.

Innocence radiated from his face. "I didn't vanish. I remembered I had an appointment."

"Really. You're going with that lie."

"It's not a lie. I had someplace I needed to be. Now I'm back." His smile brought out dimples that had been hidden by his heavy beard.

I was momentarily distracted, but it didn't last long. "Your appointment was here in town? It had nothing to do with the FBI being here."

"Were they here? What did they want?"

"I don't know why I even bothered to ask. You're an expert at avoiding questions you don't want to answer, and you lie through your teeth when you do answer." I turned away before my temper had me saying something I might regret.

"Don't go away mad." Laughter lifted his voice, fueling my anger even further.

"There's no other way for me to go, since I am mad." Before I took two steps, Griff reached out for my hand, pulling me back to him. An electric shock shot up my arm at the contact.

"Did anyone ever tell you your eyes flash fire when you get mad?" He had me pressed up against his well-muscled chest, his mouth just inches from mine. I could feel his mint-scented breath on my face.

Heavy footsteps heading our way had us jumping apart, in guilt, or something else. My heart thudded against my ribs as heat crept up my face.

Misty's smile contrasted with Chad's glowering frown

when they saw us. Chad still didn't like or trust Griff. I couldn't say I blamed him. There was something going on with him. I just didn't know what.

"Nice of you to bug out just when the FBI showed up," Chad accused. "You could have answered a few questions about the guy who threatened Becca and did this." He swept his arm around the room.

"Chad, stop it." Misty took his hand, but he brushed her off.

"No, if he was really camping out for who knows how long, maybe he saw this guy the FBI is looking for. He could have helped." He stomped across the room, getting right in Griff's face. "Why didn't you stick around? What are you afraid of?"

"Actually, I'm afraid of a lot of things, but you and the FBI aren't two of them. I needed to go somewhere. I don't have to explain myself to you or anyone else." Until now, he had laughed off Chad's little jealous fits. Now his temper was riding just below the surface.

"Back off both of you. If you can't act like adults, you can leave." I glared at both of them, hoping they'd take the hint. If not, I was prepared to give them both the boot, literally and figuratively.

"Come on, Chad," Misty tugged on his hand. "Mrs. Dutton's waiting for...us." She couldn't think of anything Mom needed. Fortunately Chad didn't argue.

"He's got quite a crush on you." Griff's teasing fell flat under my dark glare. If he thought my eyes flashed fire before, they were probably ready to start a bonfire now. I was truly ticked off.

"Where were we before being so rudely interrupted?" He took a step towards me with the obvious intention of pulling me against him again.

"We were nowhere," I sidestepped his grasp. "I need to get back to work."

"What are you running from, Becca?" A teasing smile

curled his full lips into his moustache, his dimples winking out at me again.

"I could ask you the same thing, but you'd just lie, so what's the use?" Turning away, I headed for the door. I didn't trust myself to be alone with him right now, telling myself it was because I would smack him if he got too close.

~~~

Once we had the mess cleared out, Ted Kramer brought in a crew to begin repairing and replacing all the damaged shelves, counters, and walls in the store. It would take the better part of a month to get things back to normal. Warner Franklin had even managed to uproot the plumbing and rip out some of the electrical wiring. Our house would have to wait for repairs until the store was up and running again.

Ted and his wife Millie moved to Flanagan's Gap about three years ago when they retired. Ted had owned a big construction company in Phoenix. He still had his license, and kept his hand in the trade, just not full time. During the summers, their grandsons visited, and Ted was teaching them how to build and repair houses. Thank God for good friends and good insurance.

Against Megan's wishes, the insurance company moved Mom and me into Kozy Korners Bed and Breakfast. Even though we were best friends, we couldn't impose on Jack and Megan's hospitality for more than a month. The old saying "Company, like fish, begin to smell after three days," was true.

Unfortunately, Griff had decided to settle at the same B'n'B until he decided to move on. "Shouldn't you be camping out?" We had just finished one of Janice and Ernie's delicious breakfasts. Mom had gone back to our room for her knitting. Friends had supplied her with needles and yarn to give her something to do while we waited for the store to reopen.

"I'm ready for a real bed again. The ground was getting a little hard on my back." He gave a careless shrug, like it was no big thing.

"Yeah, right," I muttered. "I'm going for a walk." I turned away from him, but his next words stopped me.

"Stay out of the forest. It isn't safe."

I whirled around. Inactivity was wearing my patience and my temper thin. "What business is it of yours what I do or where I go?"

"Becca, wait. I don't want you to get hurt. Wa…" He gave a cough to cover what he started to say. "That guy warned you to stay out of the forest."

I marched up to him, getting right in his face. "You know who is out there, don't you. Don't deny it," I charged when he started to speak. "You know Warner Franklin is out there, and you know he's the one who wrecked our store." I grabbed his arm, dragging him outside so we wouldn't be overheard. "I think it's time for you to come clean. Who are you? What are you doing here?"

For a long moment he didn't deny or confirm he knew Warner Franklin was in our forest while he debated with himself. Finally giving a shrug, he answered with what appeared to be the truth. "Yes, I think Franklin is out there somewhere." He turned to look out at the forest. "I believe he's in Arizona, and has been for a while. I don't know how long. The man is about as dangerous as anyone I've ever heard of. You've managed to get in his crosshairs, so please, stay out of the forest until he's caught."

"And when will that be? Am I supposed to become a prisoner in my own town because this lunatic is here, and the FBI hasn't been able to catch him?"

"He's making mistakes he's never made before. They'll catch him. Or someone else will." His eyes grew dark. It wasn't hard to figure out he was planning on it being him.

"Do you work for the FBI? Is that why you didn't want those agents to see you, and blow your cover?"

He chuckled. "You watch a lot of television, don't you, Becca." It was a statement, not a question.

"Don't answer my question with one of your own." I

stomped my foot in frustration. We'd moved to the little shaded garden Janice and Ernie kept for their guests to enjoy. I wasn't seeing the flowers or enjoying their sweet fragrance though. All my attention was focused on Griff. Maybe he'd finally tell me the truth.

"No, I don't work with the FBI, but I did at one point. The only undercover work I'm doing now is my own."

"Why? What's it to you?" I pressed. If he was in a talking mood, I'd take advantage of it.

"Look, it's a long story, and we don't have time to go into it right now."

"I don't have anything better to do. Since you don't seem to have a job, I assume you don't either." I sat down in one of the lounge chairs, looking up at him. "Have a seat; I'm ready to hear what you have to say."

"You are one tenacious lady." It was his turn to sigh in frustration. He turned his back on me. The faraway expression in his eyes told me he was lost somewhere in the past.

Drawing a deep breath, he sat down, bracing his elbows on his knees. "I grew up in New Mexico," he stated softly. "About fifteen years ago, my whole family was killed, along with several other people in our neighborhood."

I covered my mouth to keep the gasp from escaping my lips. I was afraid I knew what this was leading up to.

"Franklin lived in our neighborhood." His voice was so soft now; I had to lean closer in order to hear him. "He was one nasty SOB. If any of the kids got in his yard, he'd come running out of his house, screaming at us to get off his lawn. If a ball or toy ended up in his yard, it was lost to us forever. When a cat or dog went in his yard, especially if they made a mess, he'd chase after them. He shot several of the neighborhood animals with a BB gun until the police put a stop to that. Everyone wanted him gone, but there wasn't much we could do. The homeowner's association was always on him about something because he refused to conform to their dictates. After one particularly nasty confrontation, the whole block blew up, his house included. Anyone in those houses died instantly. His body wasn't found in the wreckage, and everyone knew he was behind the explosion, even the FBI."

It hurt to see the obvious pain he still felt, and I reached out to take his hand in mine. Like a drowning man, he clamped onto my hand, his grip almost painful it was so tight, but I didn't pull away. "How did you survive?" I whispered.

"I'd gone camping with my Boy Scout troop. When I got home on Sunday night I had no home, no family, nothing."

"What did you do?"

"I vowed to kill that son of a b... someday." Giving himself a shake, he dropped my hand. I flexed my fingers to make sure they still worked. "Sorry about that. I didn't mean to cripple you." He gave me a weak smile. "I went to live with my aunt and uncle," he said, continuing his story. "After college, I joined the FBI. They have too many cases to concentrate on just the one I'm interested in. They took exception to my insistence that they look for Franklin. It was by mutual agreement that I left their employ."

"Where do you work now?" I didn't think he was among the unemployed and homeless.

"I started my own security company. It took me a while, but I can now pick and choose the jobs I take. I also have several employees, so I can take time off to search for that SOB." He avoided saying Franklin's name, like it hurt just saying it out loud.

"How do you know the man out here in the forest is Franklin?" If the FBI couldn't find him, how had Griff? "Have you seen him?"

"He's just a shadow among the trees. He's never let me get close enough to actually see what he looks like, but he is aware I'm here. I doubt he knows who I am though. He's beginning to make mistakes. It won't be long before he makes the one that will bring him down."

"What do you mean by mistakes? What kind of mistakes?"

"Coming to town and stealing things is a mistake. He's never stayed in one place longer than a month or two. I'm certain he's been here longer than that. Coming as close to town as he's been doing here is another big mistake. That's how I caught on to him this time. Now he did this to your place; he even left that threatening note."

"If it's really Franklin, why is he changing his habits now? If he is such a survivalist, can't he get his own food without resorting to stealing?" I realized I was arguing against the shadowy man being Franklin, when all along I had been convinced it was him. I didn't want a man capable of doing the things he did fifteen years ago to be that close to the people I care most about.

"Even the staunchest survivalist would get a little weary of eating off the land after fifteen years. He's not Moses with the Israelites either; his clothes had to wear out sometime. He's been stealing clothes in New Mexico, Arizona, and Colorado for the last ten years. Anywhere he finds clothes hanging outside, he grabs something. Now he's resorting to taking food."

"What about that body I saw in the forest? Do you think he killed someone, and then moved the body when I stumbled across it? Could it be The Hermit or that camper from back east?" I whispered the last, turning to look towards the forest that surrounded the town. I didn't want anyone else getting hurt.

This time, Griff took my hand to comfort me, his touch gentle. "If I'm right and Franklin is out there, he's capable of anything. Please, don't try to play detective, and go looking for him. He'd kill you as soon as look at you."

"I'm not playing detective." Griff lifted one eyebrow at my defensive statement. "Okay, maybe when I first saw that TV show I was. That picture they showed looked familiar, and I don't think it was because I'd seen you in town. I still think I've seen him here, even before Megan caught him in her kitchen."

"What? When? She actually came face to face with him?" I had already explained about this, but apparently he hadn't realized she actually saw him. Also, he wasn't quite as good at keeping up with the people around him as he thought. I explained what happened that day nearly two months ago. "Megan was trying to describe him for Mom to draw," I said, ending my tale. "The drawing was just one of the things he destroyed when he wrecked our store and house." I let out a sigh.

He stood up, pushing back the chair. "I need to talk to her. If she can describe him, the FBI needs to know. They need to protect her. Did she tell them about seeing him, about the drawing?" He paced across the brick patio. "If he destroyed it, he knows she can describe what he looks like now. Both she and your mom are a threat to him. So are you."

A shiver traveled up my spine. Until right then, the possibility that he could and would come after me or anyone else in town hadn't truly sunk in to my stubborn brain. Griff took my hands, pulling me out of the lounge chair. "You need to call those agents who were here. Megan needs to give them the description of that man in her kitchen. They have computer programs that can do a composite drawing of him."

His hand trailed down my arm, lacing his fingers through mine. "Come on, show me where Megan lives. We can call the FBI from her place." He started walking, tugging me behind him, not giving me any choice but to follow.

# CHAPTER NINE

It took several hours for the agents to make it back to Flanagan's Gap from Phoenix. To say they were unhappy with us is putting it mildly. "Why weren't we told about this when we were here the first time?" Special Agent Greene glared at each of us in turn.

"Hasn't anyone been listening to me?" I returned his glare with one of my own. "Everyone is so interested in preserving their own jurisdictional boundaries, afraid someone is going to get the kudos for catching the bad guys, and they don't pay attention to what is being said."

"All right, you have our attention now. Which one of you is Megan?" He glared at each of us in turn. When she stepped forward, he growled at her with barely contained impatience. "Tell me about this man you saw in your kitchen." Before she could answer, he caught sight of Griff standing on the other side of the room, his arms folded across his chest. "What the hell are you doing here, Tomlin?" he snarled. He was even surlier than he'd been before. "Shouldn't you be out raking in the big bucks protecting some fancy corporation?" Apparently the two men had a past history, and not a very congenial one.

Griff lifted one shoulder nonchalantly, slowly walking over to stand beside me. "I'd been doing some camping in these parts when I met these nice folks. I heard about their troubles, and I thought I'd give them a hand."

Agent Greene snorted his disbelief. "It's time for you to disappear now. We'll take it from here."

Not giving Griff a chance to argue or leave the room, I took his hand, lacing my fingers with his. "If it's all the same to you, and even if it isn't, I'd prefer that he stays." The agents' faces turned red at my defiance, but I didn't care. "I think he has more skin in this game than either of you, and he deserves to be in on this conversation." Griff squeezed my hand, and winked when I looked at him.

Agent Greene started to argue, but his partner interrupted. "Fine, let's get on with this." He turned to Megan. "What can you tell us about the man who was in your house?"

"I can give you a pretty good description of him, but that's about all." She lifted one shoulder as if to apologize.

"You should have told us about this when we were here the first time?" Still stuck on his outrage, Agent Greene was ready to pounce on her until Jack cleared his throat in warning.

"If I remember correctly," Megan glared at him, able to stand her ground, "Becca tried to tell you. You just don't listen very well. You were only interested in Becca's pictures so you could get out of here." Again, red crept up his neck, maybe this time there was a little embarrassment involved.

Agent Black nudged his partner, when he would have snapped out a response. "Okay, we'll get a sketch artist up here for a composite drawing."

"That's not necessary," she objected. "Dora is a very good artist." She nodded at Mom. "If he hadn't torn up the drawing, we would have one for you already."

"Yes, well, we need to have someone from the Bureau do the drawing. No offense, ma'am." He looked at Mom. "I'm sure you're a very competent artist."

In other words he figured it would turn out to be little more than a stick figure, I thought. These men couldn't be any more condescending if they tried.

Not wanting to be outdone by his partner, Agent Greene started to attack Megan again, "If you had called us at the time this first happened, maybe we could have gotten his fingerprints."

Snickers moved around the room and Griff laughed out loud. "Come on, Greene. Think about what you're saying. If the Bureau got a call about someone breaking into their home, eating the leftovers, and taking a fifty dollar pair of jeans, would you send someone out to investigate, or laugh at them?

Even the sheriff's office didn't investigate something like that." The other man was so angry; his blood pressure must be through the roof.

After some expert questioning from Agent Black, effectively cutting out his partner once more, he managed to pull a few more details from Megan's memory banks. The FBI sketch artist wouldn't be able to make it to Flanagan's Gap until the following day. Instead of going back to Phoenix overnight only to make the two and a half hour return trip in the morning, the two men decided to spend the night.

"Where do people stay around here? I don't see any big hotels." Agent Greene's negative attitude reared its ugly head again.

He was right for a change, there are no chain hotels in Flanagan's Gap, but we do have several excellent bed and breakfasts, as well as two local motels. All of them are clean and well kept. No one suggested they stay in any of them though.

When they finally walked out the door, disgruntled that they had to drive into Payson or Prescott for the night, I realized I was still holding Griff's hand. I immediately tried to pull my hand away; only to have him tightened his grip. "Will you let go?" I hissed, not wanting to attract attention to the two of us.

He shrugged, finally letting go. "You're the one who took my hand. I figured you needed the moral support. I didn't want to let you down." His teasing grin had those dimples winking at me again. What is it about dimples that cause my heart rate to climb right off the chart?

~~~

The agents returned the following morning with the sketch artist in tow. Two hours after closing themselves off in Megan's dining room, they reemerged. "Is this the man you saw in the forest?" Agent Greene asked me. He held up the drawing.

"It looks like the man on the television show. I can't say

87

for certain I ever saw him in town about the time the petty thefts started, but that's probably why he looked familiar on TV. I've been trying to telling you, all I could see of him in the forest was a shadowy figure with a beard and long hair. He always stays in the shadows." If this was the best the FBI had to offer, law enforcement in this country was in serious trouble. "He knows how to stay hidden," I stated.

"Exactly how many times have you seen him? Was it always in the forest?"

Oops, I hadn't meant to reveal so much. I hadn't even told Mom about seeing him the second time. "Um, twice," I answered meekly, "and yes, both times in the forest." I could feel Griff staring at me now, along with several others. I wasn't worried about the agents, but Griff might take exception to the fact that I'd left out this one little detail.

To defuse the tension, Mom held up a sketch pad. Her drawing was nearly identical to the one the sketch artist had drawn. "Where did that come from?" Greene snapped. I was grateful for the diversion, but knew I would have some explaining to do once the agents were gone.

"I drew it," Mom answered calmly.

"You said it got destroyed when he wrecked your store." His anger was now directed at her. He looked like he wanted to throttle her.

"The original one was destroyed," she stated simply, not backing down from his annoyed tone. "I drew this last night. Since I no longer have a store to run or a home to take care of, I have plenty of time on my hands." She made it sound like that was his fault.

Agent Black stepped forward, taking her pad. "This is very good, Mrs. Dutton. It would have saved a lot of time and expense if we knew you could do this." He sounded like he was talking to a recalcitrant child as he scolded her.

"You were told; you just didn't want to listen. Again. Since I'm not with the FBI you didn't think I would be good enough." Leave it to her to rebuke even these obnoxious federal agents.

"Um, yes, well," he stammered. "We need to get this out to all law enforcement agencies in the area." He quickly turned away.

"May I have my pad back?" Mom wasn't about to let him walk off with her drawing.

"Of course, Mrs. Dutton, I'm sorry." He started to remove the drawing, but she stopped him again.

"You have your own drawing. You don't need mine." She held out her hand. For a minute I thought he was going to refuse to give it to her. Finally he placed the pad with her sketch in her outstretched palm. His face was red, either from anger or embarrassment, I didn't know which.

The three men walked out slamming the door behind them. Before Jerry Watkins, the sketch artist, disappeared, he turned, giving Mom a wink.

The room erupted in laughter, everyone hugging Mom. "That was priceless, Mrs. Dutton," Griff said. "I know some people who would have paid big money to have seen what you just did."

Jack took the drawing from her. "Do you mind if I make copies of this, Dora? I'm sure those two don't consider the Forest Service part of law enforcement, but my team needs to know who could be out there. This is our territory."

"Just remember, the man is a murderer," Griff cautioned quietly. "He isn't afraid of killing again."

"Has anyone come across the body again?" I stopped Jack as he headed outside.

"Sorry, Becca, I've told my guys to keep an eye out, but we've been pretty tied up."

Frustrated, I had to accept his answer. I just didn't like it.

~~~

After another delicious dinner courtesy of Janice and Ernie, I wanted to walk off some calories. The insurance company had made arrangements with them to have all of our meals served at the bed and breakfast. Instead of losing a few pounds this summer like I'd hoped, I was going to gain if I kept eating Janice's calorie laden meals. With the forest off limits until someone caught Warner Franklin, I was going to have to find another form of exercise. Maybe I could join the swim team. I had plenty of time on my hands until the store was up and running again. A small gym with some work-out equipment would be a nice addition to the town.

Power walking through town helped work off some calories, and expend the unused energy I'd been storing up. With little to do but wait for the store to be back in business, I was going stir crazy.

So far, I'd managed to avoid Griff after the FBI left town. I knew he wasn't happy that I hadn't told him, or anyone else, about seeing Warner Franklin, or whoever he is, twice.

"Becca, I want to talk to you." David Graham pulled his squad car to a halt beside me. Slamming the door hard enough to rattle the windows as he got out was an indication of his mood. I gave a weary sigh. It seems someone else isn't very happy with me. "Was it your idea to call in the FBI?" he growled. A monsoon storm was brewing off in the distance, and a storm of a different nature was brewing right in front of me. He stepped into my personal space, leaning over me to get right in my face. "Do you think they'll do a better job of finding out who trashed your store than I will?"

"Back off, Graham," I pushed against his chest. "You don't intimidate me with your macho act." I waited until he moved back several paces before answering him. "I didn't call the FBI about the store. They couldn't care less. I didn't even call them; they just showed up asking questions."

"Bull!" He came at me again until I held up my hand in warning. Was it against the law to smack a sheriff's deputy? I wondered. Would he arrest me? You bet, I silently answered my own question. Was it worth taking that chance? After several tense seconds, I gave him a thumbnail sketch of what the agents had said. "They just showed up the first time. I didn't call them," I reemphasized.

"Well, they've taken over the case. They're showing a sketch of the guy you said wrecked your store, cutting my department out. They're crawling all over my station house, giving orders like they own the place. Where did they get the sketch?"

It was my turn to ignore his question. Besides, my answer would only make him angrier. "Why would they cut you out? I thought law enforcement agencies were supposed to work together."

"The feds don't play well with other agencies, especially locals. They want all the glory for themselves. What did you tell them?"

I crossed my arms across my chest, glaring up at him. "Exactly what I told you, that someone wrecked our store. I don't know who, but I can guess. It has to be the same guy who was in Megan's house."

His blank stare told me the FBI hadn't given him that information, and I forgot Megan hadn't called it in to the sheriff's department. I took a cautionary step back. "You wouldn't have sent someone out when it happened, so she didn't call," I said as an excuse.

His reddish brow lowered in a fierce scowl, but he let it pass for now. He wasn't through questioning me. "That doesn't explain why the feds showed up. How did they know what was going on here?"

I shrugged. "I have no idea. They just showed up out of the blue," I stated again. "I don't know how they knew what happened at the store."

"Who's this Griff character?" He frowned at me. "What's he got to do with anything?" He didn't seem surprised to hear about Warner Franklin, or that the FBI was looking for him. Instead, he wanted to know about Griff.

"He's just someone I met while I was hiking," I hedged. If Griff wanted to tell David about his connection to Warner Franklin, that was up to him. I wasn't going to say anything.

"So why are the feds looking here for that guy?" He finally

got around to asking about Franklin. I'm not sure if he really didn't know who Franklin was, but I wasn't going to be the one to tell him.

"Someone died, or was killed, in the forest. That's federal land, making it their case. Or have you forgotten your basic jurisdictional chain of command? Maybe they think this Franklin character killed someone."

"There's nothing for them to find since that body disappeared before I could go looking for it. For all anyone knows, the person could have died years ago. Until it's found again, we'll never know."

"And you're not going to expend too much energy looking for it either." His insinuation was clear; he didn't believe me or the pictures I took.

"As you so eloquently pointed out, it's not my jurisdiction." He smirked at me. "If the body had still been there, I would have called them in myself. But I don't need outsiders telling me how to do my job."

"If you would have called them in anyway, why are you upset about the feds being here? I would think you'd be glad to have someone else here to do your job. Or are you upset because you wanted to find that body so you could rub their noses in it? I don't really care who finds the body or the guy who's hiding out in the forest. I just want him gone so life can get back to normal. I want our store and home back!" My voice cracked a little on my last statement.

"I'm working on that, Becca, and I don't need the feds looking over my shoulder." His attitude mellowed only slightly. "I need to get back to work." He turned to go back to his car.

"What was in the box the crime scene guys took out of the store?" My question stopped him in his tracks. Since he came to me, I wanted to get some answers.

"I can't discuss an ongoing investigation." It was the pat answer given to the media when the police didn't want to divulge information. At least he didn't say 'No comment'." He got the information he wanted, now he was ready to leave.

"Wait a minute; I have a right to know what was taken out of the store." He looked like he was going to argue. This time I took a menacing step towards him.

He finally relented, looking uncomfortable. "There were explosives hidden among all the debris. The techs weren't sure if it belonged to you and your mom, or if it was left there by the suspect."

"What would we be doing with explosives?" My knees began to wobble. Franklin was going to blow up our store as he had in my nightmare. Was he hoping to catch Mom and me inside, and maybe even people from town as well? Blowing up our store would take out half of the stores on Main Street. With the homes spread out further away from the main part of town, at least they would have been safe.

David lifted one shoulder in a shrug, turning away again only to be stopped by my next question. "Did you do some kind of search online about unsolved cases involving explosives?" A very unbecoming pink crept up his neck, giving me the answer. "You came here blaming me when you're the one who inadvertently alerted the FBI. You've got a lot of nerve." Maybe I would smack the jerk after all, and hang the consequences.

Without confirming or denying my statement, he turned away. "Stay out of the forest, Becca. The feds are shutting it down until they catch this guy." That was his parting shot. He'd known all along what was going on, he just wanted someone else to blame for what happened to his case.

My temper was still boiling as I watched David's car disappear. He was probably feeling pretty smug right about now. I headed for the bed and breakfast at the opposite end of town when a loud clap of thunder sounded overhead, heralding the onset of the monsoon storm that had been hovering over the desert. If I didn't want to get drenched, I was going to have to make a run for it.

I didn't make it. By the time I stepped onto the porch of

our little casita, I felt like a drowned rat, and probably looked like one. My long hair was plastered to my head and back, even across my face thanks to the wind. The sky had turned prematurely dark, and the porch was in shadow. I didn't see someone sitting in the lounge chair until he spoke.

"Don't you know it can be dangerous walking around in a thunder and lightning storm?"

With a startled shriek, I whirled around to face whoever was there. I'd been warned enough times about Warner Franklin, and that's who I expected to see standing there. Had he come after me?

Griff stepped out of the shadow, and I sagged against the porch railing. "Are you trying to give me a heart attack?" My voice wobbled, and my hands were shaking, along with my legs.

"I'm sorry. I didn't mean to scare you." He didn't sound sorry as he took my arm, leading me over to the chair he'd just vacated. His grip wasn't all that gentle either.

"What are you doing here, Griff?"

"What were you doing out in the storm?" he countered, ignoring my question.

I was getting tired of people doing that. My questions were just as important as theirs, and deserved to be answered. "What are you doing here?" I repeated. I figured I already knew why he was here, but let him tell me what was on his mind. "Where's Mom?" She obviously wasn't inside, or she would be out here.

"She said something about going to play cards with some friends." He was still ignoring my first question. I tapped my fingers on the arm of the chair, letting the silence drag out while I waited for him to answer.

We stared at each other for several long minutes. Neither of us wanted to back down. I knew for a certainty it wasn't going to be me. By now, the strong wind was blowing rain onto the porch. I couldn't get any wetter, but I was getting colder. "I need to get on some dry clothes. Go away." I headed for the door. If he wasn't going to say anything, I wasn't going to stay out here and freeze.

"Why didn't you tell me you'd seen Franklin twice? Did he threaten you before he broke into your store?"

"It wasn't exactly a threat. He just told me to stop poking around where I didn't belong."

"But you kept looking for him," he stated, giving his head a shake.

"No, I wasn't looking for him," I argued. Not *just* him, I added silently. "I was looking for you. You were in the forest for a long time. I wanted to know if you'd seen him, or maybe The Hermit. No one's seen him for a long time. I'm kind of worried about him." In all the mess that was going on, I didn't want to forget that the dead person might be The Hermit. "Besides," I continued defiantly, "who is he to tell me to stay out of the forest? This is my home." This last was more to myself than to Griff.

I was beginning to shake with cold. The wind had picked up even more, blowing the rain further onto the porch.

"Go change before you catch cold," Griff said, his tone gentler now.

When I stepped through the door, he followed me inside. "What do you think you're doing?" I put my hand on his chest to stop him.

"Trying not to get as wet as you are."

"Well, go to your own casita. You can't stay here while I change." The small building was only one room; a bedroom and a kitchenette combined, with a separate bathroom.

"Take your clothes into the bathroom. I'm not through talking to you." His jaw was set in a stubborn line, a muscle jumped in his cheek.

I took my time changing; even blow drying my hair, hoping he'd get tired of waiting and leave. I should have known better. Instead, he'd made himself comfortable. He was sitting in the one stuffed chair with his feet propped up on the end of the bed, sipping a cup of hot coffee he'd made while he waited.

"I made coffee," he stated the obvious, handing me a cup. "I thought it might help warm you up."

Curling my fingers around the mug, I let the warmth seep into them. Even though it was the middle of the summer, the storm had brought the temperature down twenty degrees in a matter of minutes.

The silence stretched out. To my surprise, the earlier tension was gone. Now a different type of tension took its place. Something I couldn't name, or didn't want to name, I silently corrected. For some reason, nerves were attacking my stomach.

"Becca, please stay out of the forest for now." Griff spoke softly; all anger was gone from his voice. "I don't think you understand how dangerous Franklin is. I don't want anything to happen to you."

I was sitting on the edge of the bed beside his booted feet. Before I realized what he was going to do, he pulled me off the bed into his lap, his strong arms wrapping around my waist. Setting the coffee cup on the table beside the chair, his lips captured mine in a soft kiss. When he lifted his head several minutes later, my arms were around his neck, my fingers playing with the thick hair at the back of his head. With a soft growl, he lowered his head again. The kiss wasn't so gentle this time as his tongue swept into my mouth, dueling with mine.

The wind and rain had temporarily let up, and we could hear the gravel in front of the small casita crunch when a car pulled to a stop. Mom's voice trailed back to someone. "Thanks for bringing me back. I'll see you tomorrow."

I jumped off Griff's lap, swiping my hand across my mouth as the door opened. "Well, hello," Mom stopped just inside the door. "What's going on?" I felt sixteen again, caught kissing my boyfriend in our front room. She looked from me to Griff and back again. Her gray eyes traveled quickly to the bed before coming back to me. I was very grateful everything looked neat and tidy.

"I waited for Becca to get back from her walk," Griff finally spoke up. "She got caught in the storm and needed to change clothes." He gave a bare bones explanation.

For a long moment, she continued to look at us like we were a couple of bugs under a microscope. "Well, you're talk is going to have to wait until tomorrow if you don't want to get soaked going back to your room. The lull in the storm won't last much longer."

I knew he wasn't ready to end the conversation, or what had just happened between us, but there was little he could do now. Mom wasn't going anywhere.

With a sigh of resignation, he stood up. "I'll see you tomorrow, Becca. Mrs. Dutton." Mom held the door for him, and he disappeared in the dark night.

I imagined an inquisition heaping with guilt was next on the agenda. Instead, she chuckled, heading for the bathroom. "Is there anything good on television tonight?"

# CHAPTER TEN

Agents Greene and Black brought in reinforcements the next day. They were going to search "every inch of the forest." That's a direct quote from Agent Greene. I wished them luck with that endeavor in their business suits, white shirts, and ties. Even if there was actual hiking equipment in the large duffel bags they unloaded from the big black SUVs, unless they knew something about hiking through rough terrain, they were in big trouble. The forest floor wasn't flat around here.

Griff sat on the front porch of the bed and breakfast, his feet propped on the railing, watching the activity. A smug grin tilted his full lips into his moustache, lips I had kissed just last night. Now I found myself obsessing over that, and daydreaming about doing it again.

His chuckle brought my wayward thoughts back to the present. "What's so funny?" I followed his gaze to the ten or so men gearing up to head into the forest. My own laughter bubbled up. Townspeople lined the street to watch the spectacle, some of them laughing along with us. Even a few of the tourists were watching, and enjoying the show.

"Aren't there any experienced outdoorsmen in the FBI?" I asked. Agents Greene and Black were attempting to put camo pants on over their suit pants. One of the agents had pulled a pair of hip waders from his duffel. That brought more laughter. Did these men realize how ridiculous they looked?

"One or two," Griff answered with a chuckle, "but it doesn't look like any of them are here."

"They do know there are wild animals out there, don't they?"

"They're after the wildest animal alive," he answered, his tone growing serious. "Man at his worst. Some of those agents have actually fired their guns some place other than the firing range."

"I can't let them go out there without warning them of the possibility of running into a bear." I started to stand up, only to have Griff stop me.

"Don't spoil the show. Everyone's enjoying it." He tugged on my hand, pulling me down beside him. When he didn't let go, I tugged, but he just tightened his grip. "Besides," he went on, "it looks like the good pastor and your unofficial mayor are about to intervene."

He was right; Pastor Curt and Sara stepped up to a man unloading a duffel bag in the back of one of the SUVs. "What is it you're planning on doing with all this?" Pastor Curt's calm voice carried across the street.

"Step back, sir. This is FBI business." He was as pompous as Agent Greene.

"Yes, we understand that," Sara tried. "We were just wondering if you knew what you were doing." I wanted to applaud. Sara always did go right to the heart of the matter. With that, she turned to Curt. "I guess they don't need our help after all." She gave an exaggerated shrug. "They must know about the bears and wolves that roam the forest." She made it sound like there were packs of wolves and bears hiding behind every tree. They turned and walked away.

"Wait a minute," the agent called after them. His eyes were as big as saucers. "Come back here."

Curt looked over his shoulder. "Sorry we interrupted you, sir. We won't bother you again." They continued walking, ignoring the now sputtering agent.

Stepping up on the porch beside Griff and me, Curt looked back at the activity in the street. "Are all FBI agents that big of fools?"

Griff shook his head. "No, just the ones who let the power go to their heads. They don't think anyone knows as much as they do."

"But if they don't know what they're doing, they could get seriously hurt out there," Curt objected.

"With that many bumbling fools prowling around in the

99

woods, the bears and wolves are smart enough to stay out of their way." Sara gave a small laugh.

"I'm not talking about the animals," Curt said on a sigh. "I doubt many of these men have ever been on a manhunt in the woods before. They could get seriously injured just walking around. If they aren't careful, they could even shoot each other, thinking it's the man they're looking for, or a wild animal."

"Not our problem, Padre," Griff stated with little concern. "You tried to warn them. I'll bet they'll be singing a different tune when they stumble out of the forest tonight." He laughed at the prospect.

The agents entered the trees spread out ten feet apart, each holding a gun big enough to bring down an elephant. Wearing camo clothing, they would never know when one of their own men was walking ten feet away. By nightfall we might have a few casualties, and none of them would be Warner Franklin.

Once the show was over, people drifted off. I longed for our store to be up and running, and our small house to be put back together. I'd never complain again about having too much to do. Sitting around doing nothing was getting on my nerves.

Alone with Griff, an uncomfortable silence settled over us, my mind wandered to last night. Why had he kissed me? Why would he start something when he'd be leaving once Warner Franklin was caught? I didn't want to think about that. That was precisely why I never got romantically involved with any of the summer visitors. I wasn't leaving Flanagan's Gap and they weren't staying. Neither was Griff.

"How long were you out in the forest?" I asked, hoping to move my thoughts in a different direction.

"About two months before you started following me. Why?"

"Did you ever see anyone besides the casual campers out there?"

"If you're asking if I saw Franklin, I've already answered that; no, I didn't. If I'd seen that bas..." He stopped what he was going to say, and started again. "If I'd seen him, he wouldn't be harassing you now."

"Why is he harassing me? I'm not a threat to him. No one would have known he was out there if he hadn't started stealing things. If I hadn't seen that TV show, I wouldn't have thought anything about a bearded man in the forest. That picture reminded me of someone I'd seen in town. My imagination just ran with it."

"Don't you mean ran *away* with it? Why were you so sure he was here?"

"The story fit in with what was going on here at the time. The Hermit was missing, someone was stealing things, and the guy was a criminal." I shrugged. I didn't have any other explanation.

"Are you sure it wasn't me you saw here in town?" he asked. "I had deliberately tried to look like the FBI's age enhanced photo, hoping to draw him out."

I shrugged, not sure of anything now. "Until Mom said there was a younger version of Warner Franklin coming into the store, I didn't know there were two men sneaking around out there. The first time I saw you was at our softball game. Or maybe it was in Prescott." I'd forgotten all about that. "Did you ever go there?"

"Plenty of times, why?"

"I thought I saw Franklin when Megan and I were at the craft fair. Maybe it was you."

He chuckled. "It had to be me. I can't picture Franklin wandering around a craft fair. He doesn't like people, and wouldn't want to be in a crowd. If someone had accidentally bumped into him, he could have gone off like a stick of dynamite. He wouldn't take that kind of chance."

"Yet he took the chance of coming here to steal things. It doesn't make sense."

"It didn't make sense for him to blow up my neighborhood either. He was just mad because things weren't going his way, so he did it." His voice was bitter at all he'd lost at the hands of Warner Franklin. My heart went out to the young boy who had lost so much.

Turning my thoughts away from that, I kept the conversation on neutral ground. "Why hasn't he ever joined up with anti-government groups? There are plenty of them around the country, aren't there? That sounds like it would be right up his alley."

"Yeah, there are plenty of those groups around." Griff shook his head. "But it would only work for him if he could set the rules and change them whenever it was convenient for him. He doesn't like following anyone else's rules, and he certainly won't follow orders."

"Did you ever see The Hermit while you were camping out?" I was still worried that Franklin had done something to him. He's an old man; he wouldn't be able to fight off someone younger and stronger.

"The Hermit again?" One eyebrow lifted slightly. "I thought that was just an excuse to come looking for me." He waggled his eyebrows suggestively.

"Don't flatter yourself," I scoffed. "There have been stories of an old man prowling around the woods as far back as I can remember. He never hurt anyone, but occasionally when he needed something he couldn't grow or catch, he'd come into town." I explained about the little carvings he left behind. "It was the one thing Franklin didn't destroy when he wrecked the store."

"When did things first start disappearing?" Griff asked.

It took a few minutes for me to figure out when this all began. "Maybe four months ago," I finally said. "He had to be watching us, because he only went into homes when no one was there. He wouldn't have gotten caught in Megan's kitchen if she hadn't forgotten something."

He seemed lost in thought for several minutes, giving me an opportunity to study him. Without the full-face beard, he looked much younger than he had when I first saw him. His brown hair was streaked by the sun. He had the greenest eyes

I've ever seen. Maybe there was some Irish blood running through his veins.

"You like what you see?" I didn't realize he was looking at me until his words brought me out of my contemplation of his rugged features.

I could feel my face turning red, but I tried to bluff through it. "Not bad; it's better without all that hair on your face." I lifted one shoulder, aiming for nonchalance. I decided I didn't pull it off when he laughed.

"How did you know Franklin was here in Arizona, in our forest in particular?" I asked. I needed to change the subject. "What gave him away?"

He stared into the forest where the agents had disappeared. "Nothing. Franklin was raised in the mountains of New Mexico. I always figured he was still there or Arizona where he'd be most comfortable. Every year, I spend a couple of months camping out in different areas, hoping I'll find some trace of him. It was just dumb luck that I was already here when your deputy went looking for cases involving explosives. That sent up flags at the Bureau. Contrary to what Greene thinks, I still have friends there. Any time there's something new on Franklin, I know about it."

I'd been right, David had accidentally alerted the FBI himself about the possibility that Franklin was here. He just wanted the blame placed elsewhere. "So if David hadn't made that inquiry, the FBI wouldn't have warned us or any of the other towns around here that Franklin could be living in the forest. Why wouldn't they warn people?" I asked indignantly. "Were they waiting for someone to get hurt or killed before letting us know?" I paced the length of the porch. If Agent Greene was in front of me now, I just might smack him upside the head, and hang the consequences.

"They don't let people know about fugitives in the area unless they are certain of their location. That way they don't warn their suspect. I doubt they knew exactly where he was though, just the general vicinity." Now it sounded like Griff was defending the jerk, and I glared at him.

"In the last fifteen years, agents have probably crawled over nearly every forest and wooded area in the country. Franklin is always one step ahead of them. He's always been one step ahead of me, too," he grumbled.

Before I could complain further, two men stumbled out of the woods, holding another man between them. It hadn't taken very long for the first casualty. Racing across the ball field to help, I didn't know if they'd been attacked by a wild animal or Franklin.

We came to a halt in front of them, and Agent Greene glared at me. "Why didn't you warn us about the terrain out there?"

"You mean like you warned the town that Warner Franklin might be hiding out there?" My hands were braced on my hips. What kind of idiot went into the woods without first learning something about the landscape?

"Would you have listened if she tried to tell you?" Griff asked. "Aren't you supposed to check things out, and not go into a situation blind?" He turned to one of the men holding Greene up. "What happened?" We couldn't see any dripping blood so I assumed it wasn't a bear attack.

"He tripped over a fallen tree, and tumbled down a ravine. He might have a broken ankle." He didn't sound very sympathetic; more like he thought the other agent was a moron.

"Well, it looks like you might get that desk job you've wanted for years, Greene," Griff said. "Then again, they might decide to put you out to pasture." He was taunting the other man. If Greene could have stood on his own, I have little doubt he would have taken a swing at Griff.

"Where's the nearest hospital?" He turned to me instead, trying to ignore Griff.

"We have a doctor here in town."

"I said a hospital," he snapped, "not some rural doctor."

"Closest one is about forty-five miles away. You might

want to give Doc Granger a try. He can take care of just about anything right here. If it turns out to be life threatening, he'll call in the medevac helicopter. I really don't think that will be necessary today though." It was hard not to laugh at the man, and be insulted at the same time. He had a pretty high opinion of himself, and a pretty low opinion of Flanagan's Gap and its residents.

Within an hour, Agent Greene was sporting a fresh cast, and was on his way back to Phoenix. At least we wouldn't have to put up with him while they searched for Warner Franklin. The rest of the agents wandered out of the forest dirty, tired, and hungry about six o'clock, but no one else had been hurt. They'd been unsuccessful in finding the subject of their hunt. He wasn't going to be easy to find.

"Is there anywhere local we can spend the night?" Without his obnoxious partner, Agent Black was more civil. "It will save a lot of time if we don't have to travel back and forth to Prescott."

"There are several nice motels and bed and breakfasts here in town," Sara informed him. "I'm sure they can find accommodations for all of you."

"And why weren't we told about them while we waited for the sketch artist from Phoenix?" He glared at her then me.

She lifted one shoulder in a careless shrug. "Your partner wanted a fancy hotel. The closest ones are in Prescott, and I'm sure even those don't measure up to his high standards. No one wanted to strain his delicate sensibilities further. He was under enough stress as it was." Agent Black and the other agents were all aware of the sarcasm lacing through her voice.

"Okay, let's see if we can get settled for the night. Everyone is hungry. Where do we go?" He looked around for signs. In Flanagan's Gap, advertising is subtle, no giant billboards or flashing neon signs to point the way. I left it to Sara to show the men to the various motels and restaurants.

With the forest temporarily closed to townspeople and tourists alike, the whole town was suffering financially.

Restaurants and lodgings were the only businesses to benefit from the FBI's presence. Some tourists came to watch the drama play out, but it didn't take long for them to decide it wasn't very entertaining, and head on to the bright lights of bigger towns, or other camp grounds.

After the one injury, the remaining agents enlisted the help of Jack and Griff to guide them through the forest. A week later they were no closer to finding Warner Franklin than they'd been when they started. He proved to be as elusive as he'd been in the past.

They did manage to find the body that had disappeared more than a month ago. Once again, Warner Franklin had done a very poor job of hiding the body of the man he'd killed. At least I assumed he was the killer. Identification would be even more difficult now. If it was The Hermit, they might not ever be able to identify him, since no one knew who he was.

A week was all the time they had allotted for the search. Packing up their duffel bags, Agent Black made his pronouncement that it was safe to go into the forest again. "So where is Warner Franklin?" Sara asked, getting in his face. "What was this all about?"

"Most likely, he's moved on," the agent declared. "If he knew we were here looking for him, he wouldn't stick around."

"And if he's better at hiding than you are at finding? What then?" She wasn't going to let him dismiss her that easily.

"Ms. Flanagan, this isn't the only case we're working on. If you have any more trouble, call me." He handed her one of his cards. "We can always come back and try again." Without another word, he got behind the wheel of the SUV, shutting the door in her face.

"That pompous ass!" She watched the caravan of black vehicles drive away.

~~~

Sara called a town meeting that evening. She wasn't going to take the chance that Warner Franklin was still out there, and

106

would start over again, this time doing more than take food and clothing from the town or trashing our store.

"I'm open to suggestions," she began. She knew she was in way over her head.

"What about setting up a neighborhood watch group?" Bill Wheeler asked. "Only on a grander scale. We could take turns keeping watch. Most of the men here, and some of the women, know how to handle a gun."

"We don't want any gun play," Sara objected. There'd been too much publicity in the news lately about people accidently shooting someone. She didn't want to draw any unfavorable attention to the town.

"Not gun play," Bill objected. "Just protection. The law isn't going to do anything more to catch this guy." The room buzzed with everyone voicing an opinion at once until Sara pounded on the podium.

Griff had surprised me by attending the meeting. I'd expected him to pull up stakes right behind the FBI. When things quieted down some, he stood up. "Can I make a suggestion?" He'd been in town long enough that everyone knew him by now.

At Sara's nod, he walked to the front of the room. "Some of you might not know it, but I own a security company. I'm willing to station several of my people here until we can make sure Franklin really has left the area."

So that's the reason he's here tonight, I thought. Anything long term like he's talking would cost a fortune. It's just business with him.

"That's very nice of you, Griff," Sara said, "but the town can't afford to hire your company." Around the room, I could see people nodding their heads. We don't have our own police force because we can't afford to hire one. As a non-town town, Flanagan's Gap collected no taxes for itself.

"I didn't say anything about hiring my company," Griff spoke over the murmured voices. "I want to catch this guy every bit as bad as you do; maybe more." I hadn't told anyone, not even Mom, about Griff's background.

"Why would you do that?" Sara had doubts about his generosity. If it sounds too good to be true, most likely it is.

"Like I said, I want to catch this guy. My men are all experienced outdoorsmen; some are veterans. We can keep an eye on the town as well as the forest. If Franklin is still around, he'll show himself sooner or later." It was later that worried me. He couldn't keep his men here indefinitely without being paid. What would happen then? Was he hoping we would become so dependent on his men that we would agree to pay them? We had to be able to protect ourselves, and not rely on outside sources.

It took another hour of discussing the pros and cons of letting Griff give it a try before the town agreed to his proposal. At least he knew what he was up against in the woods. Maybe his men could flush Franklin out or make sure he moved somewhere else if they made it too difficult for him here. But I intended to get a little more information about his offer.

## CHAPTER ELEVEN

When the meeting was over, Griff didn't hang around for social hour. Neither did I. "Griff, wait a minute."

"What's up, Sugar? You want to walk me home?"

"You're as conceited as Agent Greene," I snapped.

"Ouch!" He rubbed his chest. "That barb hurt."

"Then stop being a jerk." We started walking again. I was on auto-pilot, heading for the store and our house in back. It was the opposite direction of the bed and breakfast where Griff had been heading.

"Where are you going?" I could see his frown of confusion even in the dark night.

"Oh." I looked down the street, wishing I had a home to go to, but that would be a while yet. Repairs in the store were almost finished. We could begin stocking the shelves in the next few days. The house was a whole different matter. Ted Kramer suggested we have it torn down, and start over from scratch. I'm not sure if Mom is going to agree to that.

Turning around, I walked beside Griff, my thoughts jumbled up with everything that was going on. Griff slipped his arm around my waist, pulling me against his side. "What's going on in that pretty little head, Sugar?"

"Stop trying to patronize me, Griff. I'm not a little girl, and I don't need a pat on the head." I tried to move out of the circle of his arms when he turned me to face him, now holding me firmly against him.

"If you were a little girl, I wouldn't want to do this." He kissed my temple, my cheek, before moving to nibble on my earlobe. "I'd get in big trouble for doing this if you were a little girl." His lips lightly skimmed over mine before settling down to take full possession, nearly stopping my heart from beating.

Fortunately we weren't standing under a street lamp when

people began to wander out of the church hall. Social hour ended earlier than usual. No one felt comfortable leaving their homes unattended the way we used to.

My head was spinning when Griff finally dropped his hands that had somehow made their way into my long hair. The pins that had held it up were now scattered in the street at my feet. How had that happened? I wondered.

Taking a shuddering breath, I took a step back, continuing on to the bed and breakfast. When Warner Franklin was finally captured or Griff proved to himself the man had moved elsewhere, he'd leave. If I didn't want to end up with a broken heart, I had to make sure this didn't happen again.

"Why did you make that offer?" At the confused look on his face, I elaborated. I guess his thoughts were elsewhere. "To have some of your men here to help look for Franklin," I clarified. "Sara told you the town can't pay you."

"I'm not looking for payment; I'm looking for the man who murdered my whole family." His voice became a growl at the mention of the fate of his family.

"What makes you think you can find him when the FBI hasn't been able to for fifteen years?"

"It's personal for me; it's just another case to them, especially Greene. He figures if he can solve a big enough case, he'll get that desk promotion that has eluded him his entire career. When he can't solve one case fast enough, he moves on to another one, hoping it will bring him what he wants."

"How would Franklin get the explosives he put in our store?" I switched the direction of the conversation, figuring Griff wasn't going to give me the real reason for his offer. "When I'd asked Agents Greene and Black, they wouldn't confirm or deny that Franklin had explosives at his disposal."

"He'd steal them, the same as he took things he needed or wanted here. He is really good at what he does." It almost sounded like grudging admiration.

"Didn't he know blowing up our store, maybe killing us

and any number of others, would get the attention of the FBI? It doesn't make sense."

"No, it doesn't, but I can't explain how his mind works. Maybe he's bored after all these years hiding out. Maybe he saw it as a challenge, or maybe he just doesn't care anymore."

Before we could discuss the matter further, Mom joined us on the porch. I was surprised to see Bill Wheeler had walked her home. Hmm, I'm going to have to think about this.

~~~

After what felt like months, but was really only weeks, Ted Kramer finished repairing all the damage to our store. Our suppliers delivered the shipment to replace everything that had been destroyed. Pallets of food, dishes, clothing, and everything else we generally carried, were stacked everywhere. I was feeling more than a little overwhelmed at the daunting task in front of us.

"How do you eat an elephant?" Mom asked, laughing at my confused look. "One bite at a time, honey. So let's take our first bite." She cut the straps holding the crates on the first pallet.

Before we could even put away the first box of crackers, our friends and neighbors opened the front door. "We're here to help," Sara announced. "Show us where you want things."

These people had their own businesses to run, their own families to take care of, but they had set that aside to help us. I love this town, and the people who live here.

"Bless you all." Tears sparkled in Mom's light blue eyes.

By midmorning, everyone was hot and sweaty even with the air conditioner on and fans going. I wiped sweat off my forehead, looking around to see which pallet of goods to attack next "When's that guy gonna leave?" Chad stood beside me, staring across the room at Griff where he was moving heavy boxes into the storeroom. Muscles rippled in his arms. Sweat plastered his shirt to his back, the muscles outlined by the thin material. Why didn't Griff look as grubby as I felt? I wondered. He'd been working as hard as the rest of us.

"Becca," Chad elbowed me to get my attention. "When's he going to leave? Doesn't he have a job somewhere?"

Turning my back on Griff so I could concentrate on Chad's question, I finally answered. "Yes, he has a job. You heard him say he was going to stick around to keep looking for Warner Franklin."

"No," Chad argued. "He said he was going to send some of his men here. They're here, so why doesn't he leave?"

I wanted to ask what difference it made to him, but I guess I wasn't ready to hear his answer. I wasn't quite sure what I would say if he said he had a crush on me. I didn't want to hurt his feelings, but I wouldn't encourage him either. "He's helping out, Chad. He doesn't want anyone to get hurt." Griff still hadn't told anyone else about his connection to Warner Franklin, so I wouldn't either.

"Huh," Chad sniffed, unconvinced of Griff's true motives.

"Can you take that box over to the far wall for me? I'll start stocking those shelves next." It was on the opposite side of the large room from where Griff was working. I didn't want the two men in close proximity until Chad could overcome his animosity towards Griff.

When we stopped for lunch, Pastor Curt and Judy brought enough food from their restaurant to feed a small army. Tears sparkled in Mom's eyes again at all the generosity shown to us yet again. Misty sat down beside Chad. Her crystal blue eyes failed to work their magic on him today. After several attempts to capture his attention, she stood up, slapping his arm before stalking away.

"What'd I do?" He looked confused, causing everyone to laugh.

At the end of the day, we set the alarm the insurance company insisted we have installed, and locked the doors. No one wanted to take a chance this would happen again. "I think I'm going to sleep here tonight," I told Mom as we made our way to the bed and breakfast. "I can borrow a sleeping bag and pillow from Megan and Jack.

"That's not going to be very comfortable, honey," Mom objected. "We're going to be back here tomorrow, and you need to get a good night's sleep."

"I'll sleep just fine. Being back in our own space will do the trick for me. Besides," I groaned, "I'm so tired, I could sleep standing up." I wasn't going to announce my intentions to anyone else, but I wanted to make sure Warner Franklin didn't try to pull something. The alarm would let us know if he tried to break in again, but I still wanted to be here.

"Going somewhere?" Griff materialized out of the shadows as I left the bed and breakfast after dinner.

"Just over to see Megan." I stopped walking; make that limping, hoping he would go back inside. "She had charge of all the little ones today so their parents could help us in the store." That meant she had the twins and five others, ranging in age from one to six. The older kids were helping us out. "I want to see how she held up. You don't have to walk me over. I'm sure you're as tired as the rest of us. Thank you for all the work you did. Another day like today, and we'll be ready to reopen."

"I'll go with you. I'd like to talk to Jack. Besides, I could use some fresh air."

How would I sneak a sleeping bag and pillow past him if he was with Jack? The man certainly knew how to put a kink in my plans.

While the men were discussing 'man things' in the den, I grabbed a sleeping bag and pillow, hoping to sneak out while they were busy. He was beside me before I got three feet from Megan's back door. He must have radar or something. "What are you planning on doing with those?" He pointed to the sleeping bag and pillow.

"I'm sleeping at the store tonight. Go back to the bed and breakfast; I'll see you in the morning."

"You're nuts if you think I'm going to leave you at the store by yourself all night. Why would you even consider something like that?" He was angry for no reason I could see.

"This is my decision, not yours. You don't get a voice in the matter. Go back to the B and B." I kept walking, hoping he'd take the hint. I should have known better.

He kept pace with my limping steps, but didn't say anything. I could feel the waves of aggravation, or frustration, or something coming from him. I didn't care. He couldn't stop me from doing this.

"Okay, I'm here. Good night. Now go away."

"When pigs fly," he grumbled. "I'm not leaving you here alone. You're setting yourself up as a target if Franklin is watching." What is it with these animal analogies today? I wondered. First Mom with her "eating an elephant"; now Griff and his "flying pigs".

"I'm staying here tonight, Griff, and you're not, so go away." I could be just as stubborn as he was.

"What do you plan on doing if Franklin shows up again?"

"What would you do?" I countered, ignoring the fission of fear that attacked my stomach.

"I carry a gun, I'd shoot him." This surprised me. There'd never been any indication that he was armed.

"Why do men always think women can't protect themselves, and they have to get all macho?"

Griff chuckled, "Blame it on the caveman gene. It's never been completely eradicated from our DNA. Now, are we both going inside, or are we both going back to the B and B?"

There would be no good way to spin the fact that we had spent the night together even if it was completely innocent. In a town the size of Flanagan's Gap, everyone would know, and some people would assume the worst, before breakfast. Heaving a sigh, I stepped down off the porch. I didn't have anything nice to say at the moment, so I kept quiet. I have to remember to pick my battles, and I decided this one I couldn't win.

# CHAPTER TWELVE

Rolling out of bed the next morning, I groaned when every muscle in my body cried out at the movement. I hurt in places I didn't even know I had muscles. Maybe sleeping on the floor last night wouldn't have been such a good idea, after all. I could thank Griff for the fact that I'd slept in a comfortable bed, but I wouldn't tell him that. His head was already big enough; I didn't need to tell him he was right, making it even bigger.

Megan had given me liniment along with the sleeping bag and pillow last night. I rubbed another layer all over, hoping it would ease the aching muscles. Where did I ever get the idea I was in good shape?

Chad wasn't in any better mood this morning when he came to help again. I wasn't sure if it was because Griff was still here or because Misty wasn't speaking to him. He tried several times to cozy up to her, only to be ignored.

Her young heart was breaking, but she wasn't going to let him sweet talk her. "Why are men so stupid?" she asked. We were finishing up in the craft room, getting ready to start lessons again next week. I wasn't certain what their argument was about, but figured it had something to do with Chad's fixation with Griff and probably me.

"I was told recently that men still carry the caveman gene," I said. "That would explain a lot. It makes them do really stupid things. I guess they can't help it."

"Does that mean they don't even know when they're being stupid?"

I laughed. "Well, I haven't figured out the male of the species, so I can't really say if they know when they're being stupid and can't stop, or they just don't want to stop."

She gave a small giggle at that. "Just because they're locked in caveman mode, doesn't mean we still have to be cavewomen. I like to think I've moved way beyond that," she said, growing serious again.

"I'm sorry, Misty." I wasn't sure what I was sorry for, other than the fact that her heart was breaking, but it couldn't hurt to tell her.

"It's not your fault Chad's got a major crush on you." Her eyes glistened with unshed tears. "At first I thought it was kind of sweet, but enough is enough. There's no way you're going to be interested in someone young enough to be your kid brother. Now he's decided he needs to protect you from Griff, when the man's been nothing but nice to everyone, including Chad."

"Whew, for a minute I thought you were going to say I was old enough to be his mother." I laughed, but I really had thought that's where she was going.

Her pretty eyes got big, and she looked at me in horror. "Oh, Becca, no! I would never say that, or even think it. You're just a few years older than us."

"I know, but sometimes teenagers think anyone older than themselves is ancient. I remember thinking along those lines not so long ago." She was able to laugh now, easing some of the tension and hurt bottled up inside her.

"Well, Chad is acting a lot younger than he is, widening that gap even further. Maybe it's time for me to look at someone older, too." She looked over at Griff. "That would really upset the apple cart." She gave another laugh. I wasn't sure if she was serious or teasing.

A few minutes later, Pastor Curt and Judy brought in lunch again. It had to be costing them a small fortune to feed everyone. Lost in thought, trying to come up with a way to repay everyone for all they've done for us, I wasn't aware Griff had sat down beside me until he spoke. "You've been avoiding me today. There seems to be a lot of that going on. I wonder why that is."

"I've been busy, just like everybody else. I didn't realize your feelings were so easily hurt." Without thinking about it, I rubbed at my sore shoulder muscles. Sitting still even for the few minutes it took to eat lunch had my muscles beginning to stiffen up.

Griff turned me around so my back was to him, and massaged my shoulders and neck. It felt so good, I almost groaned. Momentarily succumbing to his touch, I let my head drop forward, giving him more access to my stiff neck.

It took a minute for me to come to my senses, and I shifted around again. "Thanks, I'm fine now. I need to get back to work." Before he could say anything, I walked away. His chuckle followed me across the room.

"I don't like the way that guy has been sniffing after you ever since he came to town." Chad stalked over to me. He didn't bother to keep his voice down.

"Sniffing around? Seriously, Chad?" I wanted to laugh, but stopped myself just in time.

"Yes, seriously," he said, his peach-fuzzed cheeks turning pink. "You're too good for him."

This time I did laugh. "That's probably true, but it's not something either of us has to worry about. As soon as he figures out what's up with this Franklin character, he'll be on his way, and we'll never see him again." My stomach and my heart clenched a little with the thought, but I ignored both.

"What do we even know about the guy?" He wasn't ready to give up his grudge.

"We know he owns a security company, and is in charge of security for several large corporations. He's here to help us when the FBI has given up. If that guy is still in the forest, he could be waiting until we let down our guard. Then he'll start all over again, only worse.

"Right now, you have a few fences to mend." I was ready for a change of topic. "Start by doing a lot of groveling." I nodded at Misty. My heart went out to her; she looked so miserable. Every now and then, she sniffed back her tears.

"She doesn't want anything to do with me anymore. What's her problem anyway? What did I do?"

Oh boy; I wanted to tell him the answer to that knowledge was above my pay grade, but I didn't think he'd get my meaning, so I just told him to go ask her. I wasn't even certain she still wanted to be his girlfriend.

By the end of the day, the store was in shipshape. Mom and I would spend tomorrow getting ready for our grand reopening celebration to thank everyone who had helped out.

A few more items were being delivered, but these weren't for the store. Living at the bed and breakfast had been great for the short term, but staying there for the next month or more while Ted Kramer and his crew rebuilt our house was too much. We wanted somewhere to call home.

There was a full attic over the store with a set of pull down steps, which Warner Franklin had missed when he was trashing everything else. We only used the attic to store holiday decorations or items we no longer had any use for, but didn't want to throw out. In other words, exactly what most people store in their attics.

Mom had asked Ted to build a regular staircase from the storeroom into the attic, and for now we would live there. Installing the stairs and electricity was less expensive than room and board for another month; so the insurance company had agreed to foot the bill. We'd have our own beds and we could cook our own meals.

I wasn't sure if Griff was going to give me any trouble about staying here, but he didn't have a say in the matter. This was my home. I wasn't going to let Warner Franklin, or anyone else, drive me away.

~~~

Mom and I dressed festively the morning of our grand reopening. I even took the time to put on makeup and curl my hair instead wearing it in my standard issue pony tail. Instead of tee shirt and jeans, I opted for a dress and high heels. Those would probably be exchanged for flats before the day was over.

On several of the days when we were without anything to

do, Mom and I drove into town to shop. After Franklin was finished in our house, the only clothes we had were those we wore to the softball game. Our closets weren't full yet, but it was a start. We'd also picked out new furniture that would be delivered once Ted Kramer had our house finished. I didn't realize exactly how much we accumulate over a lifetime until we had to replace it.

"You're both looking very pretty this morning," Ernie complimented us as we came into the breakfast room. This was to be our last meal at the bed and breakfast. Griff stood up to pull out our chairs; his warm gaze traveling down my body was like an intimate caress.

"I have to agree, Ernie," he said. "These ladies brighten up an already pretty room." He managed to compliment us and the owners of the bed and breakfast at the same time. He certainly is smooth, I thought, reminding myself he was here only long enough to figure out where Warner Franklin was. Then he'd be gone. I couldn't let his sweet talk and stirring kisses get past the barrier surrounding my heart.

"You gentlemen are too kind." Mom gave a playful little curtsey before taking the chair Griff was holding for her. I was feeling a little nervous about the day and couldn't think of a snappy comeback, so I settled for a nod and a weak smile.

I couldn't put a finger on the reason for my case of nerves. It wasn't like a bunch of strangers would be invading our store. I'd known these people most of my life. They had worked beside us helping to get ready for this day. We weren't doing something new and different with the store, it would be the same as before, only better, I told myself.

The joy of our reopening celebration was overshadowed by an article in the paper announcing the identification of the body found in the forest as that of the camper/hiker from back east. My heart went out to the family of the young man. I was relieved, though, to know The Hermit was still out there somewhere. Or had Franklin killed him too, and his body just hadn't been discovered yet?

119

A few tourists joined in on our celebration; some were repeat customers who camped nearby on a regular basis. But most of the people who came and went all day were locals. Even David Graham showed up. "Congratulations, Becca, you've done a nice job rebuilding. I hope you're more careful in the future."

"What's that supposed to mean?" I glared up at him. He had a way of getting under my skin with just about everything that came out of his mouth. "Are you suggesting what happened was my fault?"

"Well, he did warn you to stay away. As always, your stubborn nature took that as a challenge, so you did exactly what he warned you not to do."

"You're an idiot, David. Get back on patrol and leave us alone."

"In case you haven't noticed, I'm not in uniform. This is my day off. I wanted to celebrate with you and your mom."

"So insulting me is your way of celebrating?" I lifted one eyebrow in question.

"I didn't insult you; I made a statement of fact. You're the most stubborn woman I've ever met. But like you, I enjoy a challenge." He stepped so close I could feel his warm breath on my face. I found his actions, and what he was suggesting, revolting. Even if he was the last man on earth, and the existence of mankind relied on the two of us, there would *never* be anything between us.

"Well, find your challenges somewhere else, David." I poked my finger into his chest to push him away. "There's too much history between us, and I'm not interested."

"History is a good thing, Becca. Look at Megan and Jack." He nodded to where they were standing, each holding one of the twins and still holding hands. "Their history is as long as ours."

"Maybe so, but theirs is a good history; ours has always been very contentious. Now back away!"

He glowered at me for a minute, then did as I asked. "Just

remember what I said, Becca. Stop snooping where you don't belong. Leave hunting for fugitives to the professionals." He walked off, heading for the table holding the cake and punch.

"What was that all about?" I whirled around, nearly bumping into Griff, he was standing so close.

"Just David being David, nothing to worry about. Did you have a piece of cake?" I changed the subject. "Mom makes the best cakes around." His eyes were dark as he watched David make his way across the room, but didn't pursue the subject further.

Misty was still giving Chad the cold shoulder, but he'd been able to warm her up a little. He'd taken my advice to grovel seriously. He was going a little overboard though. He couldn't seem to get a balance. At least he wasn't following me around complaining about Griff, and that was a good thing.

The day went off without a hitch, if you don't count David's backhanded attempt at flirtation, and I don't. My case of nerves was unfounded, thank You, God. Everyone in town, and many from towns nearby, stopped in at some time during the day. Looking at our shelves, I don't think many people had done much shopping while they waited for us to reopen.

Mom planned a little private celebration after we closed with some of our closest friends. I was surprised she had also invited Bill Wheeler and Griff to join us.

Bill had moved to town about eight years ago. He'd been a good addition to the town and a good friend, but I'd never seen any attraction between him and Mom until all this happened. Had I been blind, or was this something new? Either way, I was okay with it. I did wish she'd left Griff off her guest list though.

For the first time in weeks, Mom was able to cook, and she was in her glory. She could have been a chef in any cordon bleu restaurant if she had set her mind to it. Instead, she enjoyed hosting small parties like the one going on now in the back room of our store. Or was she showing off for Bill? I smiled at the thought.

"When did this thing with Bill begin?" I asked her when we had a few minutes to ourselves. He'd been sticking pretty close to her since our store had been trashed.

"You don't mind, do you honey?" A pretty blush tinted her cheeks.

"Of course not." I kissed her soft cheek.

"When he first moved here he had just gone through a nasty divorce, and was very bitter," she said. "He wanted nothing to do with another woman; he just wanted to be left alone. And of course, your dad was still with us. After he passed away, I couldn't even think about another man." She looked away, her thoughts with Dad for a moment. "Your father was the love of my life," she went on. "After he went home to Jesus..." She gave a sad little shrug and sighed. "I thought that part of my life was over.

"Bill said the town helped heal him, and when all the stealing started, he wanted to help, but didn't know how or what to do about it. When our store and home were ruined, it about broke his heart. He wanted to protect us. That's when he realized he cared about us very much. He's a very sweet man and very protective. You don't mind, do you, honey?" she asked again.

"No, of course not," I assured her again, giving her hug. "I just want you to be happy."

The subject of our conversation entered the kitchen then, preventing us from saying more. But I had my answer. Mom was happy. As I walked into the other room, I patted Bill's shoulder, giving him a wink.

It had been a long day, and the twins had enjoyed every minute. As long as they kept moving, they were fine. Sitting still to eat had been too much for them. After just a few bites of their dinner, they both fell asleep, their cherubic faces resting in their plates. Megan wanted to help with the dishes, but Mom wouldn't hear to it. "Take those babies home, and get some rest yourselves." She gave Megan a hug, placing a kiss on the twins' cheeks, before shooing them out the door, along with most of the other guests.

Then she turned her attention to Griff and me. "Go enjoy the evening. I'll clean up here. Bill offered to help." I didn't want to be alone with Griff, but any excuse I gave would look like I didn't want her to be alone with Bill.

Mom had even replaced the lawn chairs she always kept on the patio between our house and the store. Sitting there now, I searched for something to say, but I came up blank. Maybe I could plead exhaustion, and escape to our makeshift apartment in the attic.

"You look very happy tonight," Griff's voice was soft in the night. I could feel his smile more than see it in the dark. "Your celebration turned out very nice."

"Yes, it did. It will be even nicer when we can move back into our house." My voice was a little wistful.

"You still need to be careful, Becca," he cautioned. "Just because the FBI couldn't find him, doesn't mean Franklin has left the area. He's a master at hiding."

"Why are you trying to throw cold water on my happiness?" Instead of wistful, I now sounded a little waspish. "Of course, I know he's still out there. What I don't know is why he's got his sights set on me. I'm certainly not a threat to him." This was a subject we'd discussed before without coming up with an answer.

"If he's been in the forest for any length of time, he probably considers it his property, not belonging to the Forest Service or the town. He'll consider anyone from the towns around here as trespassers or interlopers. Since you're the one who has pushed the hardest to find him, he's focused on you."

"I'm still not a threat to him," I argued. "I know the forest as well as anyone in town, and much better than those agents, but there are a lot of places I've never been. Maybe even some from the Forest Service haven't been to some of them. There are a lot of abandoned mine shafts in these mountains. I wouldn't go into those for all the money in the world. If he's crazy enough to hide in an old mine shaft, I hope it collapses on him."

Griff chuckled before growing serious again. "If that happened, we'd never know about it. We'd always be looking for him. I'd rather catch him. I want him to pay for all he's done."

"Well, I've hung up my bounty hunting credentials. As long as he stays away from the town and our people, I'll leave him alone as well." That was the truth, sort of. I fully intended to protect those I love and what is ours. I just wasn't sure how to go about doing that.

"I hope you mean that, Becca. I don't want you getting hurt." He took my hand, his thumb drawing circles on the back. My stomach churned uneasily, and I pulled my hand away. He had to stop doing this.

## CHAPTER THRITEEN

"Why are you still here?" A week later I posed the same question Chad had asked me. "Your men are here to protect the town and help find Franklin. I'm sure you need to get back to running your own business."

"Trying to get rid of me, Becca?" Griff raised one eyebrow. "I wonder why that is." He seldom ventured very far from the General Store when we were open. If I was somewhere else, he dogged my steps. Most evenings he had even managed to get Mom to invite him to dinner.

"I just don't see the sense of having your men here if you're going to stay." Truth be told, he was driving me nuts. He was becoming more important to me each day he stayed here. When he finally decided to leave, my heart was going to be shattered. I couldn't tell him that, though. His ego was already the size of all outdoors.

"You don't need to worry about my business, Sugar. I've got it all under control." He didn't explain how, and I didn't ask. That would seem like I was more interested than I was. Right, I told myself. I *wanted* to know everything there was to know about the man. But I *needed* him to leave.

"Well, if your business fails, don't blame it on Flanagan's Gap." I lifted one shoulder in a shrug that I hoped said I couldn't care less.

"Wouldn't think of it, Sugar." He ran his finger down the side of my face in a soft caress.

"Will you stop doing that? And stop calling me Sugar!" I stomped my foot in frustration, accidentally stomping on the toe of the sneakers he was wearing.

"Ow!" He pulled the offended appendage out from under the heel of my shoe.

"I'm sorry! I didn't mean to do that." I gripped his arm to steady him as he stood on one foot. I should know better than to let my temper run away with my common sense. "Are you all right? Do you need to sit down?"

"No, I think I'll be fine in a few minutes." He slipped his arm around my waist, leaning on me for support, exaggerating the extent of his injury. He put on a good show, but those enticing lips twitched with the grin he was trying to hide.

"Darn you, Griff." I slapped his chest, giving him a push. "Go away and leave me alone." I turned my back on him, hoping he would go, and afraid he would do just that. What is wrong with me? I silently asked myself. I've never had trouble making up my mind before. Why now, with this confusing, infuriating, sexy, endearing man?

When the front door of the store closed with a solid thud, I sagged against the counter, burying my head in my hands. For the few minutes this scene had played out, we'd been alone. Mom had gone upstairs for something in our little apartment, and there were no customers in the store. I was grateful for both.

"Did I hear Griff leave?" Mom asked as she came into the room.

"Um, yes, he had to go...somewhere else."

Mom chuckled. "In other words, you sent him away again. The man is interested in you, honey. You might want to pay attention."

"What for? He'll be leaving soon. I have no intention of getting my heart broken." Too late for that, a little voice in my head stated. When he leaves, you're going to be devastated. Mom shook her head, but didn't pursue the subject.

Since destroying our store, Warner Franklin hadn't attempted anything else. Everyone was keeping a close watch on their own homes, and I was on pins and needles. Was he just waiting for Griff and his men to leave before attacking us again? Did he know who Griff was? Had he left the area like the FBI believed? I didn't know the answer to any of those questions.

We still hadn't heard anything from Agent Black. Were

they investigating the murder of that young camper/hiker? After the first report in the paper, there had been nothing more about it. Was the FBI so heartless that they didn't care about a murder victim?

A week later, the town turned out to watch as Griff climbed behind the wheel of a dark SUV. He'd just announced that there was nothing more he and his men could do here. The FBI was right. Warner Franklin had left the area.

"I told you he wasn't going to stick around." My breaking heart made my voice sharper than I intended. "This is precisely why I didn't want to get involved with him."

"I'm sorry, honey. I thought he was such a nice young man." Mom wrapped her arm around my waist, pulling me close.

"Yeah, he is, I guess. He just has to get back to his own life. We knew he was only here to find Warner Franklin."

"He didn't need to trifle with your affections while he was at it," she said bitterly. She was like a mother bear protecting her cub. "I thought maybe he was the man for you."

"Not hardly," I scoffed. "I never expected him to stick around." I did my best to keep the hurt out of my voice. "If everyone is right, and Franklin is gone, maybe now life can get back to normal."

"I hope they're right, and that horrible man is no longer out there in the forest."

For a long moment we were both quiet. What would we do if Warner Franklin resurfaced? No telling how much damage he could do in the amount of time it took for any form of law enforcement to get to town. "We'll just have to take care of ourselves." I tried to sound positive. "Maybe it's time for that neighborhood patrol Bill had suggested." I didn't want to think about Warner Franklin or Griff Tomlin.

Bill Wheeler had become a regular at our table in the evening. The roses in Mom's cheeks were a testament to the fact that she enjoyed his company. I knew we could count on him if things went awry, but how much could he do against the likes of Warner Franklin? I just hoped we wouldn't have to find out.

~~~

"Will things ever get back to the way they were before Warner Franklin invaded our lives?" Megan and I were sitting on the bleachers at our regular Sunday softball game. But things were anything but normal. "I feel like the whole town has lost its innocence."

"Yeah, I know," I sighed, looking across the field where men were stationed around the perimeter. They weren't watching the game; their attention was riveted on their surroundings, checking out the people watching the game, looking for any sign of Warner Franklin. "I just don't know how to fix things."

"It would go a long way to fixing everything if the FBI or someone would catch Franklin, lock him up, and throw away the key."

The 'someone' she was referring to was Griff Tomlin. Since he left over a week ago, people didn't say his name when I was around; they just talked about the anonymous someone. I nodded, but didn't comment. I had nothing to say about the man.

"How are you holding up?" I knew what she was talking about, but pretended otherwise.

"Okay. The house is almost finished; then our new furniture will be delivered, and we can move in. It'll be nice to be back in the house instead of the attic. I'm just not sure it will feel all that much like home. There won't be anything familiar, no mementos, or anything. Mom's painted a few pictures to hang up, but it won't be the same." My breath escaped on a sad sigh, and tears burned the back of my eyes. "I feel like I've lost my past. So does Mom, even if she won't admit it." Megan gave my hand a squeeze, but there was nothing she could say.

Misty had finally forgiven Chad and was sitting beside him. He'd managed to rein in some of the crush he had on me.

Without Griff around, I guess he didn't feel the need to 'protect' me any longer. At least one good thing came out of Griff's departure, I told myself.

School would be starting in a few weeks. Chad would still be going to school in town each day and Misty attended the co-op here in Flanagan's Gap. I wondered what that would do to their romance. I didn't want either of them to get their hearts broken, but that was inevitable. They were too young to get serious. They still had college to look forward to.

Concentrating on plans for the upcoming school year helped keep my mind off of other matters. I still had the pictures I'd taken of the flowers in the forest, but I couldn't use them for a class project as I'd planned.

The body of the camper hadn't been obvious when I was looking at the flowers that day, but it was perfectly clear in the picture. I'd find another nature project for the kids to work on.

Getting up to bat, my gaze drifted to the spot where Griff had always sat, even after he moved to town. My stomach rolled and my head swam for a minute. Someone was sitting there. I closed my eyes, giving my head a shake. Was I hallucinating? Surely, Griff wouldn't come to one of our games. Opening my eyes again, I focused on the figure sitting there. No, it wasn't Griff. David Graham had stopped by, inadvertently sitting where Griff always sat.

Or had he done that on purpose? Since the store reopened, he'd made a pest of himself, stopping in just to say hello, checking up on us. It had gotten worse now that Griff was gone; he came by the store almost every day.

I turned my thoughts away from all the men in my life; I needed to concentrate on the game. Unfortunately, I didn't do a very good job. I was out after just three pitches.

"Better luck next week, Becca." David joined us for ice cream after the game, but there wasn't much to celebrate. The Flanagan's Gap Elk lost, four to three.

"It's just a game, David. Someone has to lose." I turned to walk away without getting any ice cream. I'd lost my appetite.

"I'm just offering my condolences, Becca. I know how competitive you are," he teased.

"That's right, David. You know all about me, so I'm sure there's nothing here to hold your interest. Take your ice cream and go back to work." If this was how he spent his time on duty, he was overpaid. His chuckle followed me across the church yard.

"Please, God, don't let him follow me," I whispered softly.

# CHAPTER FOURTEEN

Moving day finally arrived. Mom and I were excited, but a little apprehensive. Would it feel like home? Ted did a wonderful job making our small house look like new. Mom hadn't wanted to tear it down, but we had made changes. If we had nothing from our old home, we might as well upgrade what we did have.

The few items that meant the most to us were still locked up in the tunnel under the store. Until now, I hadn't understood why Mom kept some of those things locked out of sight. What good was having them if we couldn't see them ourselves? Now I was grateful they hadn't been where Franklin could destroy them also.

Years ago I'd transferred all of our family photos to a flash drive that had been safely locked away. I'd had some of them printed for our new home. The one thing Warner Franklin, or anyone else, couldn't take from us was our memories.

I slept in fits and starts that first night in our new/old home. Again Warner Franklin dominated my dreams like he had the first time I saw his picture. This time, Griff chased him through the dense forest only to come up empty handed. Franklin taunted Griff and the rest of the town at every turn. With The Hermit still among the missing, his image and the body of the young camper occasionally changed places.

Still tired when I went down for breakfast, I wished I could get those four men out of my mind. Dreaming about them wasn't accomplishing anything. Griff wasn't coming back to Flanagan's Gap; the young camper was also gone from his family. I hoped he was a believer; that would be his family's only consolation. No one knew the fate of The Hermit. Had Franklin killed him, or driven him away from the forest? Was he buried somewhere he'd never be found?

"You look like you didn't get much sleep last night,

honey." Mom placed a steaming cup of coffee on the table in front of me. "Why don't you take the day off and get some rest? The store won't be very busy today."

I shook my head. "I need to do the things I did before this all happened. The sooner we get things back to normal, the sooner I'll be able to sleep. Won't the crafters be in today? What are we working on?" Maybe if I kept myself busy to the point of exhaustion during the day, I would be able to sleep better at night.

Megan had a better idea. "Jack is going to watch the boys today," she announced when she came in the store an hour later. "We haven't had a girls' day out for a long time. Where do you want to go?

"I can't get away today, Megan. I need to be here while Mom works in the craft room."

"Nonsense," Mom argued when she heard Megan's idea. "Everyone knows what they're working on; I don't need to watch over them. Besides, Nancy Baker is helping out with one of her projects." She was teaching some of the women how to make their own soap from her goats' milk.

"That's right." I was suddenly excited. "I wanted in on that. We can't keep our own goats in town, but I want to know how she makes the soaps and lotions." It wasn't an excuse or just something else to add to my schedule. I really wanted to know.

"It isn't a one-time class, honey. She'll be doing this for several weeks. You go enjoy yourself with Megan." Had they planned this together? I wondered.

"All right," I reluctantly agreed, "on one condition. Next week, you take a day off to enjoy yourself. Maybe you can get Bill to go to a movie in town."

Pink tinted her cheeks, but she nodded agreement. "If there are any movies we'd both like to see, I'll ask him."

"Not if, Mom. I want you to take a day for yourself." She hadn't taken a vacation since Dad passed away more than five years ago.

There were still things we needed for the house, and we

each still needed to replace clothes that had been destroyed. We agreed to split the list for the house, and we would each shop for our own clothes. Megan was excited about helping me pick out the items we needed. Spending someone else's money was always more fun.

"Why do we always wait until we're about dead on our feet before we plan a girls' day out?" Nearly bouncing in her seat, she was more excited than I was as we headed into town.

I shrugged, keeping my eyes on the road ahead. "I guess we just get wrapped up in things and forget to relax." I couldn't quell my apprehension about leaving Mom alone for the day. What if Warner Franklin knew she was alone, and decided to do something to her? That's supposing he's still around, I reminded myself. I was giving myself a lot of credit if I thought he wouldn't do something just because I was home.

I knew if Mom had any problems, Bill would be there in a heartbeat. Now that they had found each other, he wasn't going to take any chances of losing her.

Since it was a week day instead of Saturday, there was nothing going on in the Court House Square. That meant there were fewer people milling around town, and the stores were less crowded. We could take our time looking over what we wanted to buy.

By lunch, I was finally able to relax and enjoy myself. I had to admit it was fun using the insurance money to replace the things we'd lost. At least our budget wasn't going to suffer. I even found an antique table that was startlingly similar to one that had belonged to my grandmother.

With all of my new treasures safely stored in the back of the pickup, we headed home, singing along with the radio. "Think Jack will be willing to watch the twins again next month?" I asked. "We really need to do this more often." I felt more relaxed than I had in months.

"How right you are," she laughed. "As long as he has a day off the same day I'm free, it won't be a problem. He's decided the boys aren't going to break if he does something wrong."

A few minutes later there was a loud pop, the steering wheel jerked in my hands, and the front end leaned to the right. Wrestling the steering wheel, I managed to keep the big truck upright. The thump of a flat tire told me what was wrong. Pulling to the side of the road, we stepped down from the cab to take a look. The right front tire was as flat as a pancake. Not just a flat tire, but a blowout.

Still shaking from what could have been a disaster, we both drew a shaky breath before getting to the business of changing the ruined tire.

The spare was under the bed of the truck and the jack was under the back seat. At least we wouldn't have to take everything out of the truck just to change the tire. Growing up in a small town away from all the convenience of having a mechanic or tow truck close by, Dad had taught me how to change a tire as soon as I got my driver's license. I also knew how to change the oil. I just wasn't dressed for crawling around on the side of the highway, but it couldn't be helped. I wasn't going to wait for an hour or more for AAA to send out a truck to change it for me.

"Can you lift that big thing off and get the new one in place?" Megan asked, eyeing the large tire.

"I don't have much choice." I shrugged. "You might have to help me." I sounded more assured of myself than I felt. The car Dad taught me on was much smaller than this monster.

I had the jack in place, loosening the lug nuts when a car pulled up behind us. Nerves jangled along my spine. Two women stuck on the side of an empty highway could be easy prey. "Stay close," I whispered to Megan. She stood up from where she'd been crouched beside me, and gave a loud sigh of relief.

"It's okay," she whispered back. "It's just David."

He swaggered up to us, his thumbs stuck in his gun belt. "Howdy, ladies, got a flat tire?"

A giggle bubbled up in my throat. I couldn't look at

Megan, or we would both be falling down laughing. "No, David, I just thought I'd stop alongside the road, and exchange a perfectly good tire for the spare. 'Here's your sign'." I quoted Country Western comedian, Bill Engvall's CD that was popular when we were in high school that said people should have to wear a sign when they ask stupid questions.

His face got bright red and for a minute I thought he was going to explode. Finally, he turned away. "Well, it looks like you have everything under control. Have a nice evening." Stalking back to his car, he slammed the door. Gravel sprayed under his tires as he peeled away.

"Maybe I shouldn't have said that," I giggled again. "He could have helped us."

"He asked for it. That was a stupid question." She laughed along with me. "He still should have helped us. Isn't that what Sheriff's Deputies are supposed to do, 'Protect and Serve'? We could have used a little service right about now. Are you going to be able to lift that tire off?" she asked again.

Before I could answer, David's car came back around. Apparently he'd had an attack of guilty conscience, and came back to help out. Getting stiffly out of his car, he stomped up to us. "I'll do that, Becca. Move." It was an order, not an offer to help. He didn't bother with any niceties. I couldn't say I blamed him after I made fun of him.

Megan and I stood mutely by while he worked. I was afraid to say anything. If I started laughing, he'd leave and not come back.

"You're good to go." He stood up, slinging the ruined tire into the bed of the truck and wiping his hands on a rag. "Drive safely."

"Thank you, David," I said meekly. He ignored me, stomping back to his car.

As he pulled away, Megan and I looked at each other, doubling over with laughter. "I guess I don't have to worry about him flirting with me anymore." We laughed harder. It took several minutes to get ourselves under control, and back on the road.

As I pulled behind the store to our house, a smile creased my face. Mom and Bill were sitting on the patio, enjoying what was left of the daylight with tall glasses of iced tea and lemonade.

"You look like you had fun, honey." They came around the back of the truck to see what we bought.

"What happened here?" Bill asked, seeing the tire just inside the tailgate. A worried frown drew his greying eyebrows together.

"We had a blowout on the way home. I'll bring the tire over tomorrow to see if it can be repaired or if I need a new one."

Mom pulled me in for a fierce hug. "Neither of you were hurt?" she asked, her voice shaking a little. The past couple of months had been hard on her nerves as well.

I shook my head, reassuring her we were fine. "David came along right after it happened. He changed it for me." I left out the funny part, certain she wouldn't approve of my laughter.

Bill was still frowning, as he pulled the heavy tire out of the back. "This was a fairly new tire. You shouldn't have had a blowout."

"Maybe I ran over a nail or something on the road," I suggested, not understanding his meaning.

"That wouldn't have caused the tire to suddenly blow out. It would have just gone flat." My stomach churned. "I'll take this to the station now and check it over." I couldn't talk him into waiting until the morning.

"What was that about?" I looked at Mom. "Does he think there's something fishy about my flat tire?"

She shrugged. "I'm not sure. He doesn't think this thing with Warner Franklin is over yet. He's upset that law enforcement has more or less abandoned us." She released a sigh. "I tried to tell him that we're pretty self-reliant here, but he's still worried."

My stomach churned again, but I didn't say anything, not wanting to worry her any more than she already was. What would make a tire blow out like that if it wasn't a nail?

~~~

After another restless night, I stumbled to the kitchen in search of a hot cup of coffee. If this kept up, I'd have bags under my eyes big enough to use as a suitcase. I'd barely taken my first sip when someone knocked on the kitchen door.

"Sorry it's so early." Bill came in when Mom opened the door. "I figured you'd both want to know first thing what I found in that tire." His grim face told us we weren't going to like what he had to say. Mom set a cup in front of him, waiting to hear. "That tire didn't blowout on its own. Someone put a bullet in it."

Mom gasped, her face going white. "Who would do something like that? Why would they?" I could think of only one person who felt he had a reason to get rid of me.

Bill took her hand, but didn't answer her questions. Apparently, he'd come to the same conclusion I had. "You need to call the sheriff," he said quietly. "They have to know about this. Didn't the deputy even check out the tire when he changed it?"

My stomach went to my toes. "He was in kind of a hurry," I said evasively. Calling David after the way I'd treated him yesterday wasn't going to be pleasant. Maybe he'd send out someone else in his place. I could only hope.

Forty-five minutes later my hopes were dashed when David stepped out of his patrol car. "What's this about someone shooting out your tire? Who did you tick off now, Becca?" he growled at me. "Are you sure it wasn't just a simple blowout?" The hackles on the back of my neck bristled.

"I've got the bullet to prove it," Bill spoke before I could give a sharp retort. He'd been watching for the patrol car, and crossed the street from his gas station in time to hear David's comment.

David turned quickly, his hand going to the butt of his gun.

I guess he didn't like people coming up behind him. Relaxing only slightly, David ignored me. A fact I was grateful for. He followed Bill back to the station without saying anything else.

A few minutes later, he came back with my tire, throwing it and a small plastic bag in the trunk of his car. "You know many kids with a twenty-two?" His tone was barely civil.

"I suppose. What's that got to do with anything?"

"The bullet is a twenty-two. That's a kid's rifle. Probably some kids horsing around in the woods shooting at beer cans, and a shot got away from them. I'll check it out, and get back with you." With that pronouncement, he was gone.

"Kids my eye. That had to be one lucky shot for kids to hit the tire of a moving vehicle," I said to his retreating car.

"You were right, honey." Mom put her arm around my waist, pulling me close. "He is a real turd."

That made me chuckle, easing some of my tension. "If it's kids, I don't have to worry about someone being out to get me then."

"You should call Griff. He needs to know about this." She still had her arm around me as we headed for the store. It was time to open up.

"When pigs fly," I muttered, using Griff's own phrase. "You heard David; it was kids horsing around, nothing to worry about."

"You don't believe that any more than I do."

"I'm still not calling Griff." As far as I was concerned that was the end of the discussion.

# CHAPTER FIFTEEN

A week later, David pulled up in front of the store. He was clearly still carrying a grudge. By now, it must be getting pretty heavy. Through the big plate glass windows, Mom and I watched as he went to the trunk of his car, lifting out the tire he'd taken away earlier.

"It's yours, Becca. I'm just returning it," he stated, when I stepped outside, preventing him from bringing the tire into the store.

"Take it to the gas station. Bill can do whatever it is you do with old tires. He's already put a new one on the rim." He looked like he wanted to argue, instead turned to take the tire to Bill's gas station. My question stopped him from walking away. "Did you find the "kids" who shot out my tire?" I made air quotes earning a glare for my efforts.

"I asked around, but no one admitted to being out there that day."

"Did you actually go out where it happened to look around?"

"Don't tell me how to do my job, Becca," he snapped, looking like he wanted to strangle me.

"Well, I think someone needs to if you aren't even going to investigate what happened."

He let my ruined tire drop on the sidewalk. "Take it to Bill yourself." With that, he turned, stalking back to his car. "Have a good day, Becca. Be careful you don't make enemies out of your friends, or you won't have anyone to call the next time you're in trouble."

I stood there with my mouth open as he drove away. I swear he had a smirk on his face, or was it a glare on the windshield? In school, I'd never considered David a friend. More like a 'frienemy'; half friend, half enemy. I suppose now he's all enemy. I huffed and puffed for a moment before going back inside.

"What am I supposed to do with that stupid tire?" I asked Mom.

"What did he say?" she asked. "Did he find who shot out your tire?"

"No, but he didn't look very hard. Even I know you need to look at the scene before you can figure out what happened." I drew in a deep breath, trying to calm down. The man was completely off his rocker. Maybe I'd asked for some of his attitude because I made fun of his stupid question. How could he call himself a law enforcement officer though, when he didn't even investigate who had shot out my tire?

I'm not sure what Bill did with the tire, but at least it wasn't sitting on the sidewalk. I hoped for Mom's sake he was more reliable than a few of the men in my life recently.

Even though our team won the game on Sunday I wasn't in the mood to celebrate. David's words haunted me. Was I being too critical, too choosy? I wanted to have friends, to get married, and have a family. But if I drove everyone away, how could any of that happen? Had there been even a slight chance that something could have developed between Griff and me? I shook my head at that thought. I didn't want to leave Flanagan's Gap, and his life was centered on his business. At least I thought it was. What did I really know about his life? I silently asked myself as I headed home.

The narrow covered patio between the back door of the store and the front door of our home was in shadow when I came around the building. Someone was sitting in one of the lawn chairs Mom kept there. My heart went to my throat, and my stomach dropped to my toes. Had Warner Franklin come back to finish what he started when he destroyed our home?

I took a cautious step backward. Could I outrun him? "Hi, Becca." The soft voice stopped me before I could run.

Surprise left me speechless for several seconds. "Griff?" I said when I finally managed to find my voice. "What are you doing here? Did Mom call you?" I eyed him suspiciously.

"No, why would she?" The blank look on his face said he was either a world class actor, or he didn't know what I was talking about.

"Why are you here then?" I asked again.

"I never really left. At least part of me didn't go."

"Huh?" His cryptic words were so soft, I wasn't sure I heard them correctly or knew what they meant.

He gave a little chuckle. "Sugar, you captured my heart the first time you followed me into the forest."

"How could that be?" My voice was barely above a whisper. If he hadn't been standing within a hairsbreadth of me now, he wouldn't have heard me. "I didn't even see you, and you certainly didn't speak to me."

"I've always liked my women to have a little fire, a little grit. I could see that fire burning in you that day and every day since. Why do you think I kept coming back to your softball games?"

"You like sports?" I let the comment about 'his women' go for now. I certainly didn't want to be one of a long line of them.

Laughter rumbled from deep in his chest. "Sure do, but not that much. I couldn't take my eyes off you." I could feel his mint-scented breath on my lips, but he still hadn't touched me.

"If that's so, why are you standing so far away from me now?" Oh Lord, please tell me I didn't just say that out loud. I didn't even know where that thought came from. Another laugh rumbled in his chest as he closed the inch between us, and gathered me in his arms. His lips settled on mine in a mind-blowing kiss, his hands roamed up and down my back, pulling me even closer.

"If that's how you felt, why did you leave?" The question tumbled out when he lifted his head to rest his forehead against mine.

"I had to. If Franklin is still out there," he nodded his head towards the forest, "he'd never show himself as long as he knew someone was watching over you."

"So you left me hanging out here on my own as bait?" I asked indignantly. I tried to pull out of his arms, but he wouldn't let me move.

"Not even," he stated. "I've had a couple of my men in the forest the whole time. They haven't seen Franklin. Or the hermit you keep talking about?" he quickly added before I could ask. Disappointment at his last statement warred with relief over the hope that Franklin really had moved on.

"Why did you think your mom had called me? Why would she?" We were sitting in the porch swing now with my head resting on his shoulder.

"Oh, ah, she just mentioned calling you a few days ago." What would he say about someone shooting out my tire? Had Warner Franklin done that, or was it kids messing around in the woods like David suggested?

"Yeah and why would she mention calling me?" He put his finger under my chin to lift my head, forcing me to look at him.

I sputtered for a couple seconds, trying to think of something to say before letting out a heavy sigh. He began pacing, running his long fingers through his thick hair when I explained what happened.

"So he is still out there," he muttered, facing the unseen forest. "Where is he hiding that no one can find him?" He was speaking to himself now, not me.

I answered anyway. "There are a lot of places he could hide, not just the old mine shafts. There are plenty of caves in the mountains. Some of them go a long way back, and haven't been fully explored by anyone. People have tried to find where The Hermit lives and only Jack has found his place. I don't think any of the other rangers know where it is. If he can hide all these years, Franklin could probably find a way to do it, too.

"Then I need to get Jack to help me." He sat down next to me again. Gathering me in his arms, he placed a soft kiss in my hair. "I have to figure out a way to be here without letting anyone know who I am, especially Franklin if he's keeping an eye on the town."

We didn't hear Mom and Bill coming until it was too late for Griff to disappear. Mom's happy expression when she spotted him contrasted with Bill's scowl.

"Griff, it's good to see you again. Thanks for coming back. How did you hear what happened?" She placed a kiss on his cheek.

"Becca just told me." I looked at them in turn, trying to judge if they were covering up for a phone call Mom had made. "I wish someone had called me." He turned his dark frown on me.

"What do you care?" Bill asked in a low growl, "You said Franklin was gone, and left without a backward glance." He looked like he wanted to remove Griff's arm from around my shoulders. When had he become so protective of me? "Why did you come back now?" Mom patted his hand, but he ignored her.

For just a moment I could feel the tension in Griff before he relaxed against the swing, keeping his arm where it was. "I came back to see Becca. I wanted her to know I was still watching out for her."

"Yeah? How's that when you weren't even here?"

"Bill, enough," Mom whispered. "Hear him out." Bill snorted, but didn't argue while he waited for Griff to explain.

"Could we go inside?" Griff asked, before giving the explanation everyone was waiting for. "I don't want anyone else to know I'm here." Bill snorted again, but didn't argue.

Once inside, he listened to Griff, reluctantly accepting his explanation for leaving. "So what are you going to do now? You don't buy Graham's reasoning about that tire, do you?"

Griff's laugh held no humor. "Not for a minute. I don't know how that guy can even call himself a sheriff's deputy."

"Maybe he only told me that so I wouldn't worry. He might be investigating without letting me know." I couldn't believe I was defending David. He'd been nothing but nasty to me since that day on the highway. But would he deliberately let something awful happen to me just because I'd made fun of him? I couldn't answer that question. I just hoped he was a better deputy than that.

My own conscience had been giving me a little grief in the matter. I shouldn't have made fun of his question, no matter how stupid it was. I guess I owed him an apology.

Griff ignored me as he paced around our living room. "My men haven't been able to find out where the bas...um," he looked at Mom, and started again. "They don't know where he's holed up, but after that tire incident I know he's still out there. That's just like something he'd do. He isn't one to confront you head on. He'd rather sneak up behind your back to attack you."

"If he hadn't started stealing things here in town, no one would have known he was here," I pointed out. "Why did he risk being caught to steal a few clothes and some food? We had no idea who he was, all he had to do was come to the store and buy what he needed."

"He didn't have any money."

"Oh, yeah, I forgot about that." Most people have some form of payment, like The Hermit who traded his carvings for what he took. "But if this is the first time he's surfaced in all these years, why now? It doesn't make any sense," I argued. "All he had to do was stay out there, and no one would have known the difference."

"It's the first time we know about," Griff corrected. "He could have been stealing from different towns all over the west, but it never drew the attention of the FBI, or me, until now. Something must have happened to make him change his mind about hiding. If he's been close by for very long, he probably considers the forest his personal property by now. Maybe that camper challenged him on that issue." He shrugged. "I can't say what's going through Franklin's mind. I wish I could. I just know the man is dangerous when confronted." He sank down on the couch, automatically pulling me against his side, unmindful of Mom's smile and

Bill's scowl.

"So what are you going to do now?" Bill asked. "If no one can find him, no one is safe in any of the towns around here. He can come and go as he pleases, and we can't catch him or stop him." He sounded as frustrated as Griff now.

For several long minutes, Griff didn't say anything, thinking about his next move. Coming to a conclusion, he smiled. "I think I need to get a job."

"Huh?" Why would he need a job when he owned his own company?

"Do you think you can get Jack over here without letting on why?" He looked at Mom.

So far, she hadn't had much to say. Now she smiled. "Of course, I'll just ask them over for dinner." She immediately went to the phone, putting her words into action.

~~~

The next day Jack had three new rangers on his staff, but not on his payroll. It was still wildfire season, so their addition wasn't questioned. The forest service could use all the help they could get. Since Griff had stayed in Flanagan's Gap before, he had to avoid the town now, or come up with a good disguise. The fewer people who knew he was here, the better it was. The men on Jack's crew who knew Griff had been sworn to secrecy.

# CHAPTER SIXTEEN

Waiting for my turn at bat, my thoughts were a million miles away or at least few miles down the road where Griff was staying. He had been working with Jack for two weeks, and no one in town was any the wiser. He hadn't come to see me, but sent occasional messages through Jack. That was becoming embarrassing. I felt like I was back in grade school where kids passed notes back and forth behind the teacher's back.

Chad sat down beside me getting right to his point. "I'm sorry he broke your heart, Becca."

I had just taken a mouthful of Coke and I spewed it out, nearly choking myself in the process. He pounded on my back until I stopped coughing. "What are you talking about?" I was finally able to ask as I wiped away the tears my coughing spell had caused. I was afraid I knew where he was going with this, but I had to ask anyway.

"That Griff character," he elaborated. "I knew he was no good, that he'd break your heart." He kicked at the dirt in front of him. "You should just forget all about him." Since Griff left, Chad, and most of the others in town, didn't mention his name around me. Now Chad brings him up just when Griff is back, working undercover.

"Thanks for caring about me, Chad; you don't have to worry though. I'm just fine." I wasn't certain how true that was. Yes, Griff said I'd captured his heart, but what exactly did that mean? There could never be anything serious between us. We live in two different worlds.

"Then maybe you'll start looking for a boyfriend somewhere else?" He turned his statement into a question.

I gave a soft groan. Did he think he could be that boyfriend? Why was everyone so interested in my love life? I asked myself for the hundredth time. Was I really so pathetic everyone thought they needed to help me out? Instead of voicing these thoughts out loud, I patted Chad's hand. "You don't need worry about me. Just make sure you don't break Misty's heart." Fortune smiled on me right then. It was his turn at bat.

"It was a good game eh, Becca," Pastor Curt stopped beside me at our customary ice cream social after the game.

"They're all good, winning just makes them better." We both laughed. He looked like he had something more he wanted to say, but didn't know how to start. Was he the next person to suggest I find a boyfriend? This was getting beyond embarrassing. "We have a good team." I finished lamely.

"Um, I have something I'd like to show you, Becca." Curt finally broke the silence that was becoming uncomfortable. "Could you come to the church office with me?"

"Sure." What else could I say? I was resigned to the humiliation, at least for today. Even if I had to make up a boyfriend, I was determined to put an end to the indignity of this situation.

Instead of going into his office, he opened the door to the dimly lit sanctuary. Someone was sitting near the front, a ball cap pulled low over his forehead, hair hanging on his shoulders. My stomach rolled, and excitement bubbled in my veins. "The Hermit," I whispered. "Is it really him?" I turned to where Curt had been standing a moment ago only to find myself alone in the small church with this stranger. Would Curt leave me alone with him if he thought there was any danger?

The man stood up, pulling off his cap. The long hair came off with it. "Griff?" I squinted in the dim light. "What are you doing here?" My stomach churned again, for an entirely different reason. He'd shown himself to Pastor Curt, and possibly risked people seeing him by coming here. But why?

"I wanted to see you." The sanctuary had good acoustics. Even though he was standing more than twenty-five feet from me, and spoke in a near whisper, I could easily hear him. "I had to make sure you were all right."

"Why wouldn't I be? Have you been able to get a lead on Franklin?"

He shook his head; his own sun streaked hair almost as long as the fake hair attached to his cap. "My gut tells me he's still here, but I can't for the life of me find out where he's hiding." His warm gaze traveled the length of my body, setting off fireworks, causing my legs to wobble. What was it about this man that he could do more with a simple look than any other man I'd ever known?

"Did Jack take you to The Hermit's shack?" I could feel his warm breath on my face now, but he still hadn't touched me. What was he waiting for?

"He showed it to me, but he wouldn't let me go inside. Unless you're looking for it, you could walk within five feet of it and not notice it was there."

"Does Jack think The Hermit is still living there?" This was a perfectly normal conversation devoid of any personal content, when all I wanted him to do was hold me.

"There's no way of knowing without going inside, and Jack wouldn't let me do that. I would like to lift prints to see if Franklin has been there, but that's a no go." He gave a belly-deep sigh.

"I want to kiss you." His sudden change of topics left my head reeling. "But," he looked around the old building, at the stained glass windows, "that doesn't seem like something we should be doing in a church." Goosebumps moved up my arms. I really wanted him to kiss me, but I had to agree with his assessment.

"Why did you let Pastor Curt know who you are? Is that safe?"

He chuckled softly, the sound reverberating throughout the room. "If I can't trust a pastor to keep my secret, who can I trust?" He had a valid point. Curt wouldn't say anything, even to his wife Judy.

Taking my hand, he led me to a wooden pew, pulling me

down beside him, wrapping me in his strong arms. We stayed like that for several minutes without speaking. It was where I wanted to stay, but I knew it was time to put a little space between us, physically and emotionally.

"How much longer are you going to look for Franklin?"

"The rest of my life, if necessary," he said, deliberately misunderstanding my question. "I want him to pay for what he did."

"What about your business, your employees? You can't expect them to keep looking forever."

"They don't care what the work is as long as they're getting paid and it's legal."

He wasn't making it easy for me to find out what I wanted to know. "But how long can your business keep running if you aren't around to run it?"

"It doesn't matter where I am, I can do everything necessary from any remote hookup. My employees all know their jobs and what needs to be done." I knew very little about his business or how it was run, and he wasn't giving away any details.

Curt cleared his throat when he stepped through the door from the narthex. "The ice cream social is almost over. If you don't want anyone to see you, you should leave now." A small cemetery backed up to the church, but to get back to the forest Griff would have to walk through several neighborhoods. It wouldn't be dark for several more hours. If people mistook him for Warner Franklin, it could be dangerous, but it would cause quite a stir if people thought he was The Hermit the way I had.

Giving me a soft kiss, he put his baseball cap back on, transforming him into someone completely different. Anyone seeing him now would never guess he was Griff Tomlin. Curt opened the side door, checking to see if there was anyone around. Giving a nod of all clear, he let Griff out, then locked the door behind him. It was the only door to the church that Curt kept locked. Although there was a lock on the front door, he said a church should always be open for anyone to come in and pray.

"Are you going to be okay, Becca?" he asked when we were alone. The only light came from the backlighting on the cross at the front of the sanctuary and through the stained glass windows. I wasn't sure what he could read from my expression, and I was grateful for the dim lighting.

"I'm fine, thanks for asking. And thanks for bringing me to see him. I'm glad he's okay." It was my turn to misunderstand his meaning. I didn't want to discuss my feelings for Griff. I couldn't explain them to him when I didn't understand them myself.

The women and a few of the men were finishing the cleanup when I joined them. Mom gave me a questioning look, but didn't say anything. Had she guessed where I'd gone? In her usual way of knowing how I felt, she had guessed I was falling in love with Griff. Maybe she guessed Griff had come to see me. I wondered where she thought the relationship would end up.

Evenings were beautiful this time of year. Instead of going inside, I curled up in a corner of the swing, giving it a push with the toe of my shoe and pulling my knees up to my chest. Admitting I was in love with Griff didn't make it any easier to live with. Once he had put Franklin away for good, he would return to his life, and I would still be in Flanagan's Gap. I couldn't imagine living anywhere else. What did it say about my feelings for him if I wasn't willing to relocate to be with him? Of course, he hadn't said anything about me going with him, so it was a moot point.

I was still sitting there a half hour later when Mom called me in for dinner. I wasn't hungry, but I didn't have an excuse either. I didn't want to worry her. Bill had taken to helping her in the kitchen in my place. Cooking alongside her all my growing up years, I knew how to cook, but it wasn't my passion as it was hers.

~~~

Living next to a national forest means fire is always a big threat. Fire danger was still high all over Arizona, but we'd been lucky so far. Three times Jack and his crew had found evidence of campers carelessly leaving campfires untended. Each time, someone had put the fire out before substantial damage could be done. They hadn't found the culprits who started the fires or the ones who managed to douse them before they could spread.

When the smell of smoke floated on the wind, we wondered if we were we going to be so lucky this time. The plume of smoke lifting over the forest said we weren't. This time it was farther back in the forest. It would take longer for the firefighters to reach it, time for it to spread out of control. There hadn't been any rain or lightning for weeks which meant the fire was manmade.

There is no good time to have a major forest fire, but just weeks before the big end-of-summer Labor Day Festival it would hurt a lot of businesses in Flanagan's Gap and the surrounding towns. The festival begins on Friday before Labor Day and runs through the following Monday. Craft vendors come from all over Arizona and New Mexico; there are rides on the town fire engine for the kids and a hay ride in the evenings with a bar-b-que in the forest. People came from miles around to enjoy themselves. The influx of tourists helps the bottom line of all the businesses.

"Okay folks, you know the drill," Sara called out. "Grab your hoses and get to work." This was the modern version of an old fashioned bucket brigade; we called it the garden hose brigade. Those living closest the forest pulled hoses out, and began spraying the trees and bushes. Water lines had been run around the perimeter of the ball field. People were hooking up hoses to each one. If we could keep the trees wet, it might help to keep them from catching fire.

Other people in town were watering down the roofs of homes so sparks didn't set them on fire. As yet the flames were far off, but this was a precaution we could take now.

For the next few hours everyone kept one eye on what they were doing and the other on the plume of smoke that was growing bigger with each passing minute. Already the hot shot teams had been called in, and we'd seen two tanker planes flying over, dumping their load of water and flame retardant on the fire. So far the wind had been with us and remained mild, but the flames produced their own gusts, fanning the flames further. It was sort of a vicious circle. Only time would tell if the firefighters would be able to keep this from spreading.

Griff and his men worked with Jack's crew on the fire line. Fire crews from around the state were flown in to help out. People from town took turns manning the hoses. Everyone did his best to prevent the fire from coming into the town. Food and water were taken out to the crews where they worked, and they slept in shifts close enough to help if the fire took a turn.

Three days later, a cheer went up early in the morning when black smoke replaced the white smoke previously billowing above the trees. This meant the fire was dying out.

Flanagan's Gap and the entire area had lucked out again. The fire didn't come close to any of the towns or homes. Instead of fighting a fire for weeks, it had taken only five days to fully contain it, and another two days to make sure there were no hot spots that could flare up again.

Everyone held their collective breath, waiting for all the men to come home safely. There is any number of dangers when fighting a forest fire. Once the fire was out and mop up was over, the men began straggling into town, returning safe to their families. Their faces and clothes were blackened from smoke, ashes clung to their hair.

Something seemed off, though. Where was the relief, the happiness that came once the fire was out? No homes or businesses had been damaged in any of the towns. When Jack still hadn't returned several hours later, Megan grabbed one of the men. "Where are the other guys? Where's Jack?" We had no idea how many men hadn't returned yet, since we didn't know how many men had come from all corners of the state to help. But we knew Jack and Griff still hadn't returned to town. Worry was etched into her face. Every year you hear about firefighters dying in a forest fire. Logic told me if anyone had died due to the fire, the men wouldn't have straggled in without saying a word to anyone.

"Um, the fire started in The Hermit's shack." Daniel's vague answer had alarm bells clanging in my mind. He was definitely uncomfortable saying more. At Megan's prompting though, he sighed, and finished. "He's trying to find out what happened, and make sure the old guy's okay." He couldn't quite meet her eyes. I wanted to ask about Griff, but I wasn't sure who knew he and two of his men were here working with Jack.

"What aren't you telling me, Daniel? Why hasn't he radioed in?" She gave his arm a shake.

He shuffled his feet for a minute, still avoiding eye contact. She gave his arm another shake, and he sighed again.

"A couple of the men are missing; Jack and one of the new guys are trying to find them." His eyes slid over to me, just as quickly moving away. Apparently he knew who Griff was. Was Griff one of the missing men? My stomach rolled.

"Why aren't the other men helping out?" she demanded. "Why would you leave someone behind?"

"Jack sent everyone home," Daniel answered. "He stayed behind with Decker and one other guy to continue searching." His eyes slid over to me again. I didn't know what name Griff was using. Was Decker one of his men, or Griff himself?

"How could they just go missing?" I spoke up for the first time. "Did they get caught behind the fire line?" We hadn't heard yet how many acres had been burned. According to Daniel, the only structure to burn was The Hermit's shack. There weren't even any outhouses that far out in the forest.

Daniel gave a fatalistic shrug. "They were working down

153

the line from the rest of us. They were there one minute and not the next. No one saw them walk off or anything unusual."

By 'unusual' I could only assume all the firefighters had been warned about Warner Franklin. Was he behind this fire and the others? Did he have something to do with the missing men? My guess was yes, he did. My heart was in my throat. Had he killed them or just taken them somewhere? "Who are the missing men?" I finally gathered the courage to ask. I needed to know if Griff was missing.

"One of the men is from southern Arizona, the other one is one of Decker's men," Daniel's answer filled me with relief, but it didn't last long. Two men were still missing, and their families would be worried about them.

Megan paced at the edge of the forest. She wanted to go in looking for her husband, but couldn't leave the twins. If something happened to Jack while he was searching for the men, they needed to have one parent left. While we waited, Mom took care of the twins, keeping them occupied so they wouldn't know something was wrong.

It was beginning to get dark when three figures stumbled out of the trees. Like the other men, they were covered with black smoke that disguised their features. Were these the missing men, or Jack, Griff, and his employee? The entire town had been keeping vigil at the ball field. Now they rushed forward as one, but allowed Megan to reach the men first.

Jack saw her coming, and picked up his pace, grabbing her in a fierce embrace. At the same moment, Griff pulled me into his arms. Until that moment, I hadn't been certain it was him, not one of his men; his features were so obscured by smoke.

It took forever for them to tell their story, but they didn't have much more information than Daniel had already told us. One minute the men were there, the next they were gone. How could that even happen? I wondered. If Warner Franklin grabbed them, or even a bear, wouldn't they yell, causing some kind of commotion? There was no indication of where they were or what happened to them.

"What about The Hermit?" I asked quietly. "I know he wasn't your first priority, but were you able to find out if he's still..." I couldn't put my fears in to words.

Jack shook his head, sadness rivaled weariness on his face. "I have no idea if he was in the cabin when it caught fire, or if he's even around here anymore. I wish I could tell you more, Becca, but I can't." He was the only person to befriend the old man, but he was aware of my feelings for him. He was worried about the missing men as well as The Hermit. If Warner Franklin really was here, he could have done something to The Hermit, and we would never find out what happened to the old man.

~~~

In the middle of the night the church bell began clanging, rousting the entire town out of bed. It wasn't the rhythmic sound calling the faithful to worship, but the jarring clang of an emergency. Throwing on a pair of ratty sweats over my pajamas and a pair of flip flops, I rushed outside, with Mom right behind me.

The whole town appeared in the street in various stages of undress. "What's going on?" "What's the emergency?" "Is there another fire?" The questions were flying around as everyone raced to the church to see what had happened. Pastor Curt and Judy were kneeling over something or someone on the ground in front of the church.

"What happened?" Sara stepped up, taking charge as usual. The two missing men were lying on some sort of makeshift pallet or litter strung between long branches. They looked like they'd been badly beaten, and were unconscious.

"We found them here," Curt answered. "Doc's on his way." Making his way through the crowd gathered around the steps, Doc Granger knelt beside the two unconscious men. Megan joined him, working in tandem as they'd done for years.

"How did you happen to find them?" Sara asked Pastor Curt when he and Judy joined the rest of us gathered around to

155

watch. Everyone had been tucked safely in bed. How had he found the men?

"They were here when we came out to see what was going on." He looked down at the men, then looked at those of us standing around. "Who rang the bell?"

"Didn't you?" Sara asked in surprise. Curt and Judy both shook their heads. "Was anyone here when you came out?" Living next to the church, they were the first ones to reach the men.

"No, the street was empty except for the injured men. Judy checked the church. There wasn't anyone in there either." Goosebumps prickled along my arms. If Warner Franklin did this to the men, why would he bring them to town?

"Then who rang the bell?" Sara repeated Curt's question. It was rhetorical, and she didn't expect anyone to answer.

Jack was holding both boys who had fallen back to sleep on his shoulders after being awakened by the loud bell. He stood beside Mom and me watching Doc and Megan work on the injured men. "Who brought them here?" he whispered. From the angle of the leg of one of the men, it was obviously broken.

Griff was standing beside me, his arm around my waist. A worried frown drew his light brows together. One of those men worked for him. I could only imagine what he was feeling.

Stabilizing any broken bones and placing cervical collars on both men, Doc sent Megan to his office for a back board and gurney before trying to move them. He didn't want to do more harm than had already been done. Jack handed the boys to Mom and me to follow Megan. It was still very dark out; he didn't want her going anywhere alone when there was the possibility of a stranger lurking around, even one who helped the men.

"Are they going to be all right?" Griff left my side to talk to Doc Granger. "Should they be airlifted to the hospital?"

"They've already been called, Son. I'd like to get them to

my office to check them over in the light before the chopper gets here, to see what we're facing." He patted Griff on the shoulder. "We'll do our best to take care of them." He looked down at the men. "I'd sure like to know how they got here, and who rang that bell." He was talking to himself as much as to Griff now, looking into the dark forest. That was something we'd all like to know.

# CHAPTER SEVENTEEN

There was no more sleep to be had the rest of the night. Both men were in critical condition with multiple broken bones, head trauma, and second degree burns on their hands and legs. There was also the possibility of internal injuries. Neither man had regained consciousness by the time the medevac chopper lifted off with them on board.

Curt and Judy opened their café after the helicopter left and the entire town crowded inside. Mom helped out, making coffee and sweet rolls while Curt manned the grill and Judy took orders.

"Who rang the church bell?" Bill asked the question Doc and Sara had asked earlier. "How did those men get to town?"

"Who beat them to a bloody pulp?" Sara added her own unanswerable question.

"What's he doing here?" Chad whispered, nodding his head to where Griff was talking to Sara and Jack. His almost white blond hair and dark brown eyes combined with the tall muscular build were a magic combination that was hard for any teenage girl to resist, but his immature attitude was a turnoff at times. I was surprised Misty had put up with him for so long.

"Why shouldn't he be here? One of those injured men works for him."

"But he broke your heart!" he argued heatedly.

I sighed heavily. I was getting tired of his irrational jealousy. "No, he didn't." It wasn't a total lie, I told myself. If I hadn't allowed myself to fall for him, he couldn't have broken my heart.

"I thought he left town. When did he come back?"

"He never really left. He's here helping the town and looking for a killer. We should be grateful for his help."

"You still think Franklin is around here?" He sounded

doubtful.

"Yes, don't you?"

He lifted one shoulder in a noncommittal shrug. Sometimes he acted so much like a petulant little boy that I wanted to turn him over my knee and paddle his behind.

"Who do you think did that to those men?" My voice was sharp with frustration, and more than a little fatigue. I didn't know the names of the men, but I was praying for them all the same. God knew who they were.

"But the FBI said Franklin is gone, if he ever was here," Chad argued. "They wouldn't lie to us."

I snorted my own skepticism. "Of course they would if it suited their purpose. You saw how that agent acted. No one knew more than he did."

"Why would they leave us at the mercy of a killer?" That just didn't fit with his image of a federal law enforcement agency. He was still young enough to see the world through rose colored glasses.

"Warner Franklin isn't the only fugitive the FBI is looking for. I guess they have to go after the ones they know they can find." It was a lame excuse, but it was all I could come up with.

When Griff finished talking to Sara and a few others, he made his way back to me. His eyes were locked on mine as he dodged the multitude of people crowded in the small area. Until he stopped beside me, I'm not certain he even saw Chad. "Morning, Chad." He acknowledged the younger man. "How's it going?" He sounded so tired. I'm not sure how much sleep any of the men had gotten while they were fighting the fire. When the men went missing, he blamed himself for putting them in harm's way. He draped his arm over my shoulder like it was the most natural thing in the world.

A frown creased Chad's light brow for a few seconds, clearing almost immediately. In those few seconds he grew up right before my eyes. "It'd be going a whole lot better if we could catch that Franklin guy. What can I do to help?"

Griff noticed the transformation also, smiling at him. "Thanks for offering, but right now we seem to be stuck in a holding pattern." He gave a frustrated sigh. "We just have to wait for him to do something else, and hope we can catch him."

"My mom says I've never been very good at waiting for something to happen," Chad groused.

"Yeah, my mom told me the same thing." Griff's voice held a world of sadness as he relived a very hurtful time in his life.

When David Graham slammed into the café, all conversation stopped. Everyone turned to stare at him. What's his problem this time? I wondered. I didn't have long to wait to find out.

"Why wasn't I called when those men were found? Who authorized them to be moved before I could investigate? You interfered in an active crime scene." His self-important swagger raised the hackles on my back. From the grumbles coming from others in the room, I was not the only one to feel that way.

"You were called at the same time the medevac helicopter was called," Sara stepped up to face him. Her hands were braced on her hips. "I'm sorry if you were rousted out of bed to come to our aide." There were still creases on his face where it had rested on a pillow.

"And I authorized them to be moved," Doc Granger snapped. Normally a soft-spoken man who avoided confrontation, Doc was ready for a fight. "Would you rather I left them on the street to die until you could get here? That's what would have happened if we'd waited."

"Um, no. Did anyone preserve the scene?" David changed tactics, his tone now more official than confrontational.

"No one knew why the church bell rang," Pastor Curt answered the question, "including me. Everyone was more interested in helping the men." David gave a sigh of resignation or frustration.

Before he could blame the whole town for destroying evidence, Griff spoke up. "You can probably see the tracks from the litter the men were on coming out of the forest. I doubt that's going to tell you much though."

"Just who are you? What do you have to do with all of this?" The two men hadn't actually met before, and David didn't take interference into what he considered 'his case' lightly.

"Name's Griffin Tomlin," Griff answered. "I've been helping the town out with the problems they've been having." He gave away very little information about himself.

"And we're glad to have his help," Sara interjected before David could object.

"Well, this is a case for the law now, so you can stand down, Griffin Tomlin." David's tone was more snide than official now, and he ignored Sara's comment.

"Hasn't it always been a case for the law?" Griff asked mildly. "That hasn't helped this town very much." David's face turned an angry shade of red, but Griff ignored that. "Seems to me the sheriff's department, as well as the FBI, has turned their back on the people here."

"What are *you* planning on doing to help us, David?" Sara questioned before he could argue with Griff. "Someone has been stealing from this town for months. A business and home were trashed, fires have been set in the forest, and now two men were critically injured. Whoever is doing this probably killed that young man from back east. Shouldn't someone be looking into all this?"

"That's an ongoing investigation and the FBI is in charge. They aren't sharing any information with my department," he stated grudgingly. "I suppose they're going to take over this too, since those men were beaten on federal land." He didn't sound at all happy about that prospect.

"You didn't answer my question. What are you going to do to help us? Or do we have to help ourselves yet again?"

"You can't take the law into your own hands. You need to let law enforcement handle this."

At that, everyone started talking at once. Bill's deep rumbling voice could be heard above the clamor, quieting the others down. "We've been waiting for the law to do something. So far, it hasn't done us much good. Are you suggesting we should just sit on our hands, waiting for something else to happen? Or maybe you want to use us as bait. That way you can ride to the rescue so you get credit for capturing this guy the FBI has been looking for all these years. You want to make them look bad." It was an accusation. All around the room, people were nodding their heads in agreement.

"That isn't what I'm saying. Crimes don't get solved overnight like they do on television." He shot a meaningful look at me, hinting that I was addicted to cop shows, especially the real life ones.

"I'd still like an answer, David." Sara stepped up to him, getting right in his face. "What are *you* going to do to help us? As the law in this area, you have the responsibility to protect the citizens of this and every town. I think we have a right to know if you're going to do that. If not, we will protect ourselves."

"Sara, if you take the law into your own hands, you will get in trouble instead of the guy out there." He nodded his head towards the forest.

"I guess that's the chance we'll just have to take since you don't seem to be able to stop him from coming after us." She turned her back on him now. Angry tears sparkled in her eyes.

"That's not what I said. I'm going to have a regular patrol going through all the towns around here. The Forest Service will have to step up its patrols of the forest." He glared at Jack like it was his fault the fires had been set, and those men were injured.

When Jack bristled, ready to retaliate, Megan put her hand on his arm to keep him from doing David bodily harm.

Ignoring Jack, David looked at Griff. "Show me where

those litter tracks are." It was more order than request. "I hope you left the litter in place. Maybe there will be fingerprints on it."

"Are you saying the person who brought those men in could be the person who beat them?" I spoke up for the first time since he came in.

"Well, who else could it be?" He waited for me to answer. I had no idea who brought them to town, but I was willing to bet the store it wasn't Warner Franklin. When I remained silent, he turned back to Griff. "You ready?" The sun was beginning to peek over the tops of the mountains, offering a pale light for them to see by. Hopefully there would be some clue for them to follow.

Doc Granger left a few minutes later. He wanted to get to the hospital to check on the men. In all the years he'd been in practice, nothing like this had happened before.

It was the middle of the morning before Griff and David came back. David didn't bother to come in the store. He probably figured it wasn't his job to tell anyone what they found. Maybe he just figured Griff would pass along any information.

"Got any of your good coffee on hand?" Griff asked Mom when he came into the store. He looked even more tired than I felt. He'd been gone two hours, and hadn't had a chance to eat before going out with David.

"Coming right up. Why don't you sit down in the back room before you fall down?" She patted his arm as she headed for the coffee pot she always kept going. I took him to the back where he could rest. We weren't very busy. After the night we'd had, people were sticking pretty close to their own homes.

I waited for Mom to come back with the coffee before asking if they found anything. Sara and Bill must have been watching for them to return, because they came in the store at the same time.

Instead of bringing a single cup of coffee, Mom brought a

163

tray with the pot and five cups. There were also several sweet rolls on the tray. We waited anxiously for Griff to finish his first cup of coffee, and take several bites of a roll. He finally sat back, releasing a heavy sigh. "We managed to follow the tracks from the litter for a while," he began without any prompting. "The further we went in the forest, the harder it was to follow though. Whoever was pulling it had quite a time. When we couldn't find any more tracks, we just wandered around trying to find something." He shook his head. "Whoever did this, managed to cover up his tracks."

"Do you think Warner Franklin brought them here?" I couldn't see the man who had blown up his neighborhood, killing several people in the process, bringing the men to safety after beating them nearly to death.

"No," Griff shook his head. "Kindness isn't in his DNA. He'd just as soon leave them out there to die or let the wild animals finish them off." That wasn't a pretty thought, causing a shiver to travel up my spine. Griff decided it was time for him to tell people his connection to Warner Franklin.

When he finished, there were several more people in the store listening. Everyone was quiet. "I'm sorry I didn't say anything when I first came here, but I really thought I could find him by staying in the forest, and keeping watch."

~~~

Doc Granger made regular trips to the hospital, checking up on the injured men, keeping the town apprised of their condition. When they regained consciousness, he made his usual report. "They were badly beaten, both men have head trauma along with other injuries." Doc stood at the front of the church hall, explaining what he'd learned. Or more precisely, what he hadn't learned. "There were pieces of wood in their wounds from the heavy branch used on them. They remember thinking they were going to die. Then all of a sudden, it was over, and they were on the litter moving through the forest."

"Why did the person stop beating them?" Sara asked.

"Why did he bring them to town?"

Doc shook his head. "There aren't many answers right now. The men might not ever regain a full memory of what happened. They have no idea who brought them here." He shrugged.

If David was investigating, he gave out very little information. The patrol cars passed through town several times a day as he promised, but seldom stopped. I'm not sure what good that did. If Franklin was watching, he would know they never stopped. He'd waited fifteen years before coming out of hiding; he could wait until the sheriff's department gave up their protection detail to finish what he started here. I just wish I knew what prompted him to take revenge on Flanagan's Gap. Was it my fault?

# CHAPTER EIGHTEEN

The Labor Day Festival finally arrived, and as the old saying goes 'I was as nervous as a cat in a room full of rocking chairs.' If past festivals were any hint of what the weekend would be like, there would be thousands of tourists in all the nearby towns. Would Franklin try something? He could create a lot of damage by blowing something up. He'd used explosives in the past and had tried to blow up our store. Would he try again with all the tourists in town? Each morning, I said a prayer for protection and each night I thanked God for protecting us.

This was one of the few times we kept The General Store open on Sunday. Mom had the back room of the store set up with her drawings, baked goods, and crafts made by the people in our craft workshop. Nancy Baker, Chad's mom placed her goat's milk lotions and soaps there as well. We even did a brisk business in the store itself. It always surprised me that people would go camping without all the essentials needed.

Each person who came in got scrutinized to make sure he wasn't Warner Franklin in disguise. Of course, there were more women than men, so that helped narrow down the ones I needed to watch.

By Monday evening when the last of the tourists left and the vendors were beginning to head home, everyone was exhausted. I was never so glad to see the end of a festival weekend as I was that night. There hadn't been any problems in Flanagan's Gap. If all was well in the surrounding towns, I considered it nothing short of a minor miracle. Warner Franklin had left us alone.

If he was the one who set the fires and beat those men, maybe he had decided to move along when his plans were thwarted. We couldn't say positively he was the one doing all that, but I couldn't think of anyone else who had it in for our town.

"Do you think he's gone?" I asked Griff the impossible question. We were sitting on the patio between the store and house, which had become our custom in the last few days. Evenings were cool this time of year, and he had his arm around me to ward off the chill.

"There's no way to second guess Warner Franklin," he answered with a shake of his head. "He was a bitter, cruel man when I was a kid. He always thought he was right, no matter what he did. I can't see that would have changed any in fifteen years. If anything, I would think he'd be even worse now. If he got it in his head that somehow he's been wronged, he won't give up or move on."

"I wish I'd never seen that television show about him," I whispered. "None of this would have happened."

He turned me to face him. "You can't know that. He'd been stealing from all the towns for months. Eventually, David Graham would have had to do something to put an end to it."

"But then he wouldn't be taking it out on our town." I sighed.

"You can't know that either. Everyone who complained when things were stolen would be on his radar. The fact that Megan caught him in her kitchen put a target on her back." A chill passed through me that had nothing to do with the temperature. He could have hurt her, or worse, just for that alone. "That show only brought things to a head sooner, rather than later. What's been happening isn't your fault."

Logically, I agreed with him; emotionally, I wasn't so sure. If not for my stubborn insistence that I find him, maybe he would have gotten tired of the limited offerings here and gone to greener pastures.

~~~

School began bright and early the next morning. During the next several weeks there wasn't time to worry about Warner Franklin other than to keep a close watch on the forest.

He tried to burn us out once, he could try again. I hadn't gone hiking since this all started. Would I ever feel comfortable hiking in my own backyard again?

Growing up, I had spent long hours hiking in the forest, looking for The Hermit. After I came home from college, I was so busy setting up the co-op, helping out in the store, running crafting classes with Mom, I didn't have time for hiking. Then I learned about Warner Franklin, and I rediscovered my love for the forest. Or was it the searching part I liked so much? Now I was afraid to go in the forest for fear of stirring up more trouble for the town. I missed all of it.

"This will get sorted out, honey." Mom wrapped her arms around me. We were ready to close up for the day, and I'd been lost in thought, staring towards the darkening trees. "Griff won't let anything happen."

"How do we know that, Mom? We don't even know if he's okay." He and John, his one remaining employee here with him, were working with Jack again. There had been a rash of small fires all over the area. It had to be Warner Franklin, but as yet they couldn't prove it. I hadn't seen Griff in almost a month. Even Megan had seen little of Jack in that time.

"We have to have faith that God is with them, and will bring them back safe and sound."

"Right now my faith is a little shaky," I admitted. "I try to turn my worries over to God, but within five minutes I take them right back." I gave a heavy sigh. "What kind of faith is that?"

"It's human faith," she laughed. "Unfortunately we all do that at times. We just need to keep praying."

"Do you think The Hermit is still out there?" This was another one of my worries. My gaze returned to the trees that hid so much.

Mom sighed now. "That's something we may never find out. He hasn't wanted to be a part of the town for a good many years. I want to believe that if he wanted to avoid Warner

Franklin, he would know how and where to do just that. I don't want to think Franklin is smarter than a man who has been able to avoid human contact for most or all of my life." We stood there looking into the forest for five minutes or fifty minutes. Our thoughts were lost with what might be happening to people we cared about while they worked in the forest.

"Are you ladies about done for the day?" The bell over the door jangled as Bill came in, jarring us out of our reverie. Since this all began, he had become a permanent fixture in our lives. I couldn't say I was sorry about it either. He was a good man, and he made Mom happy. That's all I could ask of anyone.

Locking up the store, the three of us linked arms, and went out the back door. We had taken to putting the day's receipts in the old mine shaft beneath the floor boards instead of leaving them locked up in the store. I'm not sure if things would be safe there if Franklin used explosives on us as he'd planned, but it would keep them safe if he tried to steal things again.

~~~

Softball season was over, and Sunday ice cream socials were now held in the church hall. Before long we'd change from ice cream to hot soup. Chad was still a part of the youth group, and becoming more involved in the town than he'd been before, thanks to Misty. The thought brought a smile to my lips. He was a good kid.

I still hadn't heard from Griff. When he wasn't working with Jack he was camping in the forest. Or so I assumed. For all I knew, he'd given up looking for Franklin, and returned to his business and his life. Fires were still cropping up and being extinguished almost as fast as they started. We had no proof of who was involved. Everyone surmised that Franklin was to blame though. Was he just toying with us until he could do something as devastating as the explosion he used on his old neighborhood in New Mexico? My prayer was that judgment would come on him soon so he couldn't hurt more innocent people.

The busiest part of the tourist season was almost over. Only the hardiest of campers would be camping out once it began to snow. If Griff and John continued camping throughout the winter, how would they survive? I've never been certain how The Hermit managed to make it through the winter all these years. For that matter, how had Warner Franklin survived?

Coming out of the church hall the following Sunday afternoon, Griff and John were standing in the street in front of the building. "Griff!" My heart gave a leap of joy until I saw who was standing right behind them. "Are you all right?" I stood rooted to the step, unable to move as I stared at Warner Franklin. This was the first time I'd actually seen his face, but I had no doubt who he was. People bumped into me as they came outside. I still couldn't move.

"Get up there with the rest of them." Franklin growled, nudging the men in the back to get them to move. "You always were a troublemaker." When Griff failed to move, he hit him on the back of the head with the heavy branch he was carrying in one hand. In the other, he held a very lethal-looking gun. When Griff staggered to his knees, I took a step towards him. "Stay right where you are." He moved the gun in my direction. "You're as big a nuisance as he is."

Mom gasped, reaching out to me, and Bill gripped my arm to keep me from stepping forward.

"Help your buddy up." Franklin poked John in the back. "Now get moving! Everyone, back inside." He shouted his order. Griff was unsteady on his feet, but at least he was upright.

Pastor Curt stepped forward, his soft voice shaking slightly, but still holding authority. "You've done enough damage to this town. If you leave now, we won't call the sheriff."

Franklin gave a harsh laugh. "I'm going to make sure you don't call the sheriff. Everyone put your cell phones on the ground as you go back inside." A few cell phones were placed on the step, but not enough to appease him. "I said everybody put your cell phones on the ground," he shouted again, "or I plug this nosy bitch right here." He pointed the gun in my direction again.

"Do it, folks," Pastor Curt said. "We don't want anyone getting shot." Franklin wasn't satisfied with the number of phones on the ground, and he began pointing his gun at the crowd. "This is a church." Curt took another step forward. "Not everyone brings their phones here."

Franklin looked doubtful for a minute, then he gave John a shove. "Search them! And bring me the 'ladies' purses'." He said it like it was a dirty word. There weren't enough purses to satisfy him either, and for a moment I thought we were all dead when he started waving his gun around again, shouting at us.

"There aren't any more purses," John insisted. "I guess they don't bring them here.

Franklin appeared to think about that before nodding his head. "Just get back in there." He nodded to the doorway, nudging John in the back with the gun and Griff with the branch. Reluctantly, they moved forward. Everyone was paralyzed with fear. We outnumbered him, but trying to rush him could prove fatal for one or all of us. I waited for Griff to reach me, putting my arm around his waist. He still seemed dazed from the blow to the back of his head. "You just had to keep poking your nose into my business," Franklin growled at me.

"You were stealing from us." I couldn't stop the words from spilling out of my mouth.

"Yeah, so what?" He snickered.

"So what?!" I whirled around, unmindful of the big gun in his hand. Mom grabbed for me again to keep me from launching myself at him. "You trashed our store, our home. You were going to blow it up. Why? Why didn't you just leave?" If he was going to kill us, I figured he owed us some

171

kind of explanation. Maybe he would be distracted enough for Griff or John to overpower him.

"I wasn't ready to move on yet." He shrugged, like that was all that mattered. "I needed to get a few things first, but you just had to keep poking at me, snooping around."

"So you're saying this is my fault?" I asked indignantly. From the corner of my eye, I could see Griff edging away from the rest of us, trying to get the jump on Franklin. Maybe his dazed act was just that, an act. I had to keep talking.

"Well, isn't it? If you had paid attention to my warnings, none of this would have happened."

"Didn't you know trashing our store and home, blowing them up, would bring the sheriff, the FBI? "

"Well, some risks are worth taking." He shrugged. "You just pissed me off with your snooping."

"I pissed you off?" I took a step towards him to keep his attention on me. Griff was almost close enough to jump him. "That's your explanation for what you've done?"

My ruse didn't work. Franklin whirled around just as Griff rushed him. They struggled for what felt like forever, then the gun went off. For several long seconds neither man moved. Then Griff crumpled to the ground. Pandemonium reigned with screams and shouts. People who hadn't been at the ice cream social came running.

I dropped down beside Griff, covering his wound with my hand to stop the flow of blood. Megan and Doc Granger tried to push their way forward to help, but Franklin wasn't having any of it.

"Stay right where you are." He waved his gun around, stopping everyone in their tracks, motioning for the newcomers to join the rest of us.

"I'm a doctor; I need to help this man." Doc took a cautious step forward.

"You can help him inside. Now shut up." He pointed at John. "Get your buddy inside." Hauling me up by my arm, he waited until John had Griff inside the heavy doors of the church. He gave me a shove hard enough to propel me through the doorway with the others. I stumbled, landing on the floor beside Griff. Blood still seeped from the wound on his shoulder, but he was conscious. That's a good sign, I told myself. The solid doors slammed shut, we heard something slide through the sturdy handles on the other side.

Griff tried to push himself into a sitting position, but Doc wouldn't let him move. "Stay still, son, until I see what the damage is."

Bill and John pushed on the heavy door panels, but they only moved an inch before stopping. Breaking through wasn't an option.

While Doc worked on Griff's shoulder, I held his hand. Pain was etched on his face. The bullet had gone clear through. From my television knowledge of cop shows, that was a good thing. At least, Doc didn't have to go digging for it. Judy brought clean dishcloths from the kitchen to use as bandages and wrapped another one around his shoulders to hold them in place. Without any antibiotics, infection could be a problem, depending on what Franklin was going to do with us. If he decided to blow up the church with us in it, infection was the least of Griff's worries.

Finished, Doc stood up, allowing his patient to sit up. "Is anyone else hurt?" He scanned the crowd. Shaken but unhurt, everyone shook his head.

"What are we going to do now?" Megan voiced everyone's concern. "How do we get out of here?" She held the twins to her side; fear clouded her brown eyes, turning them nearly black. Her thoughts were on Jack. If Franklin had captured Griff and John, what had he done to Jack and his crew?

If we went out the side door, would Franklin be waiting on the other side, picking us off one by one? The gun he had used so callously on Griff filled my mind. Did he have more explosives to blow up the church with us in it? Or was he just going to set it on fire?

The twins started squirming, jabbering in their special language. Since no one could understand them, we didn't pay attention.

"Looky, man." Jacob and Caleb spoke as one. These were the first words they had said that everyone could understand. We all stared at them until they repeated the words, pointing to a corner of the room.

Following the direction they were pointing, a collective gasp went up while they continued to chant, "Man, man," doing a little dance and pointing at a grey-haired man. All we could see were his head and shoulders sticking out of a hole in the floor boards.

"The Hermit," was whispered around as everybody stared at him. Quickly, we started talking at once, until he held a grubby finger to his lips and issued a loud "Shhh."

"How did you get in here?" Curt was the first to gather his wits and ask a coherent question.

"Through this here mine tunnel. Town's riddled with 'em under ever' old buildin'. Now let's stop jawin' and get ever'body out of here 'fore he decides to come back, and do to this here church what he done to my shack."

An old kerosene lantern hung on the wall of the tunnel, giving off a dim light. Once everyone was in the mine shaft and the trap door closed in the floor of the church, The Hermit took the lantern down, leading the way deeper underground.

"Where does this go?" Bill's deep voice echoed against the walls.

"Sum place that bastard, 'scuse the cussin' ladies and young'uns, don't know 'bout," he finished his sentence.

"What's he going to do up there?" Sara voiced the worry the rest of us were feeling. "Not everyone in town was at the church. What's he going to do with them?"

"That thar, gunshot brought most of 'em. If'n the rest don't know he's runnin' round doing his dirty work, he might leave 'em 'lone."

"And if they try to stop him?" Sara pressed.

In the dim light, I could see him lift his shoulders, but he didn't say anything. The remainder of the walk was accomplished in near silence. The kids with us thought this was an adventure. The adults tried not to let their fears seep into them.

Bill was holding Mom's hand, offering what little comfort he could. Would we get out of here only to find our town no long existed, all of our friends not with us, gone?

The air got chillier the longer we walked, and I began to shiver. Where exactly was he taking us? Griff laid his blood stained jacket around my shoulders. I tried to summon up a grateful smile, but I'm not sure I pulled it off.

When the twins began to fuss at being cold, The Hermit stopped, stooping down in front of them. "Not much longer, young'uns. Then you be toasty warm." He looked at the rest of us. "My spot ain't far now." He didn't explain what 'his spot' was. The mine shaft under the church was connected to other shafts by natural tunnels, some parts narrower than others. True to his word, a few minutes later, he hung the lantern on a nail, and started climbing an old ladder braced against the wall.

This end of the mine shaft came out in a part of the forest I'd never seen before. "We be here," The Hermit announced proudly.

"Here where?" Looking around, there was nothing but the sloping side of the mountain and lots of trees.

The Hermit gave a cackling laugh. "He cain't burn down my new home. 'Course, he'd hafta find it first." He gave another cackling laugh.

Blinking in the relatively bright light after being in the tunnel, I was able to study The Hermit for the first time. A matted beard, that was more grey than brown, hung down to his waist. His weathered face was wrinkled, looking like dried-out leather. If we weren't in such dire circumstances, I would be thrilled to see him. Looking at our surroundings, I tried to figure out which way the town would be. How far had we walked underground?

Shafts of sunlight filtered through the trees, reminding me of the picture of the sunbeam arms I'd taken the day I found the body of the young camper. I sensed the same feeling of peace as the sunbeams wrapped their light around me. Everything was going to be okay if we let the One in charge lead us. Did the others feel it as well?

The Hermit interrupted my thoughts when he turned to Megan, "Your man got his hands full puttin' out all them fires that…" he looked at the kids before choosing his words, "divil been startin'. I been doing what I could to he'p him. He don't know what's goin' on now. I be tellin' him."

"What about the others in town?" she asked. "We have to do something to help them. What's going to happen when Franklin realizes we got out of the church?" Everyone started talking at once, worried about those we left behind.

"Cain't do more'n one thin' at a time. He already thinks I be a ghost." He gave a rusty chuckle. "Been spookin' him purdy good lately."

"If he's rounding up the rest of the people in town," Chad asked, facing the old man, "how far out will he go looking for them? My folks weren't at the church." His eyes shimmered with unshed tears.

"Cain't rightly say, sonny. He's a nasty un, a'right. He kilt that young feller in the woods just fer the fun of it. Course, I had me a little fun, too." He looked at me. "When you was a comin' out all the time lookin' fer him, or me," his cackle reminded me of a chicken, "I made sure you found where he buried that feller. He didn't do a very good job of it."

"Did you move it after I left?"

He shook his head, his long beard swaying around his waist. "He was a watchin' you when I was a watchin' him. He tried to hide it agin, but I made sure them fellers in blue jackets found it. That gave him some pause. He couldn't figger out who kep puttin' out his fires neither." He gave another chicken cackle. He seemed to find all of this funny. I don't imagine he'd said this many words in all the years he'd been here.

Turning back to Megan, he grew serious, "I bring yer man to you soon. Fer now, you be warm and safe in thare. Kinda purdy to look at, too."

"In where?" she asked. We couldn't see anything. He turned to what looked like the solid side of the mountain, disappearing into nothing more than a crevice in the rock. Making certain everyone was safe inside a big cavern, he headed back out. I followed him. I had a ton of questions I wanted to ask. Before I could say anything, he melted into the trees. How do people do that?

Turning to go back to the cave opening, my stomach rolled over. Where was the crevice that led inside? Which one was it? When I stepped away from the opening, it had become invisible.

Groping around, I ran my hands over the face of the rock. It had to be here somewhere. The only clue was the sound of voices echoing out. It took only a minute after that to find my way back in.

"Pastor, can you make sure everyone is safe here? Keep them in the cave." Griff was speaking softly, but it was easy to hear him. During the walk through the tunnel, he had been chaffing against the fact that he hadn't been able to stop Franklin. Now he needed to do something. At Curt's nod, he turned to leave.

Before he could disappear as quickly as The Hermit had, I grabbed his arm. "You can't do anything. You're hurt."

"I've been hurt worse than this." He gingerly touched the makeshift bandage on his shoulder. I'm not going to let him repeat what he did fifteen years ago." He pulled me against him, placing a hard kiss on my lips. Just as quickly, he released me, and did his own disappearing act. John was right behind him.

# CHAPTER NINETEEN

I don't know how long we had walked through the tunnel. It could have been minutes or hours. However long it had been, Franklin could have been doing a lot of damage to our town and the people left behind. We did our best to comfort each other; Pastor Curt led us in prayer for the safety of all our loved ones.

"I'm going to find out if my folks are okay," Chad whispered to me. Even his whisper echoed in the cavernous room.

"No, you're not!" I grabbed his arm before he could move. "There's nothing you can do right now."

"I have to try!" Tears rolled down his young face. "They're my parents."

I hugged him, my head barely coming to his shoulders. Before I knew it, he was sobbing against me, leaning down to put his head on my shoulder. "I don't want him to kill them."

"I know," I said around the lump in my throat. For long minutes, we stood like that while I rocked back and forth offering him what little comfort I could.

At last, he stood away from me, wiping his face with shaking fingers. "I'm sorry, Becca."

"Don't be sorry for caring about your parents. We'll pray that they'll be all right."

The Hermit had been right when he said the cave was pretty. This was totally above ground, but the striations in the rock walls were beautiful. Misty and several others tried to keep the kids occupied, and I kept an eye on Chad. I didn't want him to disappear on me, too. He'd never find his way out of the forest. Then we'd have to send out a search party to find him.

"Megan, boys!" The words echoed through the cave long before we could see Jack and several men running down the long entrance. He caught Megan up in his arms as she ran to him, burying his face in her bouncy curls. "Thank God." Again the whispered words echoed through the cave. Setting her feet back on the ground, he took her face in his hands, staring down at her. "Are you three all right? Where are the boys?"

Just then, two little dynamos tackled him around the knees. "Daddy, Daddy." There were more reunions, with the other men finding their families safe as well.

"I haven't seen Griff and John for more than a week." Satisfied that Megan and the boys were safe, Jack finally turned his attention to me. "Has anyone seen them? Do you know where they are?"

"Franklin brought them into town when he came for us," I answered with a catch in my voice. "He locked us up in the church until The Hermit got us out." Not knowing how much The Hermit had told him, I explained about Griff getting shot, and the hike through the mine tunnel.

"We need to help the others in town," Chad stepped forward. "I don't know what happened to my parents." Worry clouded his face, while tears sparkled in his eyes.

Once again everyone began talking, giving their opinions, or stating their worries about loved ones. The noise echoed off the walls until it was impossible to understand what anyone was saying.

"If'n ya'all want the world to know where ya are, keep right on a jawin'." Silence fell in the large stone room. We looked towards the cave opening. From this side, it was easy to see where the tunnel leading outside was. It was several long seconds before The Hermit and others came into view. The acoustics of the cave were amazing.

More of our friends and neighbors crowded around and once again the noise level rose until my ears were ringing. A shushing sound reverberated around the cave, effectively silencing everyone again. "You'ns all sure likes to yammer." The Hermit shook his gnarly head. "Make me glad I live 'lone.

Yer racket be heard outside these here walls, so clam up."
He'd been enjoying himself up to now. I guess he'd had his
fill of people for a while. He started to stalk away when Jack
stopped him.

"Do you know if he's locking others up somewhere? Is
there any way we can stop him?"

The old man lifted his shoulders. "No tellin' what he be up
to. Only one thin' gonna stop sumone like him, that's bein' six
feet in the ground. You ready fer that?"

"I have to go find my parents." Tears clogged Chad's voice
again. "I don't know where they are."

"Them's the folks what owns all them goats?" The Hermit
asked. Chad nodded, wiping away a tear that had escaped.
"They's okay fer now. That bas..." Again he stopped just short
of cussing. "He got his hands full tryin' to figger out where all
you folks got to after you'ns was locked up." He let loose with
his chicken cackle, enjoying the fact that he was giving
Franklin fits. "I's still the ghost what's a hauntin' him." Again
he turned to leave, once more Jack stopped him.

"What can we do to help? Tell us what you need?" He was
letting the older man take the lead, not just playing to his ego,
if The Hermit even had one.

"I be goin' back to town, 'n' see if he gots more folks
rounded up agin. If'n you come 'long, you gots to be quiet."

"Agreed." Jack nodded his head. "What's he planning on
doing once he has everyone rounded up?" The look he
received for his question would have said, "Well, duh," if it
had been anyone other than The Hermit. From him, I'm not
quite certain what his exact thoughts were, but his message
came across loud and clear. "Right." Jack nodded again. "Let's
go."

"I'm going with you." Chad's young voice brooked no
resistance. He was going with or without them.

Jack turned back before he left. "For all the good it'll do, I
called David Graham and the FBI when I found out what was
going on. They said they'd be up. David might get here first."

The Hermit tugged on Jack's arm. "Member yer promise." Now his whisper echoed through the cavern.

Jack gave a nod, turning back to us. "If Agent Black or David get here before I get back, don't mention..." He stopped for a minute unsure what to call the older man. We still didn't know his name. With a slight shrug, he continued. "Don't say anything about The Hermit. He'd like to remain anonymous."

"Huh?" The Hermit looked at Jack, unsure what that meant.

"No one will say anything about you."

With a nod of approval, he turned away. Just that quick, he was gone. Jack and the others had to hurry to keep up.

It would take the FBI hours to get here from Phoenix, if they even bothered to come today. After all, it was Sunday. I didn't know what kind of work schedule they kept.

It was anyone's guess how many more people there were in town for Franklin to round up, or what he would do when he discovered a second group had disappeared from his grasp. I just knew it wasn't going to be good, one way or another.

"Did Franklin take you to the church?" Curt questioned softly. At the collective nod from those The Hermit had just rescued, a worried frown drew his brows together. "What did he do when he discovered we were missing?"

"He was madder than a wet hen at first." Sandy Bridges answered. "He stomped around, checking the other door and all the windows. When he couldn't find any way for you to get out, he started acting scared. I didn't think a man like him could be scared, but he was. He kept muttering about a ghost, and how he thought he'd gotten rid of him for good. It didn't make much sense, but for a few minutes he forgot about us. That's when two of the men got away."

"Why didn't you all run when you had the chance?" Bill asked.

"He had a gun," Sandy stated simply. "We figured he wouldn't miss two people, they could hide, and get the rest of us out when he was gone. They didn't get the chance, because The Hermit got us out first."

"We need to take a head count," Sara spoke up, changing directions of the conversation. We needed to start being proactive instead of just reactive. "We need to know how many more could be in danger." It took some doing to decide how to go about that. If Franklin wasn't going to the outskirts of the town, we didn't have to include those people. But how were we to know who was included in his sweep of Flanagan's Gap?

All of the small towns around us started out as mining camps. When the mines petered out, only the hard core people stuck around, living off the land the best way they could. Over time, more people came to live in the area, but never officially formed towns or even townships. According to state records, we were considered residents of the county. Flanagan's Gap, or any of the small towns close by, had no official existence in the eyes of the state.

As big as the cave was it was getting pretty crowded, and I was beginning to feel claustrophobic. The total turned out to be four hundred forty-nine. Next we had to figure out how many people lived beyond the confines of the main section of town. This was sort of Sara's unofficial job, but even she didn't have an exact count. This was all a guessing game.

Amazingly, light had filtered down through cracks and crevices throughout the cave, but it was getting dark inside now. I had no idea of the time, my guess said it was getting on to dusk outside. The Hermit had three kerosene lanterns, but they didn't give off much light. I wondered how he managed to keep fuel for them. Kerosene wasn't something people kept a supply of for him to barter for with his carvings. There was no food and the little ones were beginning to get hungry, tired, and cold. I didn't know what to do next.

"I'm going out to get food and blankets," Bill announced a few minutes later. "These little ones need to be fed, and it's going to get colder before the night is over."

Worry raced across Mom's face. She hadn't said much until now, trying not to let her fear show. "Be careful. Please." She placed a kiss on his cheek.

He hadn't been gone long when we heard laughter reverberate through the cave. Within minutes he was back with those living outside of the unofficial boundaries of town. Chad and the men who had gone with Jack were bringing people to safety.

Rex Baker, Chad's dad, explained what happened when Franklin tried to round them up, giving us our first laugh since Franklin locked us in the church. "Billy Boy took exception to a stranger coming on our property. He butted the man from behind, knocking him to his knees. Every time he tried to get up, Billy Boy knocked him back down." Billy Boy is the Bakers' rather large billy goat. He's better than a watch dog. When he takes exception to someone being on his property, he's meaner than a 'junk yard dog.'

"I'm surprised Franklin just didn't shoot Billy Boy," Sandy said. "He kept waving that gun at us." She shuddered at the memory.

"You mean this gun?" Rex asked, producing a big hand gun. "When Billy Boy knocked him down the first time, he dropped it. Nanny thought it looked tasty, and tried to eat the thing." They weren't very imaginative with names for their animals. "By the time I got it away from her, Franklin was being chased down the road by a very loud, very angry goose," he finished, laughing at the recollection. "Gus must have chased him a good mile down the road before giving up."

Relieved laughter filled the cave. "That's when we figured we'd better find out about the rest of the town. Chad and these men stopped us from going into town, and brought us here." Nancy hugged her son, tears sparkling in her eyes.

We'd gone out to meet the newcomers and were still standing in front of the cave when the throb of helicopter blades drew our attention skyward. One of the biggest choppers I'd ever seen circled over the forest. 'FBI' was emblazoned on the side. A spot light swept over the tree tops. Hopefully they were searching for us. Waving our arms above our heads and yelling over the noise the big machine was making, we tried to get their attention. Just where they were going to set that thing down, I didn't know. There wasn't enough of a clearing in front of the cave.

My heart sank when it continued moving away. Surely that big spot light had shown them we were here. There were groans, a few tears, and even a few cuss words shouted at the helicopter as it moved out of sight. I plopped down on the nearest boulder, resting my head in my hands.

It felt like we'd been here for days when in reality it had only been a few hours. I had no idea where Griff was, or if he was all right. He hadn't come back with the second group The Hermit had rescued. Were he and John safe? What were they doing?

A rustling in the underbrush nearby started my heart pounding. Had Franklin figured out where we were hiding? Was a bear looking for a captive meal? There were even mountain lions in these parts. We don't see them very often, but it wasn't unheard of for them to attack humans.

Before my heart stopped altogether, Agent Black broke through the bushes. I could have kissed him, I was so happy for the rescue. "What's been going on around here?" He didn't sound as happy to see us as I was to see him.

Everyone started talking at once until a shrill whistle silenced us. Curt stepped forward. "Thanks for coming, Agent. It seems that Warner Franklin has taken exception to us being alive, and he was trying to remedy that little problem." Was that a little bit of snarkiness in our dear pastor's voice? I couldn't help but smile; grateful it was dark enough the agent couldn't see it.

~~~

It was a long, uncomfortable night. Agent Black wouldn't let us go home until he and his men had a chance to check things over. At least they provided some food and blankets.

The cave was huge, but with close to five hundred bodies trying to find room to lie down, it was crowded. That many people also created their own heat. It was beginning to get steamy inside the cave. I needed some fresh air.

Sitting at the mouth of the cave, I hugged my knees up to my chest, resting my head on them. The Hermit had disappeared. As Jack promised, no one had mentioned him to Agent Black. He took it for granted that we had known about the mine tunnel, and followed it here. Griff and John were also among the missing. I had no idea if they were all right or if Franklin had captured them again. Had Griff's wound started bleeding again? If it had, could he bleed to death? I also didn't know where Franklin was. If Agent Black knew anything, he wasn't sharing it with us.

"Honey, what are you doing out here?" Mom wrapped her arms around me, rocking back and forth. "It's too chilly to be out here."

I gave a small laugh, trying to drag my thoughts out of the doldrums. "And it's getting a little too warm in there." I nodded my head towards the cave. "Besides, I can't sleep right now."

"What's bothering you, honey? Are you worried about Griff?"

"That and other things." How did I tell her what was weighing on my conscience?

"Those men can take care of themselves. They're going to be okay." She kissed the top of my head. "Griff is a good man. He knows what he's doing, and he isn't going to let Franklin get the drop on him again. I think he has some plans for the future, and he's not going to let that man derail them." She smiled at me.

"It's not that, Mom." Tears clogged my throat, making it hard to get the words out. "I'm responsible for all this. Everything that's happened to everyone is my fault."

"What are you talking about?" She frowned. "Why would you even think that?"

"This all started because I was obsessed with finding the fugitive even the FBI couldn't find. How big of an ego does that say I have?" Once I got started, the words poured out. "If I had just let it go, Franklin never would have come after the town. He wouldn't have shot Griff, he wouldn't have burned down The Hermit's shack, and he wouldn't have come after everyone here." Guilt weighed heavy on me. I couldn't hold back the tears any longer.

"Are you taking responsibility for the murder of that young camper? The Hermit said Franklin killed him for the fun of it. It had nothing to do with you or the town. Even if you had never seen that television show, Franklin still would have been in the forest doing his evil. Griff was also out there, and I'm grateful he wasn't killed as well. Now, forget this nonsense. Come back inside when you get chilled." She kissed me again, returning to her little corner of the cave. The opening seemed obvious now that we'd been in and out so many times.

She meant well, but I had to make this right, I just didn't know how. My mind ran in circles until I couldn't think anymore. Eventually, too tired to fight sleep any longer, I curled up beside the rock I'd been sitting on. The ground at the mouth of the cave proved to be marginally softer than the rock floor inside.

The first shafts of light filtering through the canopy of trees woke me. I remained still, wrapped in those sunbeams, enjoying the peace they offered.

"Good morning, Sunshine." Griff whispered, keeping his voice low so it didn't echo down the passage and wake everyone else up. Sometime in the night he had returned to find me asleep at the mouth of the cave like I was guarding my friends and family inside. He pulled me against his hard chest. His warmth seeped through me until I was overheated in the space of seconds.

"Are you all right? Where have you been? Did you run into Franklin again?" Turning in his arms, I ran my hands over his whiskery face, gingerly touched the goose egg-sized lump on the back of his head, and checking the makeshift bandage on his shoulder.

"Hey, Sugar, I'm fine." He captured my hands, holding them still. "As much as I'm enjoying this, we need to call a halt before we have an audience." He gave a small chuckle. "What's got you so stirred up?"

"I was worried about you, and John," I hastily added. "I thought maybe Franklin got you again." I kissed his stubbly chin before moving to his mouth, and sending up a silent prayer, grateful for his safe return. Drawing away from him only when we heard sounds of activity in the cave, I cleared my throat, hoping I wouldn't make a complete fool of myself. "How is your shoulder and head this morning?" I felt the lump on the back of his head again.

"It's a good thing I'm so hardheaded," he joked, "otherwise I might be in trouble. That branch he was using for a club was plenty hard."

There wasn't time for any further conversation as people began pouring out of the mouth of the cave. With Griff and John back in their midst, everyone began pressing them with questions. While we talked, people drifted off one at a time in different directions to answer the call of nature, but no one went far from the cave.

"Franklin has pulled his disappearing act again," Griff told our gathering. Dejection sat heavy on his broad shoulders. "I still can't find out where he's been holed up these past months. He's like a damn ghost." He took a deep breath, releasing it slowly. "Agent Black and his men are going to have their hands full for a while." Something in his expression and his cryptic words said there was something he wasn't telling us.

"Do you think The Hermit knows where Franklin is?" Sara addressed her question to John rather than Griff. From the looks passing between the two, it was my guess they had made an acquaintance long before last night. John had been working in the area with Griff for more than three months now.

187

He gave an expressive shrug. "Can't really say, since he's disappeared as well. I'd like to learn their secret; it sure would help in my job." He gave a small chuckle, looking at Griff. We had more questions than the two men had answers.

# CHAPTER TWENTY

"No one can return to town just yet," Agent Black issued the proclamation several hours later without giving us a reason. "It's going to take a few more days." With that pronouncement, he turned to leave giving no further explanations.

"Days!" The gasp resounded throughout the crowd gathered around him.

"Excuse me!" Curt's authoritative voice stopped him from going far. "We have small children here, as well as several older individuals. You can't leave us out here with no food or water; no bathroom facilities other than the trees. We need to know what is happening to our homes and businesses. Have you captured Warner Franklin?"

Agent Black gave such a put-upon sigh I would have felt sorry for him if he wasn't so totally without a sympathetic bone in his body. "This is a federal investigation, sir. You need to stay out of it."

"I don't think so!" Curt took another step towards the agent.

At that, several more agents closed ranks around their leader. "You need to step back. You're threatening a federal agent!"

"Get over yourself, Black!" Griff said as he stepped through the crowd. His arm was in a sling Doc had made after checking his shoulder. "Telling these people what's going on isn't going to hamper your investigation. They have the right to know what you found. If you don't tell them, I will," he added when Black remained stubbornly silent. "I'm the one who told you, remember?"

"I can have you arrested, too, Tomlin."

Griff laughed, "You can try. I doubt your bosses in D.C. will appreciate the backlash though."

189

"Are all federal agents that arrogant?" Someone from the back of the group spoke in a whisper. They must have been standing in the entrance of the cave, because the amplified sound was easily heard by everyone. Agent Black's face turned an angry shade of red which only grew redder when several of the agents snickered, mainly the two women working with him. His dark glare in their direction failed to produce the cowering response he wanted when they gave him a cheeky grin. They had probably been the brunt of a lot of discrimination from the 'good old boys' club.'

Trying to ignore the split among the rank and file around him, Agent Black glared at Griff before turning back to Curt. "Sir, for now it isn't safe to return to your homes. Franklin planted explosives in several homes and businesses around the town." He acted like the rest of us didn't exist, paying no attention to the gasps and questions his statement caused. Once again my nightmare was coming true. This time he was trying to take out the entire town.

"Now that wasn't so hard, was it?" Griff asked, a chuckle lifting his voice.

Black glared at him again before turning back to Curt. "We can't allow you to return until we can make certain we've found all the explosives. It's for your own safety." He tried to sound magnanimous, failing miserably.

"How long is that going to take?" The agent gave an 'I don't know' shrug, but didn't say anything. "You expect us to live in a cave for an undetermined length of time?"

"You need to make your own arrangements. It isn't the federal government's job to put everyone up." He sounded so superior, like he was looking down on a bunch of bugs. I wanted to smack him. He marched off, his little minion agents following behind him.

"I hope they meet up with a bear before they find their way out of the forest," Bill grumbled. "Maybe they'll get lost." Looking around, he asked the question on everyone's minds. "What do we do now?" Most of the people in town had nowhere else to go, no other family.

"Our house isn't all that big," Nancy Baker stepped forward, "but we can put some people up, especially those with little ones. Our barn is also clean and warm. We can put some people up there." Others from the community at large made similar offers. In the space of an hour, temporary homes were found for everyone. We were a pretty self-reliant bunch, not looking to the government to take care of us. This was no different.

~~~

"I don't care what that obnoxious man says," I muttered, "he can't keep me from getting things out of the store. If we can't go home for several days, we're going to need supplies." I marched off like I was going to war. Griff and several others fell into step beside me. The least those agents could do for us was let us get clothes and food from our own homes.

When we got close to town, we could see media vans parked on the main road. They had descended on our small township with a vengeance. Even though Agent Black wasn't allowing us to return home, he was letting the media get their story. Cameras and reporters from every news outlet, local and national, had their equipment set up on the softball field. "So this is why they didn't want us coming home," I grumbled. "That glory hound wanted all the media attention for himself."

He stood at a bank of microphones, facing the cameras, giving his statement. "This is an ongoing investigation." His voice floated across the field. "I can tell you that we have this situation under control. The residents are safe and no one living here is under suspicion, at this time, of supplying Warner Franklin with the explosives we've found."

"Damn big of him," I muttered. Was he hinting that someone here was involved? I started across the field; my hard glare was fixed on the man standing on the makeshift stage. He had planned this carefully so there wouldn't be any interference from the town populace. Well, he was in for a surprise. My guilt had been replaced with anger. By this time,

I was ready for bear.

"Do you have Warner Franklin in custody?" a reporter called out.

"I can't release any information of that nature at this time. I..." His voice trailed off when he spotted us coming towards him. He cleared his throat, trying to maintain control of the news conference. "I need you people to go back to your vehicles with your equipment for your own safety. Please leave, now." Urgency that hadn't been there just seconds ago rang loud and clear in his voice. He didn't want the reporters talking to us. He turned away from the microphone, almost running to make good his escape. The reporters milled around, ignoring his order to return to their vehicles.

"I have a question, Agent Black," I called out. Until now, the reporters and cameramen hadn't been aware of our approach. Now they swung their cameras in our direction. My attention was focused on the man heading for the closest building. "I have no problem shouting my questions with the cameras rolling." Griff's chuckle barely registered in my mind. The reporters were shouting their own questions at us now.

"Did you really expect us to stay in that cave while you got your fifteen minutes of fame at our expense? Is this how the FBI treats the victims of crime?"

He hustled across the field, gripping my arm, attempting to drag me away from the rolling cameras. I winced at his tight grip. "This is going to make a great lead in for the six o'clock news." I winced again. It wasn't all an act as he tightened his grip on my arm. "This will certainly make a better story than the one you just gave."

"Let her go, Black," Griff said with a murderous growl.

"Stay out of this, Tomlin." Black whirled around to face Griff, nearly dragging me to the ground in the process. "Agent Greene told me all about you. You'll do just about anything to catch Franklin. Would that include planting explosives to implicate him?"

"If you believe everything he says, you're as big a fool as

192

he is, maybe bigger." A muscle jumped in Griff's jaw as he attempted to keep his temper under control.

"Is this the man who tried to blow up the town?" a reporter called. The agent had been unaware that the news-hungry hoard had followed us across the field, their cameras capturing this scene.

"I have no more comments at this time. You folks need to move back to the perimeter on the road." He fought to keep his voice light. It wasn't working.

More questions were shouted at him, but he refused to answer them. Turning to the other agents, he snapped, "Get those reporters back, and take this one to the command post." He gave my arm a shake before passing me off to one of the women agents.

"I hope those news cameras are still rolling," I muttered, rubbing my arm. I could already feel bruises beginning to form.

Gently taking my arm, the woman led me away, her gaze on her superior. "I don't know what you did or said, but you sure set him off." Her voice was loud enough for me to hear, but not Agent Black. "I've never seen him so mad. By the way, I'm Julia Burton." She kept her voice low so Agent Black didn't hear her being nice to me.

I had never encountered anyone in the FBI until this all happened. I hope I never have the occasion to deal with them again once Warner Franklin is caught. Until now, Agent Black had been nicer than his partner. Maybe he'd been taking nasty lessons since he was last here.

After twenty minutes waiting for the agent in his 'command post,' I'd had enough of his rudeness. "I'm going to get the things I came for, if…" I searched for an appropriate name to call him without cussing. Coming up empty, I continued. "Tell him I couldn't wait any longer. If he still feels the need to talk to me, he can come to me." I stood up, heading for the door. Sometime in the night, a mobile home full of all kinds of equipment had been brought in to use as a 'command post.'

"I don't think that's very wise," Agent Burton said, looking cautiously at the door like she expected Agent Black to open it at any moment.

"Well, no one has ever accused me of being wise," I quipped. "Good luck with your boss." Calling him her boss didn't sit well with her, but she refrained from commenting.

"You really should wait for him. He isn't going to be happy if you leave."

"Am I under arrest?" She shook her head. "Then he can't keep me here. There are about five hundred people who need food and water, and that, that," again I searched for something to call him, finally settling on "idiot couldn't care less. We have small children who need to eat." I opened the door, stepping out into the bright sunlight.

Griff and Agent Black were nowhere to be seen; Sara and the others who came with us had made use of their wait by gathering what they could from the buildings the agents would allow them to enter. Doc's medical bag set on the ground beside him while they waited to see what would happen next.

"Are you all right, Becca?" Sara asked, a frown drawing her light brows together. "What's going on?"

I shrugged. Agent Black could probably cause a great deal of trouble for me, but I wasn't going down without a fight. The man had done nothing to help us since this all started. "Do you know where he took Griff?" Was there an interrogation trailer somewhere? I wondered.

She shook her head. "The agents ushered the press back to their vehicles, and Agent Black took Griff somewhere. Their argument got pretty heated. Maybe Griff should have just gone along quietly." I laughed at the image. He didn't strike me as someone who would back away from a fight. "We haven't seen them since," she finished.

When I headed for the store, an agent stepped in front of me. "You can't go into any of the buildings right now, ma'am."

"Why's that?" I raised one eye brow.

"We're waiting for ATF to get here to clear any buildings of explosives."

"When will that be?" He gave a shrug, his eyes sliding over my shoulder. "Why weren't they called last night?" He gave another shrug without saying anything. "Are there still explosives in or around this store?"

"Yes, ma'am." He still couldn't look me in the face.

"What have you all been doing, other than holding a press conference, since you arrived last night?"

"Ma'am, I can't discuss an ongoing case." I swear, if he called me ma'am once more, I was going to smack him. He was old enough to be my father.

"Well, someone needs to discuss something with me, because I need to get food for a whole bunch of people." Another thought occurred to me. "Speaking of feeding people, where exactly have you all been eating since you arrived?" Again his gaze slid away, causing me to bristle. "My guess is you've helped yourselves to food from the cafes and my store." I faced him angrily, my hands resting on my hips. I was beyond caring if I got in trouble. "You know that's stealing, right? Now, step aside, and let me in there!"

While he debated just what he should do, Agent Black appeared out of nowhere. Agent Burton was beside him, looking guilty for tattling on me. "Miss Dutton! I told you to wait for me in the command post." Stomping up, he looked like an angry bull.

"I got tired of waiting," I said mildly. "What did you want to talk to me about? There are a lot of hungry people waiting for us to return, so make it snappy. By the way, we *will* be sending you a bill for all the food and whatever else you've taken from the store and cafes." His face turned an angry shade of red, but he didn't argue. He knew he was in the wrong.

"I need to take your statement on the proceedings leading up to what's going on here. I'll need to talk to everyone."

I chuckled. "You're going to be busy because there are a whole bunch of people you're going to need to talk to. How long is it going to take to clear the explosives from our homes and businesses? You can't expect us to remain in that cave indefinitely." I didn't bother to tell him we had already made other arrangements. He probably wouldn't like that either.

"ATF has a bomb detail coming up. They'll be here later today."

"Why aren't they already here? You knew there were explosives here last night. Why did you wait until this morning to call them?" I didn't give him a chance to make up an excuse before going on. "I suppose you were waiting for the press to arrive first. The bomb squad in all their safety equipment makes for a good photo op; makes it look like you're actually doing something to help us."

He grumbled for a minute, but finally gave the okay for me to enter the store. "You have ten minutes to get what you need from your store. Then I'm going to arrest you for hampering an investigation." He nodded at Agent Burton to go in with me, maybe hoping we would both get blown up.

# CHAPTER TWENTY-ONE

After delivering the few supplies the agents allowed us to take, we watched as bomb sniffing dogs and agents, looking like astronauts in their special suits, moved cautiously through our homes and businesses looking for any explosives. It wasn't just the FBI swarming over our town now. Alcohol, Tobacco and Firearms agents had been called in to deal with the explosives. The reporters were still parked on the road, and we did our best to ignore them and the questions they occasionally shouted at us.

Warner Franklin hadn't gotten to the outlying homes, so they were all safe, giving the rest of us a place to stay until these people allowed us to go home. It took two days for that to happen.

The dogs and 'space men' went through every house and business in town at least three times, making sure there wasn't something more to find. No one was happy they were poking around in our homes, but we had little to say about it. From our vantage point at the edge of town we could see that only our little house, the General Store, and the church had been rigged to explode. Not exactly how Agent Black had described it.

The fact that Franklin had been planning on blowing up the church with us inside sent a chill through me. He was truly evil personified. I didn't understand why he was so set on destroying us. Or was it just me? Had I made him so mad he was willing to commit mass murder?

The media had given up after the first day. They had their film and sound bites. That would be worth several days of news, then another crisis would come up, and they would move on.

"There's nothing more we can do here," Agent Black finally announced. "It's safe to go back to your homes."

"What about Franklin?" Sara asked. "He's still out there."

"We have his supply of explosives, you're safe." He sounded like he was doing us a great favor, but there was the implied 'for now' hanging in the air.

"That's what you said several months ago," Sara argued. "Look where that got us."

"What do you expect me to do, Miss Flanagan? I can't keep agents here forever."

"What I'd *like* you to do is your job, protecting us from a criminal you haven't been able to find for the last fifteen years. What I *expect* you to do is exactly what you're doing, abandoning us to this maniac. But don't worry about this town; we learned a long time ago that in the grand scheme of things, Flanagan's Gap doesn't really count for much." She turned, stalking away.

"Miss Flanagan, you're being unreasonable," he said to her retreating back. "We have exhausted all leads here. The FBI can't remain here indefinitely. The man isn't stupid. As long as he knows we're here, he isn't going to do anything. He also knows we're keeping an eye on things. If he shows up again, we'll be back." She kept walking, ignoring him.

I wanted to applaud. He was right, though. As long as there was a law enforcement presence, Franklin would remain in hiding. It's too bad Agent Black couldn't figure out a way around that little problem.

The entire time the FBI and ATF agents were clearing the explosives, David was conspicuously absent. He hadn't come to our rescue the night Jack called him either. I half expected him to roll into town as soon as Agent Black and his men pulled out. When that didn't happen, a niggling worry crept into my mind.

He wanted to make a big splash with the press, showing up the FBI. Would he do something totally stupid in order to accomplish that? Of course he would, I answered my own question. He'd always been a showoff. That hadn't changed since high school. But if something had happened to him, why hadn't we heard about it? Why hadn't the sheriff come looking for him?

That evening Sara called a town meeting to discuss our options. "You can't stay, Griff." She started off with a bombshell pronouncement. Her words started everyone talking at once. I knew she was right, but it didn't stop my heart from aching. She pounded her gavel to gain control again. "As much as it pains me to say this," she spoke over the remaining fearful whispers, "Agent Black was right. As long as Franklin knows he's being actively sought, he's going to remain in his hidey-hole. He knows who you are, Griff, and that you're after him. He has the advantage. He can outwait you, just like he did the FBI." She drew a shaky breath, her agonized gaze going to the man sitting beside Griff. "You both need to leave." Her voice wobbled on the last words.

After a lot of arguing, Griff and John grudgingly agreed to leave. "But not tomorrow," Griff stated firmly. "Franklin would smell a rat if we didn't at least try to find him now that the FBI is gone."

Sara thought it over before finally nodding her head. "One week, then you both leave." Her heart was in her eyes when she looked at John. Love had bitten several people in Flanagan's Gap this summer.

"I'm not leaving because I want to, Sugar," Griff, pulled me against his hard chest, placing a soft kiss on my lips. We were sitting on the patio between our house and the store. "I know Sara is right. Franklin is watching us from some secret place that I haven't been able to find yet. Just know that even though you can't see me, I'll be watching out for you."

"You can't do that. If Franklin really is watching our every move, he'll know if you sneak back in town."

He gave a little laugh. "Give me some credit here. I'm a security expert with FBI training. I came to know the forest pretty good while I was camping. Jack knows it even better than Franklin does. With his help, I'll be able to lie low and still know what's going on. I'm not going to let him do anything else to you or this town." With his next kiss, we lost all track of time.

For the next week, Griff and John made a show of searching the forest during the day. At night they rigged the perimeter of the town with some kind of high tech security and surveillance. Our homes had communication and security fit for the president. Franklin wouldn't get into any home in town, even the outlying ones, without everybody knowing about it, including the sheriff. I'm not sure what all of it was, but if it kept us safe and in contact with Griff and John, I was all for it.

Rex Baker had turned over the gun he'd taken off Warner Franklin. Agent Black wasn't keeping us in the loop, but Griff's FBI contact said the gun had been reported stolen more than ten years ago. "Ballistics showed it was used in two unsolved homicides, one in New Mexico, one in Arizona," Griff announced, his voice grim. That meant Franklin was wanted for more than just the bombing of his old neighborhood and what was going on now in Arizona. Would the man ever be caught and made to pay?

~~~

Three days after Griff and John left, their high tech equipment paid off. Alarms went off in every house when David's lifeless body was dumped at the edge of town. People poured into the streets, shock and fear evident on their faces. Warner Franklin wasn't through with us yet.

Within ten minutes, Sheriff Duncan roared into town, lights and siren blaring. "What happened? Why was Graham here?" He started shouting questions before he was even out of his car.

Doc had examined David in the hopes that he was still alive. "He's been dead at least a week, Sheriff. An autopsy will give a better estimate and the cause of death, but I would say he was beaten like those other two men. Where has he been?" His tone turned accusatory. If David had been missing that long, why hadn't someone been looking for him? Why didn't we know about it?

"He asked for some vacation time." The sheriff shook his head. "Said he had some personal business to take care of. What was he doing that got him killed?" He was as puzzled as the rest of us. We had no idea David had been around here all this time.

Shock was wearing off; everyone started talking at once until he held up his hands for silence. "Doc, why is my deputy dead?"

That wasn't an easy question to answer. As Doc highlighted what had been happening in Flanagan's Gap and the surrounding forest, it became obvious David hadn't told his boss what was going on. Why would he do that, other than to catch Franklin when the FBI couldn't?

"If you've been having trouble this long, why wasn't I informed?" People looked anywhere but at the sheriff. No one wanted to speak ill of the dead. If the sheriff hadn't known, that would explain why he hadn't made an appearance while the FBI was here earlier. With the county seat on the other side of the county, the sheriff relied on his deputies in the field to keep him informed of any criminal activity. Obviously, David had neglected to do that.

"Okay," he huffed, "I get it. Now, will someone give me the details, from the top?" Again everyone began talking at once, until he gave a shrill whistle. "Pastor, you first." It took a long time to get the entire story out, but I had to give the sheriff credit for not interrupting unless to clarify a point. "So where is this Griff Tomlin? He called me with a cryptic message to get here ASAP; something happened to one of my deputies. He was going after his killer."

My stomach rolled. I thought he had gone back to wherever his company headquarters were to monitor the surveillance feeds. Instead, he'd been hiding in the forest again, hoping to catch Franklin same as David, only he had a different motive. He wanted the man who killed his family.

The debate whether to send for the FBI again or leave them out of the loop this time didn't last long. They'd done very little the three times they were here. Warner Franklin had proven to be more resourceful than they were. It was going to take someone with a little more forest savvy to find him.

I could think of one person who had more knowledge of this forest than anyone else. How to find him was the problem. No one had seen The Hermit in more than two weeks. Was he keeping track of Franklin's activities?

Two days after David's body had been left for us to find, Griff and John came in looking bedraggled and defeated. "I don't know how that man can continue to wreak havoc, and still stay out of sight," Griff grumbled. Mom placed a big plate of spaghetti in front of each man. It probably had been days since they had little more to eat than "Meals Ready to Eat." Combat food.

Our small kitchen was crowded with half the town. The other half was outside standing watch to make certain Franklin didn't creep back in to do more harm.

"Okay, folks, I need to talk to these men. Alone." Sheriff Duncan didn't bother to knock before entering. He gave everyone the fish eye; his message to clear out was obvious.

I bristled at his highhandedness. This was our kitchen, not his office. He had pretty much been an absentee sheriff until David was murdered. Now he wanted to take over.

"It isn't his fault that he didn't know what David was up to," Mom whispered, putting her arm around my shoulders, encouraging me to move to the door. "If David kept his activities to himself, the sheriff can't be blamed." Leave it to her to put a better spin on the situation than I would. Until he proved himself to be as incompetent as David had been, she would give him the benefit of a doubt.

After Sheriff Duncan finished his 'debriefing,' he left with the promise to do more than the FBI had done for us. "David was one of mine," he said. "I don't intend to give up until I have that bastard, either in my jail or in the ground."

"What were you and John doing out there?" We were finally alone after Sheriff Duncan had finished questioning them. "I thought you had gone…" I stopped, unsure where he had gone.

"We needed everyone to believe we had really left." We were sitting on the porch swing now, his arm holding me against him as though he was afraid I'd get away if he let go. "If Franklin had even suspected we might still be here, he'd never come out of hiding." He gave a weary sigh. "I just never expected him to do this. I had no idea Graham was out there. He must have gone into the woods right after I called him about Franklin taking you all hostage."

He looked off into the distance, reliving the chase Franklin had led them on through the trees. "I don't know how long he's been out there, but he knows just about every hiding place there is."

"Did you see him at all before he brought David's…?" I had to stop, letting my sentence trail off. He knew what I meant.

Griff shook his head, looking more miserable than ever. "We never saw him. I don't know where he was the whole time. The first time we saw him, he was bringing David here. We tried to give chase, but he's like a ghost. Home office let us know he was coming this way."

"How did you keep him from seeing you?"

He gave a small chuckle. "Once we were dug in, we didn't move out of that spot. After a while, I thought bugs had taken up residence in my clothes." He scratched at a spot on his side.

"Did you see…anyone else?" I didn't want to start repeating the questions I'd asked him when we first met, but I wanted to know if The Hermit had been out there. He shook his head, guessing who I was talking about. He seemed to share my worry for the older man.

There was nothing more we could do but wait for Franklin to strike again, hoping this time he could be stopped before someone else was hurt or killed.

We sat in silence for several minutes, each lost in our own thoughts. When he finally spoke, his voice was soft.

"Thinking I could catch Franklin when the FBI couldn't for fifteen years makes me no better than Graham. I've let my ego replace common sense."

"It isn't ego that's been driving you."

"No? Then what is it?"

"You've been centered on catching the man who destroyed your family. Maybe you need to take a step back, concentrate on other areas of your life for a while."

"You mean my love life?" His eyebrow lifted slightly before pulling me into a tight embrace, his lips grazing mine. He took his time exploring my lips, moving on to the sensitive spot below my ear.

Goosebumps traveled up my arms as a shiver shook me. I knew I was a goner. It didn't matter that he would take my heart with him when he finally left for good. I would live for the here and now, and let the future take care of itself.

# CHAPTER TWENTY-TWO

David was ten and twelve years younger than his two brothers. Because of the age difference, they had never been close. Right after graduating from high school, they moved away. I'm not sure if he had any contact with them after that. His parents left soon after David graduated.

No one bothered to come for a funeral or memorial, just requested his ashes be shipped to his parents in Florida. I found that rather sad. Maybe that was the reason David had tried so hard to build himself up, trying to prove to them, and himself, that he was worth something.

Griff and John made no more attempts to fool Franklin into thinking they'd left. They were here for the duration. I wondered what was going to happen to Sara and John's romance, as well as mine and Griff's, when they finally left. I doubted she would leave Flanagan's Gap any more than I would. We could cry on each other's shoulders when the time came.

My head kept telling me to put some distance between Griff and myself. But my heart wasn't listening. All I could do was wait for the inevitable to happen, and hope to eventually recover.

"Fire season is almost over, but that isn't going to help the Forest Service any." Megan flopped down on the sofa in the back room. Students would be arriving for class in a few minutes. This would be the only time to relax for the next few hours. "With Franklin still out there, the men are on constant alert. It still isn't safe for campers. Why isn't the FBI doing more to find him?" We'd been grousing about that for what felt like forever. "He knows FBI is aware he's here. Why doesn't he just go somewhere else? If he's avoided detection all these years, what made him decided to come after us?"

I'd been asking that since this started, and I could only

blame myself. I wished more than anything that I'd never seen that television show. Maybe he would have moved on after stealing what he needed if I hadn't started pursuing him. I had become a nuisance that he needed to get rid of. There was nothing I could do to change that now though. We had to stay vigilant because letting down our guard could be dangerous.

"How are we ever going to know if he's finally moved on?" I asked rhetorically. "Do you think The Hermit is still around?"

She shrugged. "Jack's been trying to find the cave where he took us, but so far he hasn't been able to find it or The Hermit. One part of the mountain looks pretty much like another. He certainly picked a well camouflaged place to settle after his shack was burned down." If no one could find Franklin's hiding place, it was even more difficult to find where The Hermit called home.

～～～

"I's sorry that divil kilt yer sheriff," The Hermit told Jack. He had surprised everyone by showing up as we left the Sunday morning service. Instead of coming inside the church, he preferred to remain outside. He didn't seem quite as skittish around a crowd as we always assumed he would be. Maybe after saving the town three weeks ago he had decided to be our friend. Even so, he shifted from one foot to the other like a little boy doing the 'potty' dance. Focusing only on Jack helped his tendency to shy away from the rest of us.

"It weren't like he din't ask fer sumthin to happen," he continued, with a shake of his grizzled head. His long, matted beard swayed across his brawny chest. "I seed him sneakin' 'round lookin' fer that divil, made nuf noise to wake them that's ded, he did. He weren't much fer the outdoors. Din't know his way 'round the woods a'tall." He shook his head again. "Thought lawmen was sposed to be smarter 'n that."

Well, most of them are, I thought. David just thought more of his abilities than he should have. Maybe it isn't nice to speak or think ill of the dead, but it was the truth. I just hoped he had put his faith somewhere other than in himself.

"I comed here to say you'ns need to be real keerful cuz that divil is a gettin' more crazy ever'day, and that be part my doin'."

"Why is that?" Jack kept the conversation going, hoping to find out what Franklin was up to.

The old man let out with a cackle. "That divil thinks he bein' haunted agin. I knows where ever shaft and tunnel ever been in these parts. I keeps a poppin'up to skeer him. It a workin', too." He cackled again. "That divil think I be dead cuz he burnt down my shack. He don't know it was a sittin' over a tunnel like that thar church." He pointed to the building behind us.

"Can you show us where he's hiding?" Griff stepped up beside Jack. "Maybe we can catch him before he hurts anyone else."

The Hermit shook his head, his thick beard waving around again. "He don't stay in one place long nuf fer ya to ketch him. 'Sides, he knowed who you is. Keeps a sayin' you should be dead right 'long with yer folks." Color drained from Griff's face, only to turn red with suppressed anger seconds later. "You gots to be keerful. He gots it in his mind to come git yer girl cuz she bringed them men in the blue jackets here." My stomach rolled. How much more was Franklin planning on doing to us?

"I be goin' now. Jist wanted to tell ya that." Trying to keep him from fading into the forest was useless. He was better at it than Griff was. Like he said, he knew where every mine shaft and tunnel was.

Everyone started talking at once, but no one had any good suggestions.

We didn't have long to wait to find out what Franklin's next move would be. Two days later, Megan called. "Becca, can you come over to my place?" Her voice sounded strained. "I need to show you…something," she finished.

"What's wrong? Are the boys sick?" My heart was in my

throat making it difficult to talk. Those boys were precious to me. "They aren't hurt, are they?" The Hermit's warning rang in my mind. If he was after me like The Hermit said, he would use any method to get me, even Megan and the boys.

"Just come over, Becca. Please. Right away." The line went dead before I could ask any more questions.

Mom was with Bill, and there wasn't time to go get her or even write a note. Something was wrong at Megan's. Without thinking about it, I ran out of the house.

I skidded to a stop at steps of her front porch. Something was wrong with this picture. The house was dark, not a single light was on. It was only seven o'clock, but already getting dark out. I knew Jack was working with Griff and John somewhere. Since this all started Megan didn't like being in the house without some lights on.

Cautiously stepping up on the porch, I avoided the squeaky board I knew was there. Whatever was wrong, I didn't want to give a warning that I was here. Why hadn't I brought my whistle or walking stick? They would have provided some protection or warning.

Opening the door a crack, there was just enough outside light for me to see Megan and the boys sitting in the dark. Her eyes were wide with fright. "What's going on?" I came further into the room, touching the light switch beside the door.

Before I could take more than a step away from the door, someone slammed it shut again; a strong arm circled my neck. Even without seeing who was holding me, I knew it was Warner Franklin. Who else would do something like this?

Megan gasped and the boys let out a whimper, other than that, they didn't move. With the light on, I could see her hands were tied with heavy cord. He hadn't thought to tie up the boys; after all, what could two little boys do to him? Obviously, he didn't know kids very well. Thank You, God.

"Don't make a sound, bitch," he growled in my ear. "I've had enough of you to last a lifetime." He shoved me down on the couch beside Megan and the boys.

Without thinking of the consequences, I popped back up, ready to fight. He hit me with his doubled up fist and the lights went out again. At least for me. Several minutes later, or maybe longer, I opened my eyes again to find my hands tied like Megan's. I also had tape over my mouth. My head was throbbing, and the coppery taste of blood was in my mouth. Franklin was talking to someone on Megan's phone. It took several seconds before I got the meaning of his words.

"I've got your woman here, Tomlin, along with that ranger's woman and her two brats. How about coming to get them?" He listened for a second, his face turning an angry shade of red. "You aren't calling the shots here, I am. If you want to see them again, get over here." He listened again, getting even angrier. "I don't give a damn where you are! I said to get over here now. You escaped what you had coming a long time ago. Now you're going to pay." He slammed the phone down hard enough to shatter the receiver. What he was left holding, he hurled across the room.

Turning around, he glared at me. "I've had my fill of you, too. Every time I tried to blow you up, and you got away scot free. You know what they say about the third time being a charm." He gave a nasty laugh. "You aren't going to get away this time."

I wanted to ask what I'd done that had been so wrong, but all I could do was mumble around the tape. "Shut up," he shouted. He was rapidly losing any control he might have once had over his temper. In his anger, he hit the lamp, sending it crashing onto the floor. The room descended into darkness again.

A slight noise in the corner of the dark room drew everyone's attention. A strangled scream escaped Franklin's throat as he stared at an unearthly glow. He began to hyperventilate, his breathing harsh in the otherwise silent room. "It can't be you. You're dead. I killed you. Why are you coming after me?" He backed away from the light, bumping into the wall. "Leave me alone," he whimpered.

Haunting the person who killed you sounded justified to me. I wasn't sure how he was doing it, but The Hermit made a very convincing ghost. He didn't say anything, but the light remained a flickering glow hovering just above the floorboards.

Was there a mine shaft under the house like at the church and the store? Did Megan even know about it? Could the old man scare Franklin into letting us go? Before that could happen we needed to get our hands free. My thoughts swirled around in my mind.

While Franklin's attention was riveted on the glowing light, I tried to move my hands to loosen the rope. It was no use. He knew what he was doing when he tied me up. I scraped my face against my shoulder, hoping to work the tape free; at the same time I managed to get the tip of my tongue between my lips. If I could moisten the tape enough, maybe it would come loose that way.

"All right, Franklin, I'm here," Griff called from the back of the house. I didn't know how he had gotten here so quickly. I thought the three men were somewhere deep in the forest hoping to find where Franklin was hiding. They'd been looking in the wrong place. "Let's talk."

Franklin looked towards the kitchen while remaining where he was against the wall. He wasn't going to let the apparition out of his sight for fear it might come after him. "I'm done talking, Tomlin. I told you to get in here. Now do it." His voice held very little threat and no punch now.

"I'll come in when you send the women and boys out." Griff managed to sound calm, almost like this was no big deal.

"This isn't a negotiation," Franklin yelled, backing away from the glowing light towards the kitchen. His temper was beginning to override his fear of the ghost. Until the 'ghost' showed up, he thought he had the advantage. Doubt was beginning to creep in now. "No one's getting away from me this time."

"I'm not trying to get away. I'll come in. Just let the

women and boys go."

From where we were sitting, I couldn't see into the kitchen, but The Hermit could when he lifted the hidden trap door in the floor.

"Come here, young'uns." The Hermit's voice was little more than a breathy whisper. "Git this here knife an' cut yer mama loose." The boys silently shook their heads, burying their faces in Megan's side. This was beyond scary for them. In the glow from the lantern he kept below floor level, his craggy face had an ethereal glow. He did look like a ghost.

The boys were so little, so young, even if they got the knife from him, would they understand what they needed to do with it to cut Megan free? At two and a half, they were little more than babies.

Leaning over as far as her bound hands would allow, she whispered first in Caleb's ear, then Jacob's, urging them to obey the voice. For several long seconds I was afraid they would be too scared to move. Finally, scooting off the couch, they moved together across the room, getting only close enough to the figure coming out of the floor to grab the knife before returning to Megan's side.

How was she going to make them understand what she wanted them to do? It took a little convincing, but finally Caleb moved the knife between her hands, sawing at the cord holding them tight. Her jaws were clenched, and blood seeped onto the cord. Caleb's small hands didn't have enough control of the big knife to avoid cutting her.

Please God, let those cuts be superficial, and the cord weak enough for him to cut through, I prayed silently.

After what felt like hours, but in reality was little more than seconds, she was able to pull her hands free. Giving the boys a quick hug, she took the knife, cutting through the cord holding me prisoner.

I had been concentrating so hard on what was happening in the living room, I hadn't heard the commotion in the kitchen. Griff was still arguing with Franklin, keeping him occupied. Was he aware The Hermit was helping us escape?

Moving as silently as possible, we slipped below the floorboards into the shaft. The soft click of the lock moving into place sounded like a gunshot as it reverberated through the tunnel. The Hermit's lantern gave off the wavering glow that had looked so ghostly in the living room.

"No!" The scream could be heard just above us. Franklin had discovered we were gone. His heavy footsteps stomped above us as he moved around the room, bumping into furniture in the dark. "Where are you? You can't get away again." I was grateful he had no idea there were secret tunnels and mine shafts below the buildings.

The Hermit gave his signature cackle. "The ghost be a hauntin' him." He cackled again.

"Shhh, you don't want him to hear you." I tried to shush him, but he cackled some more.

"Yep, I do." He kept his voice low when he talked to us. "That thar divil been doin' his dirty work long nuf. Time for him to get some back." He continued to cackle while Franklin screamed above us about the ghost. The man sounded truly demented.

"Git them young'un outa here," he whispered to us between cackles. "Jist down the way thar be a ladder to take you up to yer menfolk."

"We can't leave you here. You need to come with us. What if Franklin figures out where you are?"

The Hermit shook his head. "I be safe like I has been all my life. Git goin'." He turned away to continue haunting Franklin above him.

I reluctantly followed Megan and the boys. Just as he said, a ladder wasn't very far away. The shaft led to a heavy board covering the opening. Even before we pushed it aside we could hear Griff trying to get Franklin's attention in the house, and Franklin's continued screams.

Jack and John stood silently beside Griff; worry was etched on each man's face. They hadn't known The Hermit was in the tunnel. "Daddy!" Jacob and Caleb had been strangely silent while in the tunnel. Now they ran to Jack, who scooped them up, crushing them to his chest and drawing Megan in for a group hug. Tears sparkled in his eyes.

In an instant, Griff grabbed me, holding on like he'd never let go. After several tear-filled minutes, the men started asking questions: What happened? How did we get away? Franklin's tormented screams receded to background noise until a loud boom captured our attention and a fireball rose above what had been Megan and Jack's home.

"No, The Hermit is still there!" The scream tore from my throat. I wrenched myself away from Griff, running for the tunnel, but he pulled me back.

"You can't go down there, Becca."

"But The Hermit," I objected.

He shook his head. "If he was right there, you can't do anything for him now."

"He came to our rescue. We can't just leave him down there." Tears streamed down my face unheeded.

People poured out of their homes, hoses were brought over to begin the "garden hose brigade." Even though we always kept the trees and brush away from the buildings, some were beginning to catch fire from the sparks flying from the burning house. Jack called in the volunteer firefighters, but there was nothing they could do to save the house. They could only prevent any others from burning.

It was our turn to put Megan's family up at our house. Long after midnight the boys finally fell asleep from sheer exhaustion. The fire crew worked the rest of the night making certain the fire was completely out.

Once again the FBI descended on us, and they took over the investigation. It was the next afternoon before they could go into what was left of the house looking for Franklin's remains. They determined that explosives had been set around the house. Most likely Franklin had set them off to rid himself of the "ghost" haunting him.

My heart was broken. I wanted to go into the tunnel to find out if The Hermit had made it out safely, but Griff prevented me from doing that. It wasn't safe. Would I ever learn if he'd made it out?

# CHAPTER TWENTY-THREE

The only good thing to come out of all this was we were finally free of the FBI and agents Greene and Black. It would take weeks to get the final results back, proving the remains had belonged to Franklin, but there was little doubt. He couldn't have made it out.

"When will you and John be leaving?" Once things began to settle down, I finally got up the courage to ask. We were sitting on the swing on our porch. It had been a week since the explosion and fire. I knew it was only a matter of time before they went back to their lives and business. Can you die twice as fast with a twice broken heart?

My head was resting on his shoulder, and it moved up and down as he gave a careless shrug. "I have to check in at headquarters, make sure everyone is doing what they should. You know the saying, "when the cat's away, the mice will play." Then I..."

"I know you have to get back to your work," I interrupted. "I was just wondering when you planned on leaving." I couldn't look at him. I didn't want him to see the pain I knew was written on my face.

His chuckle rumbled against my ear, and I held on tight to my temper. I didn't want to leave him with a harsh memory of me so he would be glad to be rid of me. I'd rather he regret leaving me behind.

Placing his finger under my chin, he forced me to look at him. "I told you once that you captured my heart the first time you followed me into the forest. I've never said that to another woman. If you need it said in words of one syllable, that's fine, here goes. I love you. I've only said those words to one other woman, and she was my mom." Before I could sputter out a response, he lowered his head, placing his lips on mine, his arms wrapped around me, crushing me to him.

215

Three days later, Griff and John left for Albuquerque, New Mexico, with a promise to Sara and me. "We'll be back. The success of my business doesn't depend on me being in the office every day. That's why I have trusted employees. As long as I'm in contact with them, things run smoothly. I will have to do some traveling, but I'll never be away for long." His kiss was achingly tender, holding a promise.

"Do you think they were telling the truth or just blowing smoke?" Sara asked, tears shimmering in her dark eyes as she watched the big SUV disappear.

All the doubt I'd had when Griff first came into the store surfaced again. His tender words and kisses managed to override them though. "I have to believe them. Pastor Curt tells us God lets things happen for a reason. Maybe they are the reason Franklin was here."

"So much has happened, but what do we really know about them?" she argued. "We haven't known them all that long. Feelings get intensified when facing danger. How do I know this is for real?"

"I know I love Griff," I stated simply.

"Love doesn't conquer all," Sara argued again.

"No, but it's a good place to start. They came through for us when the FBI left us high and dry. We can work on the rest. We don't have to rush into anything."

Griff called me every night. John was calling Sara just as often. It would take several weeks before they'd make it back to Flanagan's Gap. Until then we both kept busy getting on with our lives.

I couldn't dislodge the lump in my stomach whenever I thought about The Hermit. He had been part of the lore of Flanagan's Gap for many years. It was hard to conceive of future generations knowing nothing about him. I felt like I'd lost a friend, even though I didn't really get a chance to know him.

After the turmoil of the past months, the calm and quiet of life as we'd always known it felt strange. I didn't know quite what to do with myself, even though I was doing all the things I normally did during the school year.

"I'm going for a hike, Mom. I'll be back before lunch." Because of Franklin's threat, it had been months since I went into the forest. It was time to get back out there. Her face clouded with worry for a split second before relaxing again. It was safe. With Franklin gone for good, we no longer had to worry whenever someone went for a hike.

Her only comment was, "Be sure to bundle up. It's getting cold."

I hiked as far as the log I'd sat on almost six months ago, taking pictures of the wild flowers. There were no flowers this time of year. Pine cones littered the ground where that poor camper had been half buried. My heart went out to his family. Warner Franklin had been truly evil.

The sun filtering through the branches above me left the same lacy pattern on the ground as it had that day. Looking up at the tall trees, a shaft of sunlight shot down on me, surrounding me with the same feeling of peace and love. This was a different time of year, a different time of day, but the feeling was the same. In this setting, how could I not feel the love of God surrounding me? Pulling my phone off my waistband, I snapped several pictures. I wanted to capture the feeling to take home with me.

The snap of a branch behind me set my heart racing. Logically, I knew it couldn't be Franklin, he was gone. That didn't mean it wasn't a wild animal.

"Don't be skert, Girlie. It jist be me." The Hermit stepped out of the underbrush. "I stepped on that thar branch so's you knowed I be thar. I din't mean to sker you."

I wanted to hug him, but figured that would scare him as badly as he'd just scared me. "How did you make it out of that tunnel alive? I was sure you died along with Franklin." He sat down on the log beside me.

With that cackle I'd come to know, and even like, he gave my hand a pat. "When you had them young'ns outa the tunnel,

I kep makin' that divil think he be haunted. Got him so worked up, he be thinkin' he could git rid of me for real by blowin' up the place." He cackled again. "He forgit he'd be blowin' hisself up, too. I runned down that tunnel jist 'fore he blowed up the place."

"Why did you let us believe you were dead? I was worried about you." I reached out to touch his hand this time.

"I knowed, and I's sorry. I jist don't like them lawmen what comed around. They always be askin' more questions 'an I want to answer. Figgered it best if'in I jist go way for a spell. Now I's back." He smiled at me with his gap toothed grin. "Where be yer man? Hain't seen him 'round lately. Kinda miss playing hide'n'seek with you'all." All these years of us looking for him he had thought it was a game. Go figure.

Sitting there with him I lost all track of time. It was like talking with an old friend I hadn't seen in a while. Turns out he wasn't such a recluse after all. He just didn't like people poking into his business. After so many years living alone, he'd forgotten what his parents had named him. But he knew the nickname the town had given him, and sort of liked it. "Sounds kinda nice," he said, his cackle echoing through the tree tops. "Jist call me Herm fer short." He gave another cackle. He was truly glad to have someone to talk to after all these years.

"Can I tell the others that you're alive? Everyone will be happy to know."

He thought about it for a long while before nodding his head. "That be all right, long as it ain't no lawmen. They jist get in the way."

# EPILOGUE

Christmas was happier than it had been since Dad passed away. Mom and Bill were planning a small June wedding. Sara and John were still working out the logistics of a relationship with him traveling for work and her living here, running her small business and our town.

It was fun watching Chad and Misty, their budding romance evolving from puppy love to something more permanent. Chad would be graduating from high school in the spring; Misty had one more year of school in Flanagan's Gap before joining him in Flagstaff at the university. Time would tell if they managed to make it all work for them.

Megan and Jack had a new house after theirs had been blown up. The insurance company was glad there wouldn't be any more claims thanks to Warner Franklin.

The Hermit was now a real part of town life instead of folk lore. He still lived somewhere in the forest. When he needed something from town, he came in to barter with his carvings instead of leaving them behind after taking something. They were even selling in the craft section of our store.

Griff and I also had a wedding to plan. No date was set, but we both knew it wasn't far off. God had answered my prayer for a handsome man to swim into our little pond and decide to stay.

# ACKNOWLEDGEMENTS

I thank God for the many wonderful gifts He has given me in this life, among them are my wonderful family. He has answered my prayers, allowing me to tell my stories and publish my books. I am so blessed.

My thanks and gratitude also goes to Gerry Beamon, Sandy Roedl, and KaTie Jackson for their suggestions, editing skills and encouragement. I can't forget about all the information retired Phoenix Police Detective Ken Shriner has given me on police procedure. Thanks for your patience with me, and for answering my many questions about law enforcement. I apologize to Ken for taking literary license with police procedure in an effort to move the story forward. Patricia Young, a retired RN, has helped me with all things concerning the activities in the hospital. Again I took literary license to move the story along. Any mistakes or exaggerations were mine, not Pat's. Thanks to everyone who helped me through this process.

## OTHER BOOKS BY SUZANNE FLOYD

Revenge Served Cold
Rosie's Revenge
A Game of Cat and Mouse
Man on the Run
Trapped in a Whirlwind
Smoke & Mirrors
Plenty of Guilt
Lost Memories
Something Shady
Rosie's Secret
Killer Instincts
Never Con A Con Man
The Games People Play
Family Secrets

Suzanne Floyd

Picture That
Trading Places
Chasing His Shadow
Rosie's Legacy

Dear Reader:

Thank you for reading my book. I hope you enjoyed reading it as much as I enjoyed writing it. If you enjoyed Lost Memories, I would appreciate it if you would tell your friends and relatives and/or write a review on Amazon.

Follow me on Facebook at Suzanne Floyd Author, or check out my website at SuzanneFloyd.com.

Thank you,
Suzanne Floyd

P.S. If you find any errors, please let me know at: Suzanne.sfloyd@gmail.com. Before publishing, many people have read this book, but minds can play tricks by supplying words that are missing and correcting typos.

# ABOUT THE AUTHOR

Suzanne is an internationally known author. She was born in Iowa, and moved to Arizona with her family when she was nine years old. She still lives in Phoenix with her husband Paul. They have two wonderful daughters, two great sons-in-law and five of the best grandchildren around. Of course, she's just a little prejudiced.

Growing up and traveling with her parents, she entertained herself by making up stories. As an adult she tried writing, but family came first. After retiring in 2008, she decided it was her time. She still enjoys making up stories, and thanks to the internet she's able to put them online for others to enjoy. When Suzanne isn't writing, she and her husband enjoy traveling around on their 2010 Honda Goldwing trike. She's always looking for new places to write about. There's always a new mystery and a romance lurking out there to capture her attention.

Made in the USA
San Bernardino, CA
17 May 2020